Keith & Elsie
Martin

DUMALA

D0890691

DUMALA

JOYCE MARIE TAYLOR
& MIKE MULLIS

DEDICATION

This book is dedicated to all of humanity, but especially to those who have strived to make our planet a safer, better and cleaner place to live.

ACKNOWLEDGEMENTS

It is our distinct honor and pleasure to re-introduce a dear friend, Danette Paris, who most assuredly deserves recognition for her outstanding poetry. Within the pages of this book, you will find small snippets of her insightful Cinquain and Haiku poetry as a prelude to each chapter.

The poetry she wrote that was included in *Sailing on Love* was so impressive that we asked her if she'd like to be a part of *Dumala* by featuring more of her fine creations and we got another exuberant "Yes!"

Rather than giving all those dead, albeit brilliant poets more notoriety by including their famous quotations in our book, Danette will be the one getting some well-deserved exposure for the entire world to enjoy. Mike and I are certain you will appreciate her poetry as much as we do.

Danette Paris grew up in a Northern Virginia suburb of Washington DC. Her love of all things romantic (including novels and poetry) began in her early teens, but it wasn't until she was in her forties that she began writing. Her poetry is based on real life experiences and often laced with metaphors, humor, love, lust, dreams and sometimes, even sarcasm.

CHAPTER 1

Fishing
the morning mist lifts
a glorious day unveiled
just right for fishing
©dp

"Whoa! Did you see that?" Ben shouted. "Larry, look! What is that?" he continued yelling, as he pointed to the edge of the riverbank.

Ben and Larry were out doing what they always did on a brisk Saturday morning, fishing for bass. Even though they knew it was the wrong time of year and the wrong part of the river, they had heard reports from other fishermen down at the Elk's Lodge that the bass were running earlier this year and these two country boys wanted in on the action.

For the past two weeks it had been raining nonstop and all the rivers in the Suwannee Valley were on the verge of reaching flood stage again, which they'd been doing on a much too frequent basis for the last ten years. Being avid fishermen and confident boaters, though, the threat of rising waters didn't deter Ben and Larry in the least. They knew the time was ripe for catching a boatload of fish, especially since the rain had stopped falling sometime during the night. Heavy rains, they both knew, always brought the fish closer to the surface and easier to spot, making the sport seem almost effortless.

"It looks like an entire school of largemouth bass," Larry said, still staring off to his right. "Only problem is they're all upside down. Dead," he added, with his mouth agape, as he stared at the carnage.

It was still quite dark out, since the sun hadn't risen

above the early morning cloud cover yet, but there was enough light from the waning moon to see, even with the thick, foggy mist hanging low overhead.

Surprisingly, the current, which had been dead still since they launched the boat into the river twenty minutes ago, rapidly picked up. Before either one of them realized what was happening, the boat made a rapid 180-degree turn and they found themselves facing upstream, directly in the path of a six foot wave, which was something unheard of on the river. In fact, they both knew it was impossible, yet there it was aiming straight for them.

"Holy crap!" Ben shouted. "Get us out of here!"

Larry had been sitting at the stern of the boat, manning the small outboard motor, which he had shut off just minutes ago, but try as he might, it just wouldn't start. The more he pushed on the foot control, the more the engine sputtered and spit, draining the battery of its juice.

"I'm trying! I'm trying," Larry yelled, but it was no use. The engine just wouldn't crank over.

Seconds later, as they both stared dead ahead, the huge wave suddenly split in two and then it rushed past them on either side of the ten-foot bass boat. As they watched in stunned horror, the huge waves continued racing downstream, while splattering a misty, sulfur spray of water against their faces as it passed by them.

"Holy God Almighty!" Ben shouted. "I know we put down a case of beer last night, but I didn't think I was still drunk! Tell me you didn't see that, Larry! Tell me I was just hallucinating!"

"I'd sure like to, my man, but..." Larry started, and then he coughed several times, trying to clear his lungs of the horrible odor.

After he spit a huge wad of phlegm over the side of the boat, he used his shirtsleeve to wipe the foul smelling moisture from his face. Soon, he was breathing freely again. Once his eyes could clearly focus, he noticed the mist that had been swirling around their heads had vanished into the atmosphere.

When he spotted a twenty-foot trail of discarded plastic bottles, plastic grocery bags, aluminum cans, used feminine napkins and plastic baby diapers floating past the boat, he drew in a sharp breath and went into another coughing fit. Ben saw it, too, and seconds later, they watched as all that garbage got swept up onto the riverbanks on either side of them.

Just then, as if a magic wand had been waved across them, the motor revved up and the boat made another 180-degree turn. They were facing downstream again when, all of a sudden, they both heard an ear-piercing scream from somewhere high in the pine trees. The next thing they saw was a huge flock of doves splashing into the water just ten yards behind the boat.

"Holy crap!" Ben screamed. "They're dead, too! What the hell is going on?!"

"I have no idea!" Larry screamed back at him.

"I don't know about you, buddy, but I say we get the hell out of here!" Ben yelled.

"I'm with you!" Larry yelled back.

The two men couldn't get out of there fast enough. Larry had the boat at full throttle, throwing huge wakes against the shoreline, as he aimed toward the boat ramp, which was now just a few hundred feet ahead.

"What the heck?" Ben mumbled to himself.

Looking ahead of him, he noticed the parking lot of the state park looked like Grand Central Station with trucks lined up one behind the other. Everyone was trying to retrieve their fishing boats and canoes from the river. At least sixteen other bass boats were trying to squeeze into the small boat ramp area at the same time. Several of the men were screaming at the tops of their lungs, threatening to kill each other with their hunting rifles if they didn't move out of the way. It seemed everyone was in a panic, just like Ben and Larry.

"Psst...Ben...hey," Larry whispered. "Do you see what I see?"

"What?" he asked over his shoulder, and then he

turned around.

Larry was nodding over toward his right where the riverbed was glowing bright yellow and sparkling against the morning sunlight that had just peeked through the clouds.

"I'm heading over there," Larry continued, and then he turned the boat around. "It's gonna be awhile before we'll be able to get out of here, anyway."

Whatever it was that had zipped down the river and terrorized all the early morning fishermen, it had left behind not only tons of waste in its wake, but also other items that had long been forgotten. Gold nuggets and precious stones were clumped together in foot-high piles along the riverbanks for a good half mile downstream.

"Is this for real, or is someone playing a joke on us?" Ben asked Larry, who had already jumped out of the boat to start retrieving as many of the precious jewels and gold nuggets as he could scoop up in his hands.

"It's manna from heaven, you big dope," Larry said, with eyes as big as some of the sparkling jewels. "Don't look a damned gift horse in the mouth! Just start loading up the boat!"

MEANWHILE, SIX HUNDRED MILES away in a log cabin in the Blue Ridge Mountains, a young woman is sitting in her den with her eyes glued to the monitor of her laptop computer, as she scribbled notes onto a well-used legal pad.

Becky Rogers had been on unemployment for close to six months already. She was one of the unlucky seven in her department who had been laid off from the local newspaper. The job she held for six years as a graphic designer – and it was a job that she truly loved – had been outsourced overseas. Finding another job with a comparable salary in the small town of Jubilee Falls was proving to be a pointless task. In fact, finding any job at all was nearly impossible, unless she wanted to work for minimum wage, but even those jobs were scarce.

Since she had so much free time, she spent the

majority of it pursuing her other passion, which was environmental activism. When she wasn't out volunteering with one group or the other, she was on her computer researching and delving into the history of mankind and his utter disregard for the planet. What truly fascinated her was the way the weather patterns had been changing, especially in the past few decades.

For weeks she had been tracking a strange chain of events within the continent of Africa. She had no idea how it all started, or why it intrigued her so much, but she felt a burning need inside her soul to figure out what was behind this weird phenomena and where it might be heading.

It began as a small dot of disturbed weather that had flared up over top of a large river near a remote village in Africa. Then, it gradually evolved into what she believed was a compact, yet deadly storm. It was the most bizarre thing she had ever seen. Just a few weeks ago, it had emerged into the ocean from a narrow river off the northern coast of Africa. It was a tiny, condensed ball of swirling high-speed winds that seemed to have three separate cores within its center.

If her tracking was correct, and she had no reason to think otherwise, this storm had set out on a direct path toward the New England States. It had been just a tiny blip on her computer screen, but it was definitely there. At that point, she was uncertain of the exact coordinates where it might strike, but all her calculations were pointing to the state of New Jersey.

After more than two dozen attempts in the last two weeks to alert the National Weather Service, however, and being told she was becoming a nuisance with her incessant scare tactics, she gave up trying to get anyone to listen to her.

"Why doesn't anyone else see what I'm seeing?" she wondered, now that she had plotted its coordinates and saw where it was heading.

Of course, she knew the answer to that question already. She had a special gift. It wasn't on the scale of a psychic or a fortune-teller. She knew that because she had tried playing the numbers in the state lottery for the last ten years, and to date, the only thing she ever won was a free ticket because she had only three out of the six winning numbers. She had no formal training in meteorology, either, which most likely explained why everyone scoffed at her.

No, her gift was on a higher plane; a different stratosphere than the rest of mankind. Strange as it sounded to everyone, including herself, she felt directly connected to the Universe on a passionate and spiritual level. It wasn't something she could truly define, either, which explained why people in authority always brushed her off as a weirdo tree-hugger or just a plain troublemaker. She was not deterred, though. There was a higher being commanding her to continue her efforts.

All the data she had been collecting about this particular storm was chronologically logged onto an advanced computer program, which took up nearly all 300 gigabytes of memory on her computer. Just last week she was forced to buy two more external hard drives to store all the information she was gathering. Plus, she had to make certain she had at least two backup copies of everything, since there was no way she was going to lose weeks and weeks of hard work and research.

"One of these days somebody is going to believe me," she said with a heavy sigh. "I just hope it's sooner rather than later."

CHAPTER 2

Drought
Year after year
The drought took control
Jobs ended
People left
The wind was all that was heard
Desolate sound
The people who abused the earth?
Their children's children died of thirst
©dp

There was a time during the 20th Century when the world at large was a peaceful place; an oasis of safety and beautiful surroundings where one could partake of the magic of nature wherever their travels would lead them. All around the circumference of the globe there were breathtaking sights to see, to explore, and to experience as an eager tourist.

Giant full moons used to light up the skies above Nova Scotia, a place where the highest tides on Planet Earth occurred. Polar Auroras, otherwise known as the Northern Lights, used to give off a greenish, red tint glow against the horizon. Those two spectacles alone were enough to inspire artists and writers to create masterpieces of paintings and poetry.

Waterfalls in South America used to glisten in the sunshine as they cascaded downward, splashing into sparkling pure pools of water that would lead to interconnecting unspoiled freshwater rivers.

Thousands of wild horses could be seen running free across the Midwestern Plains, while the American Bald Eagle nested safely with its young in the highest trees of the Northwest Country.

Rainbows and meteor showers were welcome sights for professional and amateur photographers alike, as were the schools of dolphins playfully splashing in the aqua blue waters off Florida's Emerald Coast.

Fast forward decades later, well into the 21st Century, and the landscape of Planet Earth appears completely different, not only on the surface, but down deep within its core. Subtle, yet damaging and irreversible manmade changes to the environment over many centuries have finally reached a pinnacle. These outward changes have finally caught up to the underlying reality of the situation that lay in the lithosphere level below the Earth's crust.

Earth's ecosystem had become fatally unstable and on the verge of total collapse and destruction. The oxygen that humans needed in order to exist had become toxic, causing a multitude of diseases and resultant deaths in the millions.

Air pollution, well water contaminants and massive amounts of human and animal waste are threatening to destroy life "as we know it" on Planet Earth. Years of ignoring the dangers of atomic warfare, radioactive fallout, the burning of fossil fuels and leaks from nuclear power plants have become a source of fear among Earth's inhabitants.

Countries are in battle over religious beliefs and senseless wars continue to erupt around the globe. People are dying. People are scared. They have become so frightened that many are building underground shelters to keep their families safe should World War III suddenly become a reality. It was like the Cold War all over again.

Virtually all of North America's food, cars, furniture and appliances are being imported from foreign countries, leaving the United States in a desperate time of unemployment, with more than three-thirds of the country collecting money from the government. Consequently, the national debt had reached monumental figures in the trillions of trillions.

Factories across the land lay dormant, and out-of-work employees from once-thriving industries are subsisting on welfare and handouts. The lucky ones, who had retirement savings to draw from for a short period of time, are about to join the ranks of the poor and disadvantaged, as their savings dwindle down to nothing.

All the major banks had either been taken over by the federal government or been merged into one of two remaining banking institutions that were on the verge of collapse, as well. With the unreliable banking systems, not only in North America, but also worldwide, people had resorted to burying locked safes deep underground to safeguard their hard-earned money. Many families took turns rotating guard duty day and night, hiding in the bushes with loaded guns and rifles, fully prepared to protect their remaining wealth at any cost.

Home gardens and livestock farms had become a necessity and the numbers of new farms popping up across the nation were growing by leaps and bounds. Americans were tired of being poisoned by food additives, preservatives and bacteria, especially the deadly strains of salmonella and botulism pathogens caused by careless food manufacturers in other countries.

Communal living had become fashionable again, reminiscent of the 1960's, because so many homeowners had lost their houses to foreclosure. Families were merging resources with other families and living together in a last desperate attempt to provide food and shelter for themselves and their children.

The elderly were dying off at alarming rates, due to neglect and poverty. Social Security benefits had not kept up with the rising cost of living and many senior citizens were living in squalor. Prescription drug costs had gone through the roof, and because of that, many seniors opted not to take doctor-ordered medications for their illnesses because they simply couldn't afford it.

Rather than using Earth's vast resources to cure the underlying causes of diseases and illnesses, scientists and pharmaceutical companies were instead feeding on man's ignorance by producing more and more deadly drugs to treat symptoms. The end result was that the legal professionals were cashing in on wrongful death lawsuits.

The government of the United States was at a loss, as far as coming up with solutions to any of the current problems facing all Americans.   Democrats and Republicans outwardly fought, nitpicking over inconsequential items on the latest bills trying to make it through the red tape of Congress.   Health reform measures had turned into a sick version of a three-ring circus at the White House, oftentimes looking more like Friday night at the fights with grown men and women shouting back and forth at each other. The two opposing parties of Congress couldn't agree on anything of importance, let alone how to provide quality healthcare for America's citizens.

Predictions years ago of a two-class nation had finally come to fruition. One was either extremely wealthy now or extremely poor. There was no longer a middle-class of Americans, the group of people who had held this country together for centuries.

Earth had spun into a downward tumble. The United States of America was in trouble and no one, it seemed, knew how to fix it. Times had become desperate and mankind had reached a frantic state of mind. Many were resorting to drugs and alcohol to stave off the pitiful reality of their situations. Being in a mind-altered state of mind for some people was the only way they knew how to cope with the increasing pressures of merely staying alive and the pill factories were cashing in on it.

Homegrown terrorism, with Americans being brainwashed by the growing number of dissident groups inside the country, was gaining in numbers. The Internet had been the catalyst for this new kind of recruitment, because no one knew how to police the cyber world. A monster had been created and it was impossible to stop it.

Deep below the Earth's surface, volcanic activity was on the upsweep in recent decades, especially in areas where these hotspots had supposedly burned themselves out centuries ago. Earthquakes had begun affecting major cities and towns, in areas where scientists and geophysicists had sworn were safe from such disasters. Many of those quakes triggered a backlash of tsunami waves, which devastated numerous coastal cities around the globe. Hurricanes and tornadoes had been occurring with increased strength and frequency, again, in places that typically never saw such phenomena occur.

Winters were lasting longer and temperatures continued dipping well below the freezing point year after year, especially in the southern states of the Americas. Whereas, summers had become unbearable with the mercury hovering in the 100's and above, oftentimes lasting from May through November. Gradually, the four seasons of nature had morphed into just two. There was no longer a spring or fall season; they had simply vanished. Global warming, which had its share of naysayers for decades, was not only a reality now, but it had reached a point of immense concern among the leaders of the world.

Wild animals that had been kept in captivity in zoos and amusement parks were rebelling against mankind. There were incidents of tigers and lions turning on their zookeepers and chewing them alive. Whales that had supposedly been tamed were causing scenes of terror at amusement parks by swallowing their trainers and then spitting them out in pieces.

Overzealous, greedy land developers had constructed enormous communities with houses, apartments and office buildings that took up acres and acres of land. Sadly, they were erected upon sacred areas within wildlife preservation sites, thus forcing indigenous animals out of their safe havens and into well-populated areas. Giant thirty-foot pythons and hundreds of rattle snakes were showing up in peoples' backyards. Deer were being slaughtered on busy country roads and many small animal species were in danger of becoming extinct. It was road-kill city in many previously rural towns.

It was literally becoming hell on earth. Religious fanatics were warning the masses to surrender their lives to God, to accept Christ Jesus as their Savior because the end was near. Armageddon was just over the horizon and the horizon was dark and gloomy. Their message? Sinners would be swallowed up by the Earth's crust and burn for all eternity.

Yes, that was the message being sent out around the world. Believers and non-believers alike were beginning to sit up and take notice, but was it already too late?

CHAPTER 3

Bonfire
Scent of burning wood
Mingling with the night air
Inviting, romance
©dp

"Tell me something, Dad..." Mickey started, and then he poked his head up from the book he was reading to look at his father.

"Sure, son," Brent said, smiling. "What would you like me to tell you this time?" he asked, always eager to offer an opinion, whether he knew anything about the subject or not.

Brent DeRosa was a big man in stature, towering over six feet three inches tall, with a full head of gray hair and a huge potbelly. He would be turning seventy-nine in a couple of months. Even with the progressive Alzheimer's that had been threatening his sense of memory for the last couple of years, on most days his mind was still sharp as a tack.

He loved a good meal, too, which clearly showed, not only by his oversized midsection, but also in the manner that he handled his food preparation. Right now he was delicately flipping over two large T-bone steaks. He had been marinating them in a mixture of teriyaki, garlic and pepper since around noon, utilizing a large glass pan that had been passed down through the years from his great-grandmother.

"What is your theory behind the extinction of dinosaurs?" Mickey finally asked him.

"What?" Brent shrieked, and when he swung around to look at his son, he accidently dropped a can of Swamp

Seasoning on the floor that he was about to add to his marinade. "Son, sometimes you come up with the darnedest dang questions," he said, and then he bent down to retrieve his favorite bottle of hot seasoning.

"Hey! You're the one who got me interested in all this ancient history crap, Dad. I turned into a book nerd because of you," Mickey said, laughing, as his father straightened back up, grunting and groaning while he held onto the counter for balance.

"Don't you be blamin' me for your oddball looks," Brent said. "If you'd stop shavin' that damn head o'yours, you might be able to keep more information inside that pea brain."

"Ah, so you do have a theory and from the sounds of things you must have told me before."

"Do you see them lizard tails out there, son?" Brent asked, pointing out the kitchen window toward the riverbed.

"You mean those *Saururus cernuus*?" Mickey asked, showing off his botanical knowledge, as he stood behind his father now.

"Hey! Who's tellin' this story? You or me?" Brent barked at him.

"Sorry, Dad, go ahead. I'm listening."

"As I was sayin', it was about this same time of year, almost...eh, let's say about sixty-five million years ago, when this humongous asteroid came crashing down to Earth, right smack dab in the middle of the Yucatan Peninsula," he started, as he scratched his head, deep in thought.

Meanwhile, Mickey suddenly remembered when he first heard his father relate this exact same story. It was when he was five years old. His mother had just passed away and he awoke one night around midnight after having a horrifying nightmare. His father came rushing into his bedroom, and after he tucked his son back underneath the covers, he proceeded to tell him a bedtime story...about dinosaurs, no less. Oddly, it didn't frighten Mickey, and even more strange was that the story actually calmed him down enough to go back to sleep. From that point forward he was stung by the bug to learn all there was to know about ancient history.

"Well, son, that dang asteroid was so big," Brent continued, and then he thought for a second. "In fact, it was a billion times more powerful than the Hiroshima bomb, if you can believe that. Anyway, it completely wiped out the dinosaurs. Killed 'em all deader 'an a doornail."

"I thought that was your theory," Mickey said. "I just wanted to make sure."

"You see all them squirrels chasin' each other through them pine trees?" he asked Mickey, now pointing to the row of long leaf pines that dotted the banks of the Suwannee River, just beyond the barn.

"Oh, yeah, I see them."

"Well, that's what's left of them dinosaurs. They've been reduced to irritatin', pine cone stealin' varmints. I got me about two hundred dents on the hood of my old pickup because of them rascals," his father continued ranting.

"Whatever you say, Dad," Mickey said, trying not to laugh.

"You don't believe me, do you? Well, I'll tell ya somethin' else and this is somethin' you don't want to hear, but I'm gonna tell ya anyway."

"I can take it, Dad," Mickey said, patronizing him.

"One day soon here, real quick...somethin' big is gonna happen. It's gonna be somethin' so colossal that nobody ever seen the likes of yet," Brent warned him. "And you can take that to the bank."

"Well, all righty, then. In that case, I'd better get these T-bones on the grill before the sky falls," Mickey told him with a straight face.

"Yep, you best be doin' that, son."

As Mickey was walking out the door with the pan of steaks and a big two-pronged fork, it was all he could do to keep from laughing. He loved his father, but the old man had one of the most vivid, outrageous imaginations of anyone he'd ever known in his life.

Granted, he had some of the facts straight about the extinction of dinosaurs, at least according to the history books, but his imagination always seemed to get the better of him the more he talked. If nothing else, he was a source of entertainment and he always kept Mickey on his toes.

Now that he was outside and far enough away that his father couldn't hear him, he let out a huge belly laugh. Once he stoked the coals on the outdoor barbecue pit and placed the steaks on the burning hot grill, he walked over to the shed to retrieve another ice cold Miller from the refrigerator. Then, he pulled up an old lawn chair and he sat down to wait out the cooking process, while soaking in the beauty of the river.

His folks had bought this old farmhouse nearly fifty years ago and between it and the surrounding land they owned somewhere close to four-hundred acres. Much of it was being utilized as a tree farm, which is how the family made their fortune throughout the years.

The house was old, but it had been built quite sturdy, sitting up almost twelve feet from ground level on concrete stilts. It was actually made to look like a log home, even integrating the use of wooden pegs rather than nails and screws for all the joints. For the most part, the entire structure was safe from flooding should the river decide to go haywire and rise to harrowing heights.

Mickey had spent a small fortune remodeling the entire inside of the house to meet modern safety and energy standards. With his father becoming more physically feeble every day, he even went so far as to install an elevator two years ago that serviced all three levels of the home.

Now that his dad was getting up in age, and seemingly losing a lot of his faculties in the process, Mickey felt it was time for him to start thinking about what he was going to do when his father was no longer around.

The foreman, Jockey Joe Smith, was doing a decent

job keeping the farm, the cattle and the pine straw business running efficiently, but he, too, was getting older by the minute. Jockey Joe had been a godsend from the beginning, restoring Mickey's faith in a higher, supernatural power, even though it had been years since he had stepped foot inside a church. The last time he went was the day of his mother's funeral.

Joe's story was a sad one that left him with a prosthetic leg from the knee down, but he never complained, and unless he showed you the plastic leg you'd never know he was disabled. After a near fatal accident, riding one of the fastest horses in the Preakness back in the early 1980's, Joe wound up on Mickey's doorstep one day, begging for a job. Thirty years later, business couldn't have been better.

"Jockey Joe...what a guy," Mickey thought with a heavy sigh. "Who would have thought that a washed up old jockey could turn a half-assed farm business into such a success? And then he goes and marries himself one of the prettiest Japanese women I've ever laid my eyes on. Then, she gives him four beautiful children and six amazing grandkids. God bless him."

Mickey, meanwhile, at forty-two years of age, was beginning to wonder if he was doomed to a life of bachelorhood. Living in a small town where most of the girls left the area right after high school, meant there weren't many decent looking women left behind to choose from. In fact, most all of the female population of Fishbend Creek, unless they married a local guy right after graduation, either went to college out of state or they made permanent moves to larger cities like Atlanta, Jacksonville, Tallahassee and even Gainesville, in order to secure decent paying jobs.

Not that he was proud of it, but Mickey could count the number of girls he had dated on one hand. Only one of them, Darlene Whipley, had even the slightest possibility of being wife material. Unfortunately, she got knocked up by one of the Yeager brothers after sneaking off to a mud bog party one night, so that was the end of that relationship.

About that same time was also when he decided to start shaving his head. He had no idea why, but ever since that incident with Darlene, he felt compelled to rid himself of his head hair. It was almost as if he was cleansing himself from backwoods females. The habit of shaving his head everyday just seemed to be a natural part of his daily ritual now and one that he had no intention of stopping, no matter how much his father ribbed him about it.

"Holy crap!" he suddenly shouted when he heard something out on the river. "What in the hell was that?"

The Suwannee River, which was normally quiet and peaceful at this time of year in late spring, had suddenly come alive. It was making sounds like a groaning bear that had just been snared by a hunter's trap.

"Good God! Is that a whitecap?" he gasped, as he stared out across the river. "Nah...that's ridiculous. We don't get whitecaps on the Suwannee River. Maybe I've just had one too many beers," he thought, since he was on number six already, and then he laughed out loud.

The fire underneath the steaks suddenly flared up about two feet in the air, as grease from the fat of the meat dripped down onto the coals. Mickey snatched the fork from the old wooden table beside him and he flipped them over, enjoying the crackling sounds as they baked on the grill.

It reminded him of simpler times when he was just a young squirt playing in the yard with his brothers and sisters, while the old folks gathered on the back porch to gossip. He remembered their conversations were loud and animated, especially after they drank a bit too much beer or wine. Most of the gossip, as he recalled, was about all the neighbors who weren't part of their little clique, but a lot of it leaned toward complaints about the way the city was being run. Everybody had an opinion, it seemed, especially his father.

The small town of Fishbend Creek along the Suwannee River was officially a part of Hamilton County, although, one would never know the town even existed unless they owned a swamp buggy or a four-wheel-drive vehicle. That's what was needed in order to access the area. Consequently, the small community of less than two hundred residents had developed their own ruling government that was based on the barter system and just plain good neighborliness. Even all these years later, their system seemed to be working out better than any city-run government could ever hope to accomplish.

Jeremiah "Butch" Meyers, the mayor of the city, had never ventured anywhere close to their little town in the twenty years he'd been in office. It was almost as if they were the forgotten community, but that suited Mickey and all his neighbors perfectly fine.

Mickey was born and raised in Fishbend Creek and from the looks of things he was going to die here, as well. He tried getting out once and it was good while it lasted. The eight years he spent in the state's capitol going to college were the best times of his life. He had majored in ancient history and archaeology and minored in language studies, coming away with four different Masters Degrees and being able to speak more than a dozen foreign languages fluently.

After five years of mild fame, showing off his acute knowledge of ancient history during hundreds of speaking engagements at different colleges and universities across the U.S., he began to tire of all the traveling. Living out of a suitcase for weeks on end was becoming quite uncomfortable, as well as lonely as hell.

He wanted to settle down somewhere; somewhere other than Fishbend Creek, that is. He also wanted all the usual things a man wants; a wife, two-and-a-half children, and a steady job with benefits. He didn't think that was too much to ask for.

He was all set to start living that dream when he was offered, and then accepted a teaching job out in San Diego, when tragedy struck. It was the day before he was going to drive out to California from Tallahassee, where he was still living in the same apartment he'd been renting since his first year in college. He had a U-Haul trailer already attached to the back of his brand new Dodge pickup. It was stuffed front to back, and up to the ceiling with all his earthly belongings.

When the dreaded phone call came in at seven o'clock that evening that his father had just suffered a major stroke, Mickey felt as if his world and his future had come to a crashing halt. It seemed so unfair at the time.

The doctor assured him that his father would be fine in time with the proper rehabilitation, but with no one at home to take care of him it would have meant hiring a full-time, live-in nurse. It would have cost an arm and a leg, too, because his father's insurance didn't cover such things. Mickey was forced to make a life-altering decision right there on the spot, but in all honesty, he had few regrets, anymore, if any.

He hated to admit it, and he would never say it out loud to anyone, but he actually liked living in Fishbend Creek. The town was nestled along the banks of the unspoiled Suwannee River, and just a mile or so to the south of the DeRosa residence was a place called White Sulfur Springs. It was a pristine natural spring and the wooded area surrounding it was like visiting a slice of paradise. Over the years, it had provided him with many fond memories.

The spring had loads of history behind it, too, which had always fascinated him. It was said to have been a place of refuge for the Timucuan Indian tribe way back in the 1530's. Mickey had dug up many relics from the area, which were now proudly displayed throughout the house. One time he had collected enough shards of one piece of pottery to glue it all back together, making it look as if it had never been broken. Over the years, he also found a slew of ancient Indian hunting and cooking tools, as well as a few handmade weapons that were buried deep into the soil.

Back then, the Suwannee River in this particular area used to be the boundary line between the Timucuan Indians on the east side of the river and the Apalachee's on the west. White Sulfur Springs, at that time, was considered a sacred healing ground where warring tribes would come to bathe, as well as drink the mineral waters, all in the name of peace.

Unfortunately, the spring had dried up several years back and the area was closed off. One of the city councilmen propositioned the state to proclaim it as an historical site. They did so a year later, although, no one had been back since to attempt cleaning it up. It was just left to the forces of nature. Now, it was laden with hundreds of overgrown trees that eventually hid what was left of the spring underneath layers and layers of dead pine branches and brush.

Being a history fanatic and a lover of nature, as well as a devoted son, Mickey had learned to appreciate living in Fishbend Creek with his father, even as nutty as his old man could be at times.

Both of Mickey's sisters had moved away to Texas right after high school. Since they were twins, they mistakenly felt as if they should stay joined at the hip and do everything alike, which always made Mickey cringe. Neither one of them seemed to be able to think on their own.

One day a couple of cattle ranchers were in town visiting relatives and one thing led to another. Soon, both girls were knocked up and a double wedding ceremony followed weeks later. Then, they were whisked off to Austin and Mickey hadn't seen them since.

One of his brothers was a lifer in the Army and he'd been living overseas in Germany for the last twenty years. His other brother was serving a life sentence in prison for murdering his wife and child. So, the only one left to care for Brent was Mickey, and over the past fifteen years he had only left Fishbend Creek twice.

The first time was when he got drunk as a skunk on two pitchers of Margaritas and he decided to hop a plane to the Caribbean Islands in the middle of the night. He spent two glorious weeks scuba diving the coral reefs and taking photographs. The second time was a quick trip to see a woman up in Tennessee. Her name was Suzanne Johnson, whom he had met through an online dating service.

The first trip was relaxing, enjoyable and fulfilling, not to mention something he desperately needed after caring for his father day and night for close to two years. The second one, however, nearly scared him to death.

The so-called woman he went to meet turned out to be a hermaphrodite. All the details of that fiasco had been permanently wiped from his mind now, or at least whenever he was sober. After throwing down a few too many beers, however, those memories would oftentimes come back like gangbusters to torture him. Even now, he found it difficult to rise above the shame and the feelings of stupidity. After all, she was one hell of a fine looking woman...or whatever he/she/it was.

"I wonder if Suzanne is the reason I swore off women," he thought, as the memory of her flashed across his mind.

As he pondered that thought, his left hand happened to brush across the lump in his pants pocket, so he reached inside and took out his key ring.

"Ahh, yes, there you are," he said with a heavy sigh.

Among the house keys and the vehicle keys, there was one special item that to this day still had him puzzled. As he slipped the small gold ring around his pinky finger, his thoughts drifted back to his childhood again.

While digging around White Sulfur Springs, there was one item in particular he had found that he had never shown to anyone, not even his father. He was thirteen years old at the time and just discovering his sexuality, as he entered the awkward, scary world of puberty.

What he found was an old ceremonial Indian ring that had three inlaid jewels. What kind of jewels they were he had no idea, but all three of them were exactly the same size and shape in brilliant shades of purple. When the sunlight hit them just right he could see a distinct matching design in the middle of each stone.

There was also an inscription on the underside that when translated meant, *"To my true love. You have found me."*

It had touched him on a deep, spiritual level, although, back then, he didn't understand its true meaning. In fact, he didn't translate the inscription until his second year of college, after studying the ancient Mayan language. A couple of the new words he had learned immediately triggered memories of the words written in the inscription on the ring.

He still wasn't sure he knew the significance of it, or even if it truly was an ancient tribal ring, but he liked to think it was. Something in his subconscious mind told him to carry it with him at all times, but to also keep it a secret until the perfect moment presented itself. He was still waiting for that moment. Meanwhile, he had kept the ring on his keychain ever since then, as a reminder that there was someone out there who was meant for him. He simply hadn't found her yet.

All of a sudden, the screen door slammed shut. When Mickey turned around, he saw his father standing at the edge of the porch. He was flailing his arms in the air and yelling like a madman.

"You makin' shoe leather out there, boy, or what? You know how I like my steak! I wanna hear it moo when I slice into it!" he screamed. "I only got about four good teeth left and I'd like to keep 'em in my mouth, if ya don't mind!"

"I'll be right in!" Mickey yelled back to him, stifling his laughter as best he could.

"Well, hurry up! I'm starvin'! Make sure you put that fire out, too! I ain't in no mood to play Smokey the Bear, puttin' out a damn blazin' forest with a dadgum garden hose!"

With that, he stormed back inside and the screen door slammed shut again with a thunderous bang.

"You crazy old coot," Mickey said, now laughing so hard that he could barely scrape the steaks off the grill.

Dinner that evening turned out better than he had hoped. The steaks were cooked to perfection, the coleslaw his father made was mouthwatering and spicy with the dash of Swamp Seasoning mixed into it, and the fresh greens that Mickey had been simmering on the stove for hours tasted like a fine delicacy.

After Brent turned in for the night just after ten o'clock, and after Mickey cleaned up the kitchen, it was time to head upstairs to the den to catch up on the news of the day. Since his father refused to have a television in the house, Mickey had to resort to the Internet to keep up with current events.

He didn't mind it much because he hated watching the boob tube even more than his father, especially all the news stations that only reported what the government wanted the public to hear.

The Internet offered better, more in-depth news and less opinionated drivel, as far as he was concerned. It was more believable than the crap that all those too-handsome jocks and jockettes on any given television news station could ever report.

While he waited for his computer to power up, he changed into his pajamas and brushed his teeth, all the while still having thoughts of Suzanne, the he-she that he couldn't seem to shake off. Suddenly, life seemed oh-so-dull and he wished he had the nerve to make a break for it and go search out some excitement somewhere.

The string of events that were about to transpire next would set all sorts of strange phenomena into motion; they were things that had been stirring amid the atmosphere and underground for centuries. Mickey didn't know it yet, but he was about to be thrust into the thick of it.

CHAPTER 4

Silent is the Stream
Patience the rocks that lie beneath
Wicked winds whisper to the stream
Flow faster and you will wear them down
The silent stream rages like the river
Saying nothing
The rocks become smooth and beautiful
The wind drifts away
Silent is the stream
©dp

"Are you ready to go, Jamal? We need to go now before the sun rises," Wakulla urged his younger brother, speaking in his native tongue of Creole.

"I'm ready," Jamal said, and the two of them set off on a journey to find food for their families.

The seas were flat and slick as glass as they meandered out into the Gulf of Mexico from an inland marshy river in the western Everglades. It was an isolated area in southwest Florida that few people ever ventured into and this morning was no different.

What they were about to embark on was illegal and if they got caught they would both be charged with poaching. They'd also be deported back to their homeland of Haiti, so the risks were extremely high and dangerous.

Six months ago, the two brothers had sneaked into the country and they set up a makeshift home made from old timber and discarded automobile tires they had found in the swamps of the Everglades. It wasn't the Taj Majal by any stretch of the imagination, and it was risky, due to the large alligator and snake presence in the area, but it was better than living in a mud hut in their earthquake-devastated country of Haiti. At least here they had food to eat, even as gamey as it oftentimes tasted.

After the fifth 8.0 earthquake in less than two years struck the battered nation of Haiti, they, as well as thousands of other Haitians, had fled the country to seek a safer environment for themselves and their families. Legally entering the United States had become an impossible task because of strict new immigration laws. Those who did make it ashore were eventually sent back to the country after being held in outdoor prison camps for weeks, enduring despicable treatment, while government officials processed tons of red tape paperwork.

Wakulla and his wife, Maji, had four young children and Jamal, who lost his wife in the last earthquake, had three kids, all under the age of seven. Between them and Wakulla's two elderly uncles and aunts, Maurice, Shala, Benka and Mariah, they were crammed like sardines onto a twenty-foot motorboat for the three-day trip across the Atlantic. Miraculously, they made it safely into the country and completely undetected by the Coast Guard or immigration officials.

The Everglades, where they now called home, had been almost completely stripped of all the native wildlife and plants by hungry land developers over the years, before the government finally put a stop to the projects. Unfortunately, it would take years before the area would replenish itself.

After a while, Wakulla and his relatives began to tire of eating alligator tails, snake meat and an occasional dove, if they were lucky enough to capture one. They sorely needed more nutritional food to eat and Wakulla was determined to find it.

Today, their mission was to steal from the lobster and shrimp traps that the local fishermen from the Big Bend area of Florida had set two months ago. Wakulla had discovered that those fishermen weren't scheduled to return to the site until next week, so now was the perfect time to pilfer a few of the delicacies. Aside from the shrimp and the lobster, he was also hoping to bring back some oysters.

He despised thieves and he had never stolen anything before, but times had become futile and he saw no other way around it.' He and his family desperately needed to eat something healthier and different from what they'd been subsisting on for months.

Wakulla's two uncles would be staying behind in their swampland home to protect the women and children, until Wakulla and his brother could return, which he told them might be two or three days.

"It's a beautiful day, isn't it?" Wakulla asked Jamal, seeming more than eager to be on his way.

"Ahh, yes, it is," Jamal said, as a broad smile spread across his face. "I can tell from the smell of the ocean and the color of the sky that it is going to be a good day. Yes, a very good day."

Wakulla wanted to agree with his brother, but he had a nagging feeling in his soul that something dreadful was about to happen. He tried brushing it off as just plain fear of getting caught and he hoped he was right. Before long, he found himself reminiscing about days gone by.

His roots were complex and he often felt as if he didn't belong to any one specific culture. His great, great-grandfather came from an ancient Aboriginal Indian tribe in a remote area of Australia. His people had migrated over the years to Indonesia, then to Algeria, and finally, years later, they settled in a small town near Morocco, very near the borderline of Spain.

As the story went, he and his family had been taken – or kidnapped, if you believed his great great-grandfather's version of the story – by a Christian missionary group and transported to Port Au Prince, Haiti. It was a total upheaval for the entire family, who suddenly had to learn a new language, as well as a new culture.

As the decades went by, though, everyone adjusted to their new surroundings and most of them felt as if they truly did belong to the country of Haiti. All except Wakulla, that is, who had studied under his great-grandfather's tutelage for several years until the old man died of lung cancer and heart disease at the age of 102. He had learned the culture and the language of his ancestors, although, he had forgotten much of it in recent years.

"Wakulla, are you still awake?" Jamal suddenly piped up from where he sat at the stern of the boat.

"Oh, I'm awake all right," he assured him, and then he increased the speed of the outboard motor to prove it.

As the sun began to rise, an eerie silence surrounded them. Other than the low rumble of the motor there were no other sounds. No birds, no airplanes flying overhead, no other boaters within sight, and the waters of the ocean seemed to be standing still.

It had been nearly three hours since they first entered the waters of the Gulf and they were so far out at sea that they couldn't see land.

"Are we there yet?" Jamal asked, laughing.

He had come up behind Wakulla, looking over his shoulder at the vast expanse of wide-open sea ahead of them. Wakulla ignored his question and instead he looked down at the compass, checking to be certain he was on the correct heading toward the undersea traps.

"It stopped working!" Wakulla shouted, shrieking so loud that it made Jamal jump backwards, nearly toppling overboard. "The damned compass stopped working!" he shouted again.

He was in a panic now, banging the side of the device with his fist, trying to make the needle move, but it was stuck.

"What do we do now?" Jamal asked, as he scraped himself up off the deck. "Are we lost?"

"No, we're not lost...not yet, anyway," he said, and then he put his finger to his mouth and shut the motor off. "Shhh," he told Jamal. "Listen..."

Just then, out of nowhere it seemed, a massive twenty-foot wave arose from the sea behind them. Before either one of them had time to react, it splashed over top of the boat, soaking both of them with acrid smelling saltwater.

"What the hell was that?" Jamal hollered.

With his eyes clamped shut, he held onto Wakulla's arm with one hand, while wiping the stinging moisture from his eyes with the other. Wakulla's eyes, however, were wide open.

When Jamal opened his eyes again, he looked over at his brother. It was clear to him that Wakulla had been spooked by something and it wasn't just because of the huge wave that had crashed into the boat. He had seen that look before and he knew it wasn't good. The last time his brother acted this way he wound up going into convulsions, flailing his arms and legs around on the floor, as if the devil himself had taken over his body.

"This is not good," Jamal muttered. "This is not good at all."

All of a sudden, there was a low, guttural roar and the sea opened up about ten yards ahead of them. Within seconds, the water spread out and down, creating a large circular crater filled with dark green, gaseous fumes.

Foreboding, hideous black clouds rushed in, surrounding them in pitch darkness, as the tiny boat edged forward toward the gigantic gaping hole in the sea. Both Jamal and Wakulla were coughing and gasping for air.

"Dumala! Dumala!" a deep raspy voice shouted to the heavens from beneath the sea. "Dumala!" it yelled again, only much louder this time.

As the boat inched closer to the black hole in the ocean, more foreign words were being shouted to the heavens, getting louder and louder by the second. It was an unknown language to both of them, or at least that's what Wakulla told Jamal, as the two of them cowered in each other's arms on the deck of the tiny boat.

"Who's there?" Jamal screamed. "Who's there and what do you want?"

All he got in return was more ear-piercing shouting

and more crazy sounding words being spewed toward the heavens.

Wakulla suddenly stood up and Jamal watched in horror as his brother faced the beast. He could barely see through the dark fog, but he knew it was happening again. Wakulla was going to succumb to violent convulsions at any second. He was already in a trance. As the beastly voice continued shouting from the depths of the sea, Wakulla's arms and legs began to shake.

Just then, another huge wave of seawater crashed against the side of the boat, this time tipping the craft over to a ninety-degree angle. Both Wakulla and Jamal were tossed into the sea, which brought Wakulla back to his senses. Neither one of them were wearing life vests and Wakulla watched in horror as his brother fell helplessly into the crater of nothingness, which was now only inches away from the overturned boat.

"Dumala!" the thing shouted again. "Dumala! Dumala!"

In a flash of bright purple light the boat suddenly up-righted itself. Seconds later, the sea closed up again and returned to a flat, motionless body of water. Wakulla began swimming back toward the boat, finally grabbing onto the motor, so he could hoist himself onboard.

"Jamal! Jamal! Where are you?" he cried out. Jamal!"

Frantically, he searched the waters, but there was no sign of his brother. Two heart-wrenching hours later, he finally gave up looking. His brother had simply vanished into some otherworldly place; some evil, dark place beneath the sea.

Wracked with grief and scared out of his wits, Wakulla had no choice but to head back home. All thoughts of poaching lobsters and shrimp had been banished from his mind. Only one thing mattered now. He had to get away from this wicked place out in the middle of the sea. He had to get home to save his family from certain doom.

As he neared the coastline three hours later, still in a

state of shock and mumbling words that he thought he had long forgotten, a frightening sight appeared just ahead of him. It was a Coast Guard patrol boat with four gun barrels aimed at his head.

CHAPTER 5

Natural Beauty
stirring my soul with longing
my words are useless
no description brings justice
to the way you make me feel
©dp

"Well, hey there, Becky. You caught me on my way out the door. What's up?" Carl asked, sounding anxious to get off the phone.

Carl Edwards was the handsome weatherman from WNCN News in Charlotte and he and Becky had been telephone friends for more than nineteen years. They had never met in person, but one would never know it from the way they conversed with one another.

"Did you hear the news? Are you going to Miami?" she asked him, sounding enthused, yet frantic at the same time.

"What's going on in Miami? Another hurricane?" he asked, laughing. "Come on, Becky, it's too early for hurricanes. It's only the middle of May."

"No, silly, it's not a hurricane...not yet, anyway," she said. "It's some crazy Haitian they found out in the Gulf, who keeps babbling about some evil spirit that sucked his brother down into the sea."

"Ohhh, I get it. My producer put you up to this," he said, obviously not believing her for a second. "Look, Becky, I'm really in a hurry. If I don't get to the restaurant in time, my girlfriend will have my 'you know what' for dinner, instead of steak and lobster. I really gotta run. You go take care of that crazy Haitian and get back to me with your findings. Later, kid," he said, and he hung up.

"Aaghhh!   Carl, you idiot!" she screamed, as she slammed down the receiver. "Why won't you *ever* learn to trust me?!"

Becky Rogers was a beautiful, vibrant young woman in her early thirties and for the past twelve years she had been a staunch supporter of Greenpeace, the world's leader in environmental protection issues. She had been actively and personally involved in their campaigns for the last six years. Her main fascination, however, was the subject of weather patterns and their effect on the environment, which had been undergoing drastic changes over the last century.

Many hours were spent with her eyes and ears glued to the television set, watching and listening intently to global warming issues being argued back and forth by scientists, scholars and naysayers.   She had also done extensive research on the Internet, as well as read dozens of books on the subject that were available at the local library.

Another thing that had her spellbound was the Brad Pitt-lookalike weather forecaster, Carl Edwards. She had fallen in love with him when she was a child, watching the evening news with her parents.   Their relationship, of course, was purely a platonic one and even though she had begged him on the phone hundreds of times to meet in person, he would never succumb to her requests. Since he was twenty-four years older than her, she figured that fact alone probably had a lot to do with him not wanting to meet her up close and personal.

From time to time, over the years, she would contact him, either by phone or e-mail, and ask him questions regarding his weather predictions and insights, especially when she disagreed with him.   On more than a few occasions, she adamantly contradicted his forecasts, and to his admitted amazement afterward, her predictions turned out to be correct.

The first time she called him at the station was two days after her thirteenth birthday.   At that time, Carl was fresh out of college and he had miraculously landed the lead weather anchor spot at WNCN, North Carolina's premier weather channel. She found out years later that his uncle owned the station. One day he broke down and told her what had happened the first time she called him.

Being his first day on the job, Carl merely thought someone in his department was playing a joke on him. After all, he thought, a little girl calling in to correct him about one of his weather predictions?   It was preposterous.

"Ha!" he thought at the time, and he blew it off as just that, a practical joke on the new guy.

After work that day, he had stopped in at his favorite sports bar to have a few drinks with his old cronies from college and he got a kick out of telling them that someone had put a little kid up to calling in with a ridiculous weather prediction. The next day, however, when her prediction proved to be true, he felt duly humiliated, yet totally impressed.

"Impossible!" he told everyone at the station. "How could she have known?!"

He told her he was on pins and needles waiting for her to call back, but it was weeks before he would hear her voice again. Even though there was that wide age gap between them, he eventually took her under his wing when he realized she was somehow making profound connections that he couldn't explain.

For years he had told her that she was just a child, who had a special sense of the weather and the earth, and that her environmental convictions were extremely noble. He also told her that the world could use more people like her. He called her gift a unique spiritual connection to the universe, because she had no formal training in meteorology.

"It's just instinct," he had insisted from the beginning.

There was one thing he was certain of, though, and he had told her time and time again.

"You truly love the planet, because to you, it is a

living, breathing entity, responsible for sustaining life to all humanity and animals," he told her. "Without a healthy, thriving planet, the civilized world will eventually crumble. That is what you believe, Becky."

She, on the other hand, felt that it was a gift from God that she possessed. It was her calling; one that she had received from the Holy Spirit. She had always been keenly aware of how dangerously close mankind was to damaging the planet, especially when she started doing her own research as a teenager. She knew that soon the environment would be beyond the point of no return, and she wasn't afraid to speak her mind.

Aside from her parents and Carl's occasional pep talks, there was one person in particular who had shaped Becky Rogers into the woman she was today. He was a remarkable man by the name of Abraham Gutierrez, who lived just a few miles from her on the other side of Jubilee Falls. She first met him when she was ten years old and they became instant friends.

Not only was he the minister of her church, but he was also a missionary, who had unorthodox theories about God and the Universe. Aside from teaching her the literal meaning of the Bible, he also taught her about Rhema words, which are sudden inspirational words that give insight into spiritual matters. Those teachings alone, she felt were most likely the reason behind the majority of her thoughts and actions.

There had been many times over the years when she had resorted to unorthodox methods herself, in order to garner the attention of individuals or corporations that were harming the planet.

Many officials in high places were well aware of her unconventional ways of gaining attention for environmental causes. Now, when she was trying to convince the media, as well as the government that something prodigious had been happening completely unnoticed right before their eyes for years, all they were doing was ignoring her. Most of them simply chalked it up as Becky Rogers, the troublemaker, trying to pull off one of her old tricks again. Thus, they all dismissed her as a fanatic and a freak and a few of them even threatened to have her thrown in jail.

All she was trying to do was save the planet from certain ruin. She longed for the olden days when her ancestors, the Native American Indians, roamed North America and lived with the earth as one, only taking what was needed and not wasting a thing. They respected their natural world and they only killed animals for food to sustain life, not for the thrill of the kill, or just for sport. Humanity throughout the years since then had been reeling out of control for much too long, and it was time to put a stop to it.

"Mom, I'm leaving! My cab should be here any minute!" Becky shouted up the staircase the following morning. "Come say goodbye!"

While she waited on her mother to come down, she decided to grab a sweater from the downstairs coat closet, just in case the weather decided to turn cold again. It had been hard to tell lately what the weather was going to do. One day it would be a steamy ninety degrees and the next day it would dip down into the fifties.

About two minutes later, her mother came rushing down the stairs, huffing and puffing, holding a dust rag in one hand and a bottle of Pledge in the other. In the mean time, Becky had gone into the kitchen to wolf down the remainder of her breakfast.

"Rebecca Suzanne Rogers," Ida started, which always made Becky cringe when her mother called her by her full name. "Where on earth do you think you're going this time?" she asked.

"Mom, didn't you hear anything I said last night? I'm going to Miami," she reminded her, after she swallowed her daily dose of vitamins with a glass of orange juice.

"But, honey, we've got the church social tomorrow afternoon. Will you be back by then?"

"I'll try to be, Mom, but quite honestly, I don't think so."

"Oh, dear," her mother fretted, as she twisted the

dust rag into a knot. "Well, I suppose I could get Lilly over here to pick me up. She's half blind, you know, and she can only hear out of one ear."

"Mom, quit worrying. Lilly can drive through these mountains blindfolded. You two will be just fine," Becky said, stifling a laugh.

Becky and her mother lived alone in a sprawling four-bedroom log cabin in Jubilee Falls, North Carolina, just off the Blue Ridge Parkway. Twenty three years ago when Becky was ten years old, her parents had decided they wanted to move away from the noise of the city, since they had both grown up in the country and they missed the quiet and the privacy that went along with it.

So, after months and months of house hunting, they both fell in love with the spacious log cabin, especially the way it was constructed against the side of the mountain. It was a bit isolated with only about five other neighbors nearby, but for Becky, as a young child, it was also like living in Heaven on Earth.

The forests surrounding them were filled with an abundance of virgin hemlock, white pine, hickory, oak and birch trees, as well as colorful varieties of dogwood trees. Then, there were also the gorgeous violets and assorted wildflowers in every color of the spectrum. During springtime, especially, Becky felt as if she was living in the middle of Sherwood Forest, or at least one of those forests she had read about in storybooks when she was a child. Everything was in bloom and the mountainside looked as if it had been spray painted in vivid rainbow colors.

Over the years, she had hiked every single wilderness trail in the surrounding three counties at least once. Her photo albums were jam packed with pictures of the magnificent scenery, along with the different species of wildlife that roamed through the mountains and the thick wooded valleys. Her favorite shots, though, were the ones of the numerous waterfalls in the area, especially Jubilee Falls, which was less than half a mile from the cabin.

As far back as she could remember, her father had always said he wanted to know what it would feel like to glide down the forty-five foot drop into the lower falls area. Of course, it was much too dangerous with all the sharp rocks jutting out, so he never attempted it, as far as she or her mother knew.

Two years ago he died of a sudden stroke. It was totally unexpected because he had always been in excellent health and it truly devastated both her and her mother. His final wishes were to be cremated and then he wanted half of his remains scattered across the upper pond of Jubilee Falls. He told Becky that was the only way he would ever get to experience the thrill of the fall, as he referred to it. The remaining ashes, he had told both his wife and daughter, they could do with as they pleased, since he had no preference.

So, on a beautiful spring day when all the trees and flowers were in full bloom, Becky trekked up to Jubilee Falls with the urn in one hand and a small shovel in the other. Her mother told her she would have to handle things alone because there was no way she could hike up the mountain with her arthritic knees. Becky wasn't pleased about handling it by herself, but she told her mother she understood. In all honesty, she knew the real reason was that her mother simply wasn't up to it emotionally.

It was probably the most difficult thing she had ever done in her life, but she managed to get through it without totally breaking down. That is, until she watched his ashes free fall forty-five feet down into the pond below her. Then, it was big time waterfall city, as tears streamed down her face nonstop for a good thirty minutes afterward.

It was Becky's idea to bury the remaining half of his ashes in a shallow grave about thirty yards from the falls. Since her mother didn't object, that's what she set out to do next. As she was digging the hole, she happened upon a shiny gold object deep in the soil. It was solidly in the ground and she really had to tug on it to release it from the intertwining roots of a nearby tree. Just as she was about to give up and find a different place to dig the hole, whatever it was that was buried in the dirt, finally pulled free completely intact.

It turned out to be a gold neck chain and dangling from it was a round pendant with three inlaid stones. The chain was dirty and tarnished and twisted in knots, and the chain links were encrusted with dirt and residue, but she thought it looked as if it might be 18-carat gold. On the back side were the initials M.D., along with some other words that had been scratched through until they were illegible. It made her wonder if it was some sort of medical alert identification necklace that someone had lost. To find its owner, she knew would be an impossible task, especially since she had no idea how long it had been buried. So, she decided to take it home, clean it up, and wear it herself, since it truly was a stunning piece of jewelry.

Once she properly buried her father's remaining ashes, she said a prayer and she returned his empty urn to her mother, who then placed it above the fireplace mantel in the living room. It remained in the same exact spot to this day.

While Becky was washing her breakfast dishes and still listening to her mother complain about Lilly and her driving, a horn suddenly honked out on the street in front of the cabin.

"Ohh, there's the taxi, Mom. I gotta go," Becky said.

After she dried her hands, she gave her mother a quick hug and a kiss before grabbing her purse and her luggage, which she had stacked by the front door.

"Well, you be careful, young lady," her mother warned her, as she was walking out the door. "And stay out of trouble this time."

"Mom, you worry way too much. I'll call you when I get settled into my hotel room," Becky said, and with that, she rushed out to the waiting cab.

"Bye, sweetheart! I love you!" her mother shouted to her.

"I love you, too, Mom! Bye!"

Becky knew her mother had no clue what she was up to and she figured it was better that way, at least for the time being. She rarely showed any interest in the environmental issues that Becky had been involved with over the years, but she knew if she told her about this latest weather phenomenon she was chasing it would have freaked her out. Consequently, she kept quiet about it.

After tracking this storm for weeks, using a variety of sources, including the Internet, she was certain that something deadly was about to happen. She was even more certain when she heard about the crazy Haitian's claims that the sea had not only swallowed his brother alive, but that it also spoke to him.

Becky's problem was, and had always been, that she couldn't get anyone to listen to her, or even take the slightest interest in any of her findings. Everyone she had spoken to about this storm, including the dashing Carl Edwards, told her she was insane, but in her heart, she knew her facts were accurate, no matter how outrageous and farfetched they sounded.

With the sophisticated computer program she bought on the black market last year from a fellow tree hugger, who worked for the E.P.A., she was able to track the freak storm that had formed off the northwest coast of Africa near Morocco; a place that historically had never spawned a hurricane.

It wasn't an ordinary hurricane, though. Only thirty feet in circumference, it had some sort of divine power to go unnoticed by climatologists, but it also had even more unexplainable powers, the likes of which no human had ever witnessed before.

As it was gathering steam within its core, it stayed in a stationary position in a remote river pond in the jungles of Africa. Once it gained the power it needed for its journey, it began slithering westward, crawling across the North Atlantic Ocean at less than one mile per hour towards the United States, its ultimate target. Weeks later, the tiny eye of the storm wormed its way into the Manasquan Inlet off the state of New Jersey, miraculously doing so against the currents.

Then, it traveled south down the Intracoastal Waterway at tremendous speed, until it met up with the Okefenokee Swamp just above Fargo, Georgia, utilizing an unknown underground aquifer. From there, it traversed down through the winding Suwannee River, feeding off the high nutrients in the water, until it exited into the Gulf of Mexico, a few miles north of Cedar Key. That was the last time Becky could get any readings, until yesterday, when it suddenly reappeared out in the middle of the Gulf of Mexico, before falling off the radar again hours later. When she heard Wakulla's unbelievable story, she knew it was connected to this storm somehow, some way.

"Why won't anyone believe me? Do they really think I'm just a kook? Dammitall!" she thought, as the taxi sped down the narrow, winding road into town.

She was on her way to Avery County Airport to catch a puddle-jumper over to Raleigh-Durham for the trip down to Miami. Even now, as she re-hashed the entire scope of this strange phenomenon, she had no doubts as to the legitimacy of her vision, as well as the accuracy of her tedious research, especially after she watched an in-depth story on Fox News last night about the Haitian's oddball claims, as they referred to it.

During those weeks tracking the storm, she was awestruck at the continuing saga of events that seemed to be following it. All the while the storm was threading its way through the southeast sector of the United States, it was terrorizing boaters, canoeists and river rafters. When those people were interviewed, however, all of them wound up retracting their statements. Most of them admitted to having too much to drink and that they must have been hallucinating. The media, of course, agreed with them, but they obviously thought it made for interesting news coverage.

Then, there were the extraordinary phenomena's,

such as river currents suddenly shifting course, fish that were racing the wrong way upstream, and sudden spurts of hail on a cloudless, scorching hot day that never made it into the mainstream news. They were all over the Internet, though. Nobody, however, had the sense to inter-connect all these events to this one powerful storm. They were all treated as separate incidents, and most of the stories were regarded as phony tales from drunkards or druggies. It amazed her that people could be so stupid. It also astounded her that no one had even the slightest inkling about the power of this storm or its fatal intentions.

"Am I the only one with a functioning brain in this country?" she wondered. "Am I the only one who can see this storm and what it's trying to do?"

CHAPTER 6

Shattered
A whole piece shattered
A thousand splinters scattered
Irreparable
©dp

"**H**oly crap," Mickey mouthed, as he read through an article on CNN's news website. "What in God's name is going on?"

It had been reported by several eyewitnesses that off the southeastern coast of the United States and all along the Florida straits, sunken ships were rising to the surface. More than two dozen decades-old military vessels and pirate ships that had been sunk out in the ocean to serve as artificial reefs were floating to the surface in huge chunks of twisted metal and rotting wood.

Dead fish were washing up along the beaches and strange looking birds that no one could identify were free floating in the surf, scaring away beachgoer's and prompting the closing of all the beaches along the coast from the Florida Keys up to Nova Scotia.

Another headline that caught his eye was an article about an illegal Haitian immigrant who had been rescued out in the Gulf of Mexico yesterday. It only took a few sentences before Mickey got completely caught up in the story.

The photo of the forty-four-year-old man was frightening to look at. He was thin and haggard, and he looked as if he was a hundred years old, especially around the eyes. The reporter who wrote the story said that the guy's name was Wakulla. That was it. No last name, no nothing, just Wakulla.

As Mickey got deeper into the story, his interest skyrocketed. Seconds later, when he saw the word Dumala, though, his heart skipped a few beats. Dumala, in ancient Aboriginal dialect meant Armageddon.

Armageddon, of course, was synonymous with "end of time" prophecies; the place, according to ancient Hebrew literature, where an epic battle would take place before the Millennium. The Battle of Armageddon, fire and brimstone, Satan...it was all too Biblically frightening to even think about.

Just then, his eyes drifted down to the bottom of the computer screen.

"Oh, crap," he said, when he saw the date on his computer monitor. "Today is May twenty-first, 2012."

Nostradamus, the most famous author of prophecy, had predicted the end of the world to be December twenty-first of 2012. Mickey had done extensive research on the man and his prophecies when he was in college, and he had a fair amount of respect for all his predictions, many of which had come true.

"Hey, Mickey! Come down here!" Brent yelled from the kitchen.

"Oh, shoot," Mickey mumbled. "What now?"

"Son! Get your ass down here now!" his father continued shouting.

"I'll be right there!" Mickey yelled back to him, wondering what all the hoopla was about this time. "Sheesh, Dad, I'm not deaf," he muttered, as he rushed down the spiral staircase.

As soon as he stepped into the kitchen it was clear to him why his father was freaking out. Through the six-foot wide shadowbox window he could see water lapping up against the barn, which was only forty yards away from the back porch.

"What's going on, son?" Brent asked. "I ain't seen the river this high since 1986. And hell, it ain't rained in days."

"I don't know, Dad, but there certainly seems to be a

lot of strange things happening lately."

Against his better judgment, he told his father about the whitecap he thought he saw the night before, and just as he figured, his dad blamed it on the beer. When he told him the story about what was going on down in the Gulf of Mexico, though, his father changed his tune.

"What did you say that man's name was? Wakulla?" Brent asked him.

"Yeah, Wakulla. Why?"

"Well, there's a county by that name over near Tallahassee."

"Yes, I know," Mickey said.

"It was named after a word that the Timucuan Indian tribe used. It stands for 'spring of water'."

"It also means 'mysterious water', Dad," Mickey interjected.

"Now, how do you suppose a man from Haiti wound up with a name like that?" Brent asked.

"That's a very good question. Kinda spooky, if you ask me."

Just then, the phone started ringing and Mickey went into the living room to answer it.

"Well, I'll be darned! Johnny, you old coot! I haven't heard from you in what? Ten years?" Mickey asked his old college buddy.

"Something like that," Johnny said.

He and Johnny Evans used to be best friends and drinking buddies when they were attending Florida State University. Right after graduation, Johnny got a job working at an insurance firm in downtown Tallahassee. That was where he met a sweet, young girl named Jill Stevens. They dated for almost six years before he finally popped the question. Then, no sooner did Jill have the ring on her finger, than she whisked Johnny off to her hometown of Kansas City, where they proceeded to have one baby after the next. Mickey hadn't heard from him since.

"How many kids do you have now?" Mickey asked him, laughing, and expecting to hear him say at least twelve.

"Oh, we stopped at five. The last two were twins, a boy and a girl. I told Jill we couldn't afford any more after that surprising birth."

"You mean you didn't know you were having twins?"

"Nope, Jill wouldn't allow the doctor to tell us. You know how she is. She just loves surprises."

"So, how have you been otherwise?" Mickey asked, and then he plopped down into the recliner, knowing it was going to be a long conversation.

"Why don't we just cut the crap, Mickey? Are you going to Miami, or what?"

"Ahh, so you heard, too. I don't know, Johnny. Do you think it's worth my time to go talk to some crazy man? I mean...think about it. How likely is it that a body of water could speak? He and his brother were probably out there smoking crack or whatever the latest drug craze is now."

"That could be, but what about all the other stuff that's been going on? All those artificial reefs that came to the surface, and all those sightings on the rivers and the Intracoastal."

"I read about the reefs, but I didn't hear about those other things," Mickey said. "You know how the news gets suppressed these days. Plus, you gotta remember, I live in the sticks and I don't own a television."

"Oh, yeah, that's right," Johnny said. "How can you not own a T.V.?"

"It's very simple, Johnny. You don't buy one," he said, laughing. "Oh, and you have an old man like mine, who still lives in the dark ages."

"I don't know how you do it, man."

"Sometimes I don't either," Mickey said. "So, do you think all these strange phenomena's are connected somehow?"

"Could be," Johnny said. "By the way, have you checked your yard lately?"

"Other than the fact the Suwannee River is about to become the new flooring in my house, no. Why?"

"Well, all around here in Tallahassee..." he started, but Mickey cut him off.

"You're back in Tallahassee?"

"Heck, yeah! I couldn't stand that damned cold weather one more day. Me, Jill and the kids moved back here two years ago."

"Well, what do you know? We'll have to get together soon."

"Yeah, soon," Johnny said. "Anyway, back to the yard. It seems my entire neighborhood is being overrun by moles and gophers. There's millions of them all over the place. It's like they've taken over or something. When I first saw it, I thought an army of backhoe brigadier's had just attacked the town."

"Really? Dang! That is strange."

"It's more than strange, Mickey. What's even weirder is that it all happened overnight. And that isn't all. We've been getting bombarded with bird poop from these oddball-looking birds. They almost look like Dodo birds."

"Oh, that's ridiculous. Dodo birds have been extinct since the late 17th century," Mickey told him.

"I'm tellin' you, that's what they look like. I took pictures of them. If you want, I'll e-mail them to you."

"Well, mankind made sure those Dodo's would go down in the history books as an extinct species when they destroyed the forests where the birds called home," Mickey said, wondering if his friend had been hitting the sauce a little too hard.

"Yep, mankind can certainly do stupid shit, huh?"

"You got that right," Mickey said, wholeheartedly agreeing with him. "And yes, e-mail me those pictures when you get a chance."

"Will do," he said. "I'm hitting the send button right now. So, are you going to Miami, or what?"

"After all you just told me, I may just have to. How could I pass up the opportunity to watch history in the making? And on such a grand scale!"

"Oops, I gotta run, man. That's Jill trying to call," Johnny said, when he heard the call waiting beep in his ear.

"Okay, but stay in touch. We'll get together real soon," Mickey said, and they hung up.

Meanwhile, Brent had gone out to the barn to talk to Jockey Joe, who had just pulled up with a truckload of pine straw to store in the barn.

Mickey decided to head back upstairs to his computer to check out some of the phenomena that Johnny had just told him about. As soon as he sat down, his e-mail inbox started bleeping at him. When he switched over to the program he counted about forty messages from friends and colleagues, whom he hadn't had any contact with in years, including the one Johnny just sent. Every one of them asked him the same question: "Are you going to Miami?"

"Sheesh! I guess I have no freakin' choice!" he shouted, especially after he saw the pictures of the birds in Johnny's yard.

Now, he had a decision to make. Could he really fly off to Miami and leave his father unattended? There had to be someone who could stay with him, or some neighbor's house where he could drop him off for a few days, but where?

CHAPTER 7

Soft
A soft velvet petal
Carried by a delicate summer breeze
Floats aimlessly across new mown grass
Until she fades out of sight
Unobtrusively
Her essence now becoming
A mere memory
©dp

"**H**i, Mom, I'm here," Becky said, when her mother finally answered the phone on the fourteenth ring.

"Well, it's about time you called. I was getting worried about you," Ida reprimanded her.

"I told you, Mom, you worry too much, especially about me. I'm fine. I've always been fine."

"That's a matter of opinion," Ida continued.

"All right, all right. Go ahead and worry yourself sick. It's not going to change anything," Becky told her, with a heavy, exhausted sigh. "By the way, did you get in touch with Lilly?" she asked, trying to change the subject. "I already know that I'm going to be here for a few days, so I won't be able to take you to the church social."

"Oh, I got in touch with her all right, since I knew you'd be staying down there for a while," Ida said, obviously knowing her daughter better than anyone. "She wasn't happy about having to drive a couple of extra miles to pick me up, but I plied her with some of my rhubarb pie and she caved in," she added, laughing.

"Oh, that's good news. You two will be just fine and please tell Pastor Gutierrez that I'm sorry I won't be able to make it tomorrow night. Will you do that for me, please?" she asked.

"I'll tell him," Ida said. "I'll also tell him to have a good long chat with you when you get back home. Somebody needs to talk some sense into you about all this craziness you've been involved in lately."

"Mom, I'm afraid you won't get any consolation from the preacher. He agrees with me about a lot of this stuff. Besides, you really don't have a clue what I'm working on, now, do you?"

"Hrmphh," Ida grunted, and after they both said their 'I love you's' and 'goodbye's', the two women hung up.

"Okay, now...it's time to get to work," Becky said, truly excited and anxious about what may lie ahead of her, if she could only get through to some people on the phone, that is.

It only took her a few minutes to get her laptop set up and tapped into the wireless high-speed Internet service that the hotel provided free of charge. While she waited for all her programs to load, she plugged in her wireless printer and loaded it with half a ream of paper.

Comfort Suites, where she had booked a room, was centrally located to all the places she needed to go, including the National Hurricane Center and Florida International University, where one of her friends from high school worked as a teacher. Somehow, she knew she'd be needing library resources to convince certain people of the impending danger and F.I.U. had one of the best libraries in the state.

The immigration detention facilities would be a bit of a hike farther south, but with the brand new, convertible rental car she had splurged on, it would at least be a scenic drive with oodles of sunshine beating down on her Vitamin D deprived body.

"Geez, I'm getting hungry," she mumbled, as she rubbed her gurgling stomach. "That frozen waffle I had for breakfast is long gone from my system."

Earlier, right after she checked in, and even before she unloaded her suitcases, she had tried calling the local immigration officials to get an appointment to speak to

Wakulla, but she couldn't get anyone to answer the phone. It was a maze of automated prompts for a good five minutes, until she finally hung up. She tried the local police department, too, but all they did was laugh at her.

Now, it was time to try one last person; Eric Donley, the Director of Operations at the National Hurricane Center. When the operator put her through to his office, a man by the name of Jeremy Baxter answered. She told him her name, as well as a little bit about her research and her findings on the storm she was tracking. He, too, chuckled at first. After telling him a few more details, though, she thought he at least halfway believed what she was saying. Once he drilled her again on who she was and what she wanted, she sensed that he began to relax, at least a little bit. After a while they were chatting freely, until soon, he opened up a bit about himself.

"I'm actually a NASA scientist," he told her, which immediately impressed her. "I'm just here visiting an old friend and I picked up a ringing phone. I do that a lot. I can't stand to hear a telephone just keep ringing and ringing and ringing."

"I know what you mean," she said, recalling the three phone calls she had made earlier. "Ummm, Mr. Baxter..." she started, trying a last ditch effort at name-dropping to maybe score some points with the guy.

"Please, call me Jeremy," he said, and she could actually hear the smile in his voice.

"Oh, okay...Jeremy. Do you, by any chance, know Carl Edwards, the infamous weather forecaster from North Carolina?"

"Carl? Well, hell, yeah! He and I go way back. We went to school together back in Raleigh. Hey, would ya lookie there? Small world, isn't it?" he asked her, and suddenly she could hear the southern drawl in his voice that he had been trying to conceal.

"Have you spoken to him recently?" she asked.

"As a matter of fact, I talked with him this morning," he said, and then there was a brief silence on the line. "He told me what you've been up to, in case you were wondering. In fact, he told me all about you and your *gifts*," he added, emphasizing the word 'gifts', as if he was skeptical.

"Oh, I see," she said, feeling disheartened again and expecting to be brushed off by yet another high-ranking official. "Is there any chance I could talk to the director?" she asked anyway.

"He's not here at the moment, but I'll tell you what," he said, all of a sudden sounding as if he was flirting with her. "Give me your number and I'll get back to you sometime tomorrow, okay?"

"Oh, okay, sure," she said, and she rattled off her cellular number, as well as the number for the hotel.

"Maybe we can get together over dinner," he suggested, which totally caught her off guard.

"Dinner?" she asked, in a voice that could not have been mistaken for anything other than shocked surprise.

"Sure, why not? I know some darned good restaurants in the area. Maybe Carl will join us, too," he said.

"Carl? Carl is here?" she gasped.

"He's due in late this evening, actually. Didn't he tell you he was coming?"

"No, he didn't. I didn't think he believed me about this storm."

"Eh, that's Carl for you. Never was one to admit when someone was smarter than him, especially if it was a girl," he said, laughing.

Becky laughed, too, although it was more of a nervous tic than genuine amusement. She couldn't believe that after all these years she might finally be meeting the man she had been infatuated with since she was a teenager.

Suddenly, she heard a lot of commotion going on in the background. People were yelling and cursing, and then the phone started cutting in and out with noisy static.

"Jeremy, what's going on? Are you still there?" she asked.

"Yeah, I'm here, but I gotta run. It looks like all the computers just went haywire," he said, and before she could respond, the line went dead.

"Whatever," she mumbled, as she hung up the phone. "Just don't forget to call me back tomorrow."

Her stomach started growling again, so she figured she'd better go eat something before she passed out from hunger. Earlier, the concierge had suggested she try the hotel dining room, claiming they served the best seafood in town. Rather than risk getting lost in a strange city after dark, that's where she decided to go.

First, however, she had one more phone call to make. Oddly or not, she was put through immediately to Captain Jake Richards at the Miami Beach Coast Guard Station. He was the one who had spoken to the media about Wakulla and he was the one Becky needed to speak to, in order to gain access to Wakulla at the immigration center. The captain agreed to meet with her at eight the next morning.

MEANWHILE, MICKEY DE ROSA had just checked in downstairs and he was being shown to his room on the tenth floor, which happened to be two doors down from Becky's.

Thankfully, Jockey Joe, after only some minor begging on Mickey's part, had agreed to take care of his father for a few days. At the very least, he promised to look in on him occasionally. Mickey's major concern was the rising river that could possibly strand his father out in the middle of nowhere. Joe told him not to worry and that if things got too bad he would definitely take his father to higher ground.

Mickey, of course, knew it would take at least six men and a bulldozer to get his dad to evacuate, but he also knew how persuasive Joe could be, if necessary.

"Is there anything else I can get for you?" the concierge asked, as he and Mickey stood in the hallway outside his room.

"No, I think that should do it," Mickey said, and he

handed the guy a five-dollar bill.

"Thank you, sir," the concierge said, and he turned and started back toward the elevator.

Just as Mickey was about to shut his door, he heard noises out in the hallway, so he poked his head out to take a look.

"Holy crap," he said under his breath, when he spotted Becky coming out of her room.

With her long, chestnut brown hair laying softly on her shoulders, and her toned hourglass figure clearly defined through her skintight designer jeans and rib knit sweater, he found himself getting aroused for the first time in years. Then, when she turned and smiled at him, he thought for sure he was going to have an accident of massive proportions right there in front of her.

"Whoo-whee!" he thought, as he watched her walk away. "This trip may just turn out to be halfway worth it, after all."

CHAPTER 8

Pearl
Iridescent pearl
Amidst a sea of turquoise
Elegant beauty
©dp

"Excuse me, miss, are you all right?" Jules, the waiter asked, as he passed by Becky's table.

"Huh?" she mumbled, and then she looked up at the five-foot-ten young man who was dripping in pheromones and looking at her like he wanted to do her right there on top of the table. "Oh, yes, I'm fine. I'm just fine," she said, and then she watched him walk away.

She wasn't fine, though. She was spooked. Directly across from where she was sitting in the back of the restaurant was a framed artist's painting hanging on the wall that had her mesmerized. She had been staring at it for so long that it had put her into a trance, which is why the hunky waiter asked her if she was all right.

"I must have looked like an alien zombie," she thought, as she rubbed her eyes, trying to get her wits about her again.

As hungry as she had been when she first sat down, she was having a hard time trying to swallow the broiled fish she had ordered; not that it wasn't the most delicious mahi-mahi she had ever tasted, but after a few bites, a strange feeling washed over her and she felt almost impious, as if she was desecrating one of God's creatures by eating it.

The painting was what prompted those feelings. She was sure of it. It was a rough sketch of an ancient Mayan map that was done in charcoal. Surrounding it on all four sides were at least three dozen odd-looking symbols. What caught her eye was the dark black line that weaved in and around certain areas of the map. Parts of it were shaded in varying degrees of blacks and grays.

Outlines of dolphins that were interconnected with one another formed three sides of the border, with the fourth side eerily missing something. From a distance it looked like something profound, but she couldn't quite piece it all together. She knew, of course, that the dolphins in the sketch and the dolphin on her plate weren't the same type of fish, but it freaked her out just the same.

"I have to eat something," she mumbled. "If I don't, I'll never get any sleep tonight."

With that, she pushed aside the entrée plate and instead, she concentrated on wolfing down her Caesar salad and the entire loaf of warm Pumpernickel bread that had been enticing her since the waiter set it down on the table.

After that, she picked at the rice pilaf and steamed vegetables, and as much as she wanted the fish, she just couldn't bring herself to eat it. Rather than deal with a barrage of questions from Jules as to what was wrong with the fish, she piled what was left of it inside her napkin. Then, she shoved it inside her purse, so she could dispose of it later, once she got back to her room.

After she paid her tab and Jules brought back her receipt, she figured it wouldn't hurt to ask him a question.

"Are any of these paintings for sale?" she queried him, as she pointed around the dining area.

"Oh, yes they are, miss. All of the paintings are for sale," he said, still grinning at her, as if he was undressing her with his eyes. "Is there one that you are interested in?"

"As a matter of fact, there is," she said, and then she stood up and walked over toward the one she'd been drooling over for the last forty-five minutes. "This one," she said.

"Ahh, a very nice choice," he said. "Do you know the artist?" he asked her.

"I'm not sure. Who is it?"

"His name is Andre Barringer. He lives here in town part of the year when he's not traveling."

While he was explaining about the famed artist, he was taking the picture down from the wall. On the back was the sticker showing the price of the painting.

"Are you certain you want to purchase this one? It's quite expensive," Jules told her, scrunching up his face as he read the dollar amount to himself.

"It can't be that expensive. How much?" she asked.

"Three-hundred and fifty dollars," he said. "Plus tax, of course," he smugly added.

"I'll take it," she said, even though she knew better than to put such a large purchase on her credit card.

She had to have it, though. As crazy as it sounded, somehow she knew there were answers within the drawing. Answers to all the questions she had about the freak storm playing havoc with the world.

Minutes later, with painting in hand, she hurried back to her room. Not only was she eager to get started with deciphering the drawing, but she needed to get the smelly fish out of her purse before it completely ruined the silk lining.

"Phew! This thing stinks!" she said, holding her nostrils shut, while she wrapped the fish-encrusted napkin in half a roll of toilet paper before putting it in the bathroom waste can.

After undressing and slipping into a comfy pair of pajamas, she started up her computer. As she was waiting for the wireless Internet to connect, she went into a sudden coughing and sneezing fit.

"What the heck?" she nearly screamed, wondering what brought on the attack, and then she smelled it. "That fish! That stinkin' fish is what's gagging me!"

Immediately, she went back into the bathroom and dug the wad of toilet paper out of the can. Next, she tossed it into the toilet and flushed ol' stinky down into the sewer.

"Dang! I'm glad I didn't eat but a few mouthfuls of that thing. Heck, that could be me right now, stinking up this entire room," she said, and then she started laughing. "Or tomorrow morning! Sheesh!"

She had to wash her hands three times before the odor washed away and it took nearly four flushes before all that toilet paper finally went down the pipes. There was a can of Lysol on the counter and she used up half it spraying the room from one end to the other before the smell of the rotted fish finally dissipated.

"Now, can I get back to work?" she mumbled, as she shut the bathroom door.

The next order of business was to remove the fake painting of beautiful, downtown Miami from the wall above the desk and replace it with Andre Barringer's sketch. For the next two hours, she diligently studied all her notes, as well as the minutely detailed map she had created with her graphics program. It showed the storm's path from its inception in Morocco to where it now sat idle in the middle of the Gulf of Mexico.

When she compared her map to the one in the sketch, however, she couldn't detect any similarities, other than perhaps one part of it where the black lines resembled a backward letter 'S'.

"This isn't making any sense," she said out loud. "What am I missing?"

By now, it was almost midnight and her eyes were growing weary. If she was going to make her early morning appointment on time, she knew she had to turn in and get some sleep. The last thing she wanted to do was to show up late and miss her chance to speak with Captain Jake Richards.

CHAPTER 9

Inviting

There's something in your voice
That is enticingly arousing
When you speak my name
It's much more than, inviting
If you were to seduce me
It wouldn't take much effort
Just whisper in my ear
For the undivided pleasure
©dp

"Well, Professor Wiggins, I was wondering when I'd hear from you," Mickey said through a mouthy yawn.

It was six o'clock in the morning, and after a restless, fitful night of sleep, he was finding it difficult to wake up now. For a few moments he forgot where he was, until his cell phone reminded him he was in a hotel room. He hadn't used the phone in years, other than those two times he had left Fishbend Creek. It was an older model phone, without all the fancy features that the majority of the population had been embracing for the past decade, but it served his purposes, for the most part.

"I'm sorry if I woke you, Mickey, but I need to borrow your brain for a bit," the professor said with a nervous chuckle. "It's about that Haitian guy, which I'm sure is the reason you're down here in Miami."

"Not a problem, Doc," Mickey said, addressing him by the pet name he remembered from his college days. "And you are correct. That's why I'm here."

"I hope you don't mind me calling you, especially so early in the morning, but I knew you'd be awake. You were always an early bird. I know it's been quite a while since we last spoke, too, and I'm sorry about that. I've just had a lot going on."

"Not to worry, Doc, and I don't mind the early call at all. By the way, did my father give you this number?" Mickey asked him, while stifling another yawn, and wondering how the professor knew he was in Miami.

"Yeah, and he's a feisty old man, isn't he?"

"That's as good an adjective as any I could think up," Mickey said, and they both had a good laugh.

After a quick catch-up of their lives since they last saw each other, Doc got to the point of his call.

"Would you be able to meet me at around nine o'clock this morning?" he asked.

"Yeah, sure. Where are you staying?" Mickey asked him.

"Oh, I guess I never told you. I moved to Miami Beach about two years ago. I decided to live out my retirement years in a warmer climate. Those north Florida winters seemed to be getting colder and colder every year."

"Yes, I've been kind of noticing that myself, and if it wasn't for the fact my father refuses to leave Fishbend Creek, I'd have been long gone years ago to Costa Rica, or at least somewhere closer to the equator."

"Mickey, I don't mean to rush you, but time is of the essence here. I'm going to be at the library over at the F.I.U. campus to meet an old colleague this morning, so if you could meet me there, I'd sure appreciate it."

"Sure thing, Doc. Nine o'clock it is. I'll be there."

After they hung up, Mickey ordered in breakfast from room service and then he took a quick shower. As soon as his sausages and eggs arrived, he devoured them like a ravenous wolf. Then, after he finished off an entire pot of coffee, he went downstairs to the conference center, so he could use one of their computers to check his e-mail.

Aside from not being up-to-date with a new fangled cell phone, he didn't own a laptop, either. The ten-year-old beast of a PC he used at home had always seemed to suffice for his needs, but suddenly, he was feeling out of the loop with technology, and it was beginning to disturb him.

After waiting more than thirty minutes for a computer terminal to open up, and seeing that no one was getting up to leave any time soon, he vowed to start shopping for a laptop as soon as he got back home. He even thought he might investigate his options for a new cellular phone; one that had e-mail capabilities and maybe a built-in compass, as well.

"Shoot, if I don't leave soon I'm going to be late for my meeting with the professor," he muttered, as he glared at his watch. "E-mail will just have to wait."

With that, he left the conference center and he started over toward the elevators. A quick glance outside the massive windows in the lobby assured him it was going to be a bright, sunny and warm day, which was something he'd been craving since winter set in more than six months ago.

He hadn't thought much about weather patterns lately, because the changes had been so subtle and gradual over the past several years. After Doc's comment earlier this morning, however, it made him stop and wonder for a moment if all the talk about global warming was actually becoming a stark reality.

The more he pondered the subject, the more he realized that the winters in Fishbend Creek seemed to be hanging around months longer than they used to. Years ago, it never got below fifty degrees until at least the latter part of December, and then by March the temperatures would be back up in the 90's. Lately, though, the mercury had been dipping into the mid-thirties in early September and not warming up until well into May or June.

"Hmmm...why am I just now noticing all of this?" he wondered. "Ahh...I know why. I live in Podunk. I live in a vacuous world of fantasy out in the middle of the woods," he thought, and then he threw his head back and laughed out loud, just as the elevator doors were opening less than a foot in front of him.

When the bell sounded it startled him and he jumped forward with his arms extended. The next thing he knew, he felt his hands grabbing onto something soft and warm.

"Ahem," Becky said, rolling her eyes at him, as if he was some kind of nut, standing all alone and laughing like a hyena.

When she cleared her throat again and rolled her eyes down to her chest, Mickey realized where his hands were and he immediately jerked them back. Becky then stepped out of the elevator and tugged at her blouse, straightening the collar around her neck.

"Ohh...I'm so sorry about that, miss," he said, as his face flushed a bright shade of red. "I wasn't laughing at you...and I didn't mean to grab your...I was just..."

"Whatever," she mumbled, and then she rushed past him toward the exit. "There sure are some strange people here in Miami and I just met one with a cue ball for a brain," she added, referring to Mickey's shaved head, as she hurried over to the valet.

Mickey, meanwhile, was still standing by the elevator doors with a sheepish look on his face, feeling like a complete dope, as he admired the beautiful young girl walking away from him. He soon realized that she was the same girl who was in the room two doors down from his.

"Sheesh, can you tell I'm from Hicksville?" he mumbled, and then he punched the button for the tenth floor. "Now, I'll never get her to talk to me."

Once he got back to his room, he made a pit stop in the bathroom, then he grabbed his briefcase, and he was out the door again in less than five minutes.

Aside from wanting to check his e-mail earlier, he also wanted to print out some of his old Mayan research papers that were posted on the web to take with him, so he could ask the professor some questions. Since he wasn't able to do that, he figured he'd just have to rely on his memory.

Yesterday, after he arrived at the airport, he decided

against renting a car because he didn't think he'd be in town long enough for it to be worth his while, but now he wished he had. It took a good twenty minutes after the hotel valet called for a cab before he finally saw the guy pull up out front.

Twenty minutes later, he found himself stuck in rush hour traffic, sitting in the backseat of a Yellow Cab taxi with no air conditioning, and being forced to listen to rap music that the young Hispanic driver was blasting on the stereo. By the time they pulled into the parking lot of the college campus, he had a royal headache, not to mention a much lighter wallet after forking over almost forty bucks for the chauffeured ride.

On his way up the steps to the library, his cell phone started ringing again and he was hoping it wasn't the professor calling to say he needed to cancel their meeting.

"Mickey, I'm really sorry to bother you..."

"Jockey Joe, is that you? You know, I think this is a first. You've never called me on my mobile phone before. What's up? I hope not the river," he jokingly said.

"As a matter of fact, that's why I'm calling. I've never seen anything like it before. The water is up past the back porch. It came rushing over the banks about twenty minutes ago. I got most of your stuff up off the deck, but I'm afraid your little bass boat got away. Don't worry, though. Once this water recedes I'll find that sucker."

"Holy, geez," Mickey gasped. "Is Dad all right?"

"Oh, heck, yeah, he's fine. He's upstairs with his binoculars watching all the debris as it floats down the river. Oops...I mean *up* the river."

"Huh?" Mickey asked.

"Yeah! It's the funniest thing. The water is running upstream. Don't ask me how, but it is," Joe said.

"That *is* weird," Mickey said, wondering if both Joe and his father had been hitting the sauce so early in the morning. "Can you two get out of there up to higher ground somewhere?"

"Well, we could have, if your damn boat hadn't floated away. The water's done flooded this whole area, and according to the neighbors, who haven't stopped calling for the last fifteen minutes, all the roads have been washed out, too. We're all stuck, Mickey."

"Do I need to head home?" Mickey asked him.

"I don't see any reason to. This old house is sturdy enough and high enough that I think we'll be safe. Besides, you wouldn't be able to get in here with the water up so high. Your dad's truck is floating around in the front yard, which, of course, really has him ticked him off, but heck...there wasn't much I could do about it."

"Well, if you're sure..."

"I'm sure, Mickey, and don't you worry too much. Just do your best to try and stop this thing, whatever it is, okay?"

"I'll do my best, Joe. Just keep a close eye on Dad. There's no telling what he might attempt. Just keep that BB gun away from him. You know how he acts when he gets riled up. He likes to take pot-shots at those squirrels from the upper balcony."

"Too late, Mickey. I hear him up there now," Joe said, and he started cracking up laughing.

"Oh, good God Almighty! Go up there and take that thing away from him, will you?"

"I'll try," Joe said, still laughing.

"If things get any worse, you call me, okay?"

"I will, I will," Joe said, and they hung up.

"Well, isn't this just great?" Mickey mumbled. "I knew I should have just stayed put. Damn!"

MEANWHILE, BECKY HAD BEEN trying all morning to decipher the map she had drawn, as well as the sketch in the painting, but she wasn't having much luck. Since she didn't want to lug the heavy framed piece of artwork around with her, she had taken a picture of it earlier with her digital camera and then she printed it out to take with her for her meeting with the Coast Guard captain.

Earlier, after checking on the storm's progress through her computer program, she noticed that it had completely disappeared off the radar for the umpteenth time since she started tracking it. All of a sudden, she wondered if she was just on a wild goose chase, or maybe she really had lost her mind. She was beginning to doubt herself and her gifts.

"I'll know a lot more after I speak to the captain," she said out loud, as she pulled into the parking lot of the Coast Guard base off the McArthur Causeway in Miami Beach.

She was stopped at the gate by three uniformed officers, asking her what her business was on base property. When she explained that she had an appointment with Captain Jake Richards, one of the officers went inside the guard shack and made a phone call. Seconds later, he came back to her car.

"I'm sorry, miss," he said. "The captain got called away on an emergency. He apologizes for the inconvenience."

"What? Oh, good grief!" she said. "Now, what? Can I make another appointment?"

"Yes, miss, you can. Just call the main headquarters and request another appointment," the young whippersnapper rattled off to her, as if he was a robot and had given the same instructions to hundreds of other people already this morning.

Knowing neither one of the guards was going to budge from following orders, Becky just smiled at them and said goodbye. Then, she backed the car up, so she could turn around.

"Crap," she muttered. "Dammitall! Why is nothing going right today? First that hunky-looking guy down the hall turns out to be some sort of laughing weirdo molester and now my appointment has been cancelled. What next?"

Just then, the bridge lights for the Intracoastal Waterway started flashing and traffic came to a dead stop. Soon, the bridge opened up to let four beautiful sailboats pass through.

"I wish I was on one of those boats right about now," she mumbled. "It would be a lot more fun than this crap

I'm trying to figure out."

Twenty minutes later, after the bridge was lowered and traffic started moving again, she figured she would head over to the library at F.I.U., since the morning was shot, anyway.

"History books always have the answers," she said.

CHAPTER 10

Spring's Romantic Colors
graciously lure us
into the heated passion
of summer
©dp

"Wow, this place is huge!" Becky said in awe, as she pulled into the parking lot of the Florida International University campus on Southwest Eighth Street.

The library where she was headed was located inside the Modesto A. Maidique Building and she thought it looked as if it had just recently been remodeled. Aside from the unique architecture of the building itself, the massive courtyard had been designed for outdoor seating underneath the glorious Florida sunshine, with several dozen majestic California Fan Palms offering plenty of shaded areas.

"Gee, this looks like a popular place," she said, as she walked toward the entrance. "I certainly hope it's quiet inside the library."

At least seventy-five people, ranging in age from about ten to eighty, were milling about the courtyard, loudly chatting back and forth, while another twenty or so folks were seated on benches reading books or doing homework. Several more were either coming in or walking out of the quadruple set of glass doors at the entrance. Compared to the dinky library in Jubilee Falls, this place was like a fairy tale dream come true for Becky.

Ever since she could remember she had always been fascinated with books, especially ones that taught her something new. Science had always intrigued her and in school she was often ridiculed for being such a good student, although the word her classmates used to describe her wasn't so complimentary.

"Nerdy-pants know-it-all, my butt," she thought. "We'll just see who the intelligent one is when I figure out what this storm is gonna do next."

Once inside the grandiose building, she aimed straight for the research section to look for a book on ancient Mayan history.

"Wow, look at all these I have to choose from," she quietly gasped, as she scanned three entire shelves of research books on the subject.

One of them, in particular, caught her eye because of the plain-Jane book jacket. She figured it would be a no-nonsense type of book dealing strictly with facts, which is what she needed at the moment. The subject matter, it seemed, was mostly about the language of the ancient culture. Without further ado, she snatched it off the shelf.

"Hmmm...written by Mickey DeRosa," she read out loud. "I wonder if this guy is still alive. I'd love to meet him."

Out of curiosity, she turned to the inside book jacket to see if there was an author biography and a picture.

"Oh, my goodness," she said, as she stared at the small photo. "You look awfully familiar. You're kind of cute, too."

Unfortunately, his biography didn't give any indication as to his age. All it said was that he was a native of Florida.

"Well, that helps," she mumbled. "I guess I'll have to do my own investigating when I get back to my hotel room and my computer."

With that, she took the book and she sat down at a nearby table to browse through the pages. She was thoroughly engrossed in her reading when, suddenly, loud male voices erupted on the other side of the bookshelves. The way the two guys were talking, and the things they were saying, made her think they were old buddies who hadn't seen each other in a while.

"Sheesh, pipe down," she muttered.   "I can't concentrate."

As she continued flipping through pages, the chatter going on behind her was beginning to get on her nerves. She was about to get up and go tell the noisy guys that this was a library and they should be respecting the other patrons' rights to silence, when she heard one of them say something shocking.

"Holy crap, did that guy just say Wakulla?" she asked, a bit too loud herself this time, which made the librarian glare at her. "Sorry," she mouthed to the old woman, as she continued listening to the conversation going on behind her.

When the word Wakulla came up again she knew she had to go check things out. After she closed the book, she tucked it under her arm, grabbed her purse off the table, and she quietly eased her way around the corner of the bookshelf to take a peek.

Being nonchalant wasn't one of her finer traits, so when she saw the two men sitting together, still chatting much too loud, as if they were here in the library for old home week, she couldn't resist butting in.

"Excuse me," she said, as she walked up to where they were sitting. "I couldn't help but overhear parts of your conversation..."

"Oh, I'm so sorry. I guess we were being a tad obnoxious," Mickey said, and when he turned around in his seat and saw Becky, his jaw dropped.

"You again," she said, glaring at him. "Are you always so boisterous?"

"Do you two know each other?" Professor Wiggins asked Mickey.

"Uhh...not really. We sort of bumped into each other this morning at the hotel," Mickey said, as his face flushed a bright shade of red.

"Sort of?" she mocked him, and then she folded her arms across her chest, hoping the book she was holding in her hands would hide her cleavage from this crazy dude's wandering eyes.

"Miss, I can't tell you how sorry I am. It seems you can take me out of Fishbend, but you can't take the Fishbend out of me," he said, which only made Becky look at him even more cross-eyed than she did earlier that morning.

"Hello, I'm Professor Wiggins," Doc said, evidently sensing he needed to bail Mickey out of a tight spot. As he stood up to greet her with his arm extended, he asked, "And you are?"

"Becky Rogers," she said, shaking his hand. "I'm pleased to make your acquaintance."

"I see you're interested in Mayan culture," Mickey said, when he spotted the book she was clutching. "Are you a student here?"

"Why?" she asked him, not bothering to hide the sarcasm in her tone. "Do I look like a student?"

"Well, not really. You look more like a runway model or a..." he started, but she cut him off.

"Look, I'm not here to make small talk," she said. "I just overheard something and I wanted to find out if you two guys knew something I didn't about this Wakulla guy."

"Ahh, that explains the book," Mickey said. "Are you a reporter?"

"No, I'm not a reporter. I'm just a woman who's interested in weather phenomena."

"So, why the book on ancient Mayan culture?" he asked her.

"Because I believe it's all connected somehow," she said.

Just then, Mickey's cell phone started ringing with its obnoxious Star War's ringtone, which prompted several loud shushes from people who were sitting nearby.

"Oops, I need to take this. I'll be right back," Mickey said, and he got up from his seat and hurried toward the exit.

"I apologize for my friend's behavior," Doc said to Becky. "He's normally more reserved than this. Won't you join us?" he asked, pointing to the empty seat beside him.

"Maybe for a few minutes," she said. "I'm kind of in a hurry, though."

"Yes, it seems we're all in a hurry today."

As the laughing idiot was walking away to take his phone call outside, she noticed he was wearing baggy blue jeans, a plaid shirt that he didn't bother to tuck inside his pants, and hunting boots that had definitely seen their fair share of backwoods country. It made her wonder why such a scholarly man like Professor Wiggins, who was dressed in suit and tie, was associating with such a roughneck backwoodsman.

"So, Professor, would you mind telling me what you know about this Wakulla guy? I've been trying to get someone to let me talk to him, but I'm not having much luck," she said.

"Well, I'm afraid I don't know much. That's why I asked Mickey to meet me here," he said.

"Mickey?" she asked, raising her eyebrows.

"Yes, Mickey DeRosa. The man who wrote that book you're holding," Doc said, smiling.

"Oh, I see," she said. "Will he be here soon?" she asked, not making the connection between the author and the laughing idiot, of course.

Just then Mickey reappeared and sat back down at the table.

"You look concerned," Doc said. "Is your father all right?"

"Huh? Oh, uh...I guess he is," Mickey said, seeming totally distracted.

"Don't keep me in suspense, son. Who was that on the phone?" Doc pressed him.

"It was Johnny. You remember him...my old drinking buddy. We shared a dorm together," Mickey explained.

"Ahh, yes," Doc said. "How's the old boy doing?"

"Well, he's okay, but there seems to be some strange things going on in Tallahassee right now."

"Like what?" Doc asked.

"Johnny said there was a sudden flood that came up out of nowhere. It hasn't rained there in days, which is why it seems so odd. He said it was almost as if the water came up from out of the ground, but then it quickly receded. He thought he was hallucinating at first, but then he spotted all these dead animals laying in his front yard...squirrels, rabbits, raccoons, foxes and even an anteater. Can you believe that? An anteater in Tallahassee?"

"I can believe almost anything these days," Doc said. "Did he call the authorities?"

"Are you kidding? Johnny call the cops? No way! The last time he summoned them they wound up hauling him off to jail for contempt. It seems he called one of the officers a name that didn't go over so well. So, no...he hasn't called anyone...except me, that is."

Now it was time for the professor's cell phone to start ringing, which he quickly answered.

"I'll be right there," Doc said, and he hung up. "I hate to run off, especially now, when things are starting to get really interesting, but duty calls," he told Mickey. "I'll be in touch with you soon, so stay by that phone."

Then, he left before Mickey could say anything. All of a sudden, Becky felt extremely uncomfortable sitting next to the laughing hyena, although he wasn't laughing anymore. He looked almost scared, she thought, as she eyeballed him out of the corner of her eye.

"Are you okay," she finally asked him.

"Oh, yeah, I'm fine...just a little confused at the moment."

"Me, too," she said, and she smiled at him. "Is the professor on his way to see Mickey DeRosa?"

"Huh?" he asked, wrinkling his brow.

"Yes, he said he had a meeting with the guy who wrote this book," she said, as she laid it on the table.

"Oh...uhh...yeah, that's where he was headed," Mickey said, grinning.

"Well, I suppose I should properly introduce myself

and explain why I so rudely intruded on your conversation with the professor," she said, wondering why she was being so nice to this guy all of a sudden.

"Yes, please do," he said, still grinning at her.

After she explained who she was, where she was from, and why she was so interested in Wakulla, his demeanor seemed to change right before her eyes. The more she looked at his face, the more she felt as if she knew this crazy man.

"Have I met this guy before?" she wondered.

"It's very nice to meet you, Miss Becky Rogers," he said, and he extended his hand to shake hers, after which he said, "Mickey DeRosa, here. May I take you to lunch?"

The library was suddenly as quiet as a cemetery and Becky's jaw had literally dropped to her chest, as she stared at the man seated across from her. She turned the book over and looked at the author picture, and then she looked back at Mickey. She did that about three times before finally speaking.

"You're Mickey DeRosa? The author?" she gasped.

"The one and only," he said, chuckling. "And, by the way, that's the one and only book I've ever written. Are you enjoying it?" he asked her.

"Quite frankly, I haven't had time to really get into it. I was so distracted by these loud voices behind me that I couldn't even get one page read," she said, and then she, too, started laughing.

"Well, you can put that one back on the shelf. I brought one with me. I'll even autograph it for you when we get back to the hotel."

"Really? Thank you," she said.

"So...lunch?" he asked again.

"Yeah, sure," she said, after glancing at her watch. "It's getting to be about that time, isn't it?"

"Yes, it is," he said, as he stood up from the table. "Where would you like to go?"

"Gee, I don't know. This is my first time down here in Miami. One thing I do know is that I don't want to eat at the hotel."

"Why is that?" he asked.

"They served me this rotten fish last night. God, it was horrible. I almost never got the smell out of my purse," she said, which made him look at her as if she was the crazy one now.

After she explained the entire scenario from last night, he didn't laugh. In fact, he seemed even more disturbed about something.

Once they were outside the building, Becky asked him where he might suggest they go for lunch, since they both had agreed the hotel restaurant was out of the question.

"Why don't we just hop in your car and play it by ear?" he suggested.

"My car? You mean you're going to leave yours here?" she asked, feeling hesitant to let the laughing author into her vehicle.

"I took a cab here," he said. "It was a rip-off, too. I'm glad you're here to rescue me from the taxi gods. Besides, I don't think I can listen to one more second of rap music."

After he explained his harrowing ride to the library, she softened up and agreed to be his chauffeur for their lunch date. The front seat of her car was strewn with papers, as well as the two maps she had brought along with her. When Mickey saw them his eyes widened, as if he'd just seen a ghost.

"So, these are your findings?" he asked, as he took a closer look at both maps, comparing the two of them.

"Oh, that's only one little smidgeon of all my research," she said. "The rest of it is back at the hotel and there's even more back home."

"Hmmm..." he said, scratching his chin and still examining the maps.

Becky was chomping at the bit to get inside Mickey's brain and she didn't really want to waste a lot of time going to a restaurant for lunch. She wanted to get cracking on trying to solve the puzzle of the maps and the mystery of Wakulla's claims about the talking ocean that swallowed up his brother.

"Do you like pizza?" she asked him, as she pulled out onto the highway.

"I love pizza," he said. "Can we get anchovies on the side?"

"On the side? Are you nuts? I like mine right on the pizza," she said.

"My kind of woman," he said, smiling again.

"Cool. We'll order in from Dominoes or whatever pizza joint is close by. That way we'll save some time and we can get started on that," she said, pointing to the pile of paperwork that was now on the floorboard at Mickey's feet.

"Ahhh, so you'd like my help with this?"

"If you wouldn't mind," she said. "I mean...you don't have to, but..."

"I'd be happy to assist," he said. "Home, James," he said, pointing to the roadway ahead of them.

"Huh?" she asked.

"Don't mind me," he said. "I'm just an ole country boy. I say a lot of stupid stuff."

"You got that right," she agreed, but she smiled back at him just the same.

CHAPTER 11

Affirmation
Comforting reassurance
Ubiquitously growing stronger
Putting my mind at ease
Truth
©dp

Inside the National Hurricane Center's sprawling command post on Southwest 17th Street in Miami there was utter chaos. It was standing room only and every employee of the Center, along with a slew of government officials were milling about, yelling back and forth to one another. It seemed everyone had their own opinion about what was happening out in the Gulf of Mexico.

Meanwhile, Jeremy Baxter, Carl Edwards and Eric Donley were huddled around the master computer mainframe trying to figure out what was wrong with the system. Ever since last night when things started going haywire, there had been three separate computer technicians called in from three different high-tech companies, but not one of them seemed to know how to fix the problem.

None of the radar systems countrywide were operable at the moment and all the satellite feeds had seemingly vanished into the atmosphere. The phones hadn't stopped ringing, though, with outlandish reports coming in nonstop from people all along the Gulf Coast from Florida to Mexico.

Eric himself had listened to fifty different people from fifty different locations explain that they had just witnessed a tsunami come ashore. The odd part about it was that the tsunamis were short-lived and did very little damage onshore before receding back into the waters of the Gulf.

Right before the computers died yesterday, Eric saw three massive balls of some sort of underwater disturbance on one of the radar screens. They were so huge that they filled the entire Gulf basin. As soon as he picked up his phone to summon his assistant, however, the computer screen went black. It had stayed that way ever since.

"Are you sure you saw what you saw?" Carl asked Eric, during a lull in the activity.

"Look, Carl, we've been over this a hundred times already. Yes, I'm absolutely sure I saw three distinct swirling balls of...of something out there. The Coast Guard dispatched a helicopter to check it out, but they said their sonar stopped working as soon as they got out over open waters. Visually, they said they couldn't see anything unusual. There's a Coast Guard cutter on its way as we speak."

"Has anyone checked out those eyewitness reports yet? Have they been verified?" Carl continued.

"I suppose we'll have to check with the media about that. I'm sure they're all over this story by now."

Eric then led both Carl and Jeremy into his office and he told them to have a seat while he turned on the television. Sure enough, as soon as he hit the switch and tuned into CNN, it was like a mad circus of one reporter after the next interviewing people who had seen the tsunamis. As he clicked through the channels he saw that Fox News, Headline News and all the local news stations were airing the same exact news feeds that CNN had been gathering since yesterday from the Associated Press, so he switched back to CNN.

"Shhh...listen," Carl said, as one of the witnesses was describing not only what he saw, but what he heard.

"It was scary as hell," the frightened young man said. "First, this big twenty-foot wave came crashing ashore, and then, as it was rolling back out into the sea, I heard these godawful sounds."

"Sounds like what?" the reporter asked him, as they stood together about ten feet from the shoreline.

"I don't even know how to describe it. It was some kind of foreign language...nothing I've ever heard before, that's for sure," the guy said.

"Can you describe it any better?" the reporter kept on.

"The only word I heard...at least, it sounded like a word...was Dumala. What that means, I have no idea, but I kept hearing it over and over and over," the guy said, with his eyes about to bug out of his skull.

Eric switched over to Fox News next.

"What the hell?" he gasped when he spotted a familiar site in the background.

There was a female reporter interviewing two men and they were standing on the banks of what looked like either the Suwannee or the Santa Fe River in northern Florida.

"Me and Ed were just out there fishing and all of a sudden the river stopped moving," one of them started.

"Yeah, then, just like that, the current started flowing the other way, real fast like," his buddy interjected.

"The next thing we knew, we was pulled underneath the water and we wound up here at Little River Springs...on top of the spring itself," the first guy said, clearly dumbfounded by the experience.

For the next fifteen minutes, the three of them listened to one astounding account after the next from all parts of the globe. Hundreds of rivers, springs and waterfalls in both North and South America had come to a complete stop and then slowly reversed direction. Boaters, swimmers, kayakers and tubers were being pulled backwards.

Some, just like the two guys in northern Florida, had been sucked underwater and then mysteriously swept into underground spring caverns before eventually popping to the surface. Every one of them said that it happened within a matter of seconds. Fortunately, no reports had come in that anyone had died, but there were hundreds of serious close calls.

BACK AT THE COMFORT SUITES hotel, Becky and Mickey had just finished their first slice of pizza when Becky's cell phone started ringing.

"Jeremy? Hi, how are you?" she asked, with a mouthful of pizza in her mouth.

"Becky, I need you down here at the Hurricane Center right now," he said, with a freaky urgency in his tone.

"Right now?" she asked.

"If not sooner," he insisted. "Eric would like to speak with you before Colonel Madsen gets here."

"Who's Colonel Madsen?" she asked.

"He's a hardnosed, arrogant, pessimistic military adviser who thinks all of this storm business is just a bunch of B.S. There's no telling what he'll do to try to stop it," Jeremy told her. "So, get your pretty little buns down here pronto."

"Aye, aye, sir!" she said, and they hung up. "Woo-hoo! We're in!" she screamed to Mickey.

"We?" he asked.

"Hey, you're coming with me," she said, all excited. "With everything you know, along with all my findings, they're gonna need both of us to figure this thing out."

"Hmmm..." Mickey said, as he chewed on a piece of crust.

"Well, come on! Let's get a move on!" she shouted.

"I'm right behind you, sweetheart," he said.

"Sweetheart?" she asked, as she aimed for the door. "Look, Mickey, I'm not your sweetheart, okay?"

"Whatever you say, darling," he said, and then neither she nor he could keep from laughing out loud.

CHAPTER 12

Falling Sky
pink sky falling down
surrounding the day's graces
introducing night
©dp

"Gee, talk about V.I.P. treatment, huh?" Mickey said to Becky.

As soon as she pulled into the parking lot, two armed security guards directed her to a secure area, just steps away from the entrance to the National Hurricane Center.

"You might think we were celebrities or something," she said, seeming quite amused by all the attention.

"You mean we're not?" Mickey asked her, with a serious look on his face, which only made her smile wider.

Over the past few hours, Becky's opinion of the laughing author sitting beside her had gradually changed. This man, whom she originally thought was just some redneck smartass, was actually turning out to be an extremely intelligent man, not to mention the fact he seemed to be growing handsomer each time she looked at him. Underneath his gruff, backwoods exterior was a kind and gentle soul, who seemed, on the surface, to really give a damn about the environment.

No sooner did Becky put the car in park than two more guys in security uniforms whisked them both inside the building, as if they were involved in some sort of covert, top-secret operation.

After showing their identification and after answering more than a dozen questions each, they were told to pass through a human x-ray scanner. The man behind the machine explained that it was what they referred to as a backscatter, which was the equivalent of a physical strip search.

After that, they were immediately led into Eric Donley's generously sized office. Jeremy Baxter and Carl Edwards were already seated around a fifteen-foot-long oblong shaped table and Eric Donley himself was standing beside a gigantic sixty-inch video screen. Becky thought he looked deeply disturbed about something.

Since she had already explained who Mickey was when they entered the building, word must have been immediately relayed to Eric, because no introductions were made or even seemed necessary. Eric then wasted no time in getting down to business.

"I want all of you to watch this video and when it's over I want input from each and every one of you," he flatly stated, as he glanced around the room, looking into everyone's eyes.

While he was getting the film ready, Becky glanced over at Jeremy and Carl. It was easy to figure out who was who. The handsome weatherman, whom she had been infatuated with for the last twenty years, suddenly looked like an old man, now that she was seeing him face-to-face.

"They must really pack on the makeup before he goes live on television," she thought to herself. "Look at all those wrinkles, especially around his eyes. Boy, what a letdown," she continued thinking.

Jeremy Baxter, on the other hand, she thought was a spitting image of Clark Gable with dark, bushy eyebrows, a neatly trimmed moustache, and a wisp of dark black hair draped across the right side of his forehead. Decked out in full uniform, he looked like he just walked off the set of *Gone with the Wind*, which was her all-time favorite movie.

"Psst...little lady," Mickey said, nudging her in the ribs when he saw Jeremy wink at her. "Pay attention."

It seemed Becky wasn't the only one sizing people up

in the room. She knew Mickey had been stealing glances at her ever since they first met. She had caught him on more than a few occasions just staring at her all glassy-eyed. At first it gave her the creeps, but after a while she felt flattered.

Even now, she had no doubt that he'd been watching her, as she interacted with the other men in the room, especially the charming Jeremy Baxter. As for Eric, he was all business and he didn't seem to have any qualities that appealed to her in the least. Besides that, he was wearing a wedding band, as was the dashing Carl Edwards.

"Okay, people, here we go," Eric said, and the lights in the room went dim, as the video began to play.

It was raw footage of a news story that had come in off the wires from the Associated Press earlier in the day. Eric explained that it hadn't been released to the public as of yet, but he feared that it had already been leaked over the Internet. He also told them that if they, meaning the National Weather Service, didn't come up with a logical explanation soon, this story might just cause mass panic, not only in the U.S., but on a global level.

Suddenly, all eyes were on the screen in front of them, while Eric wandered behind them, nervously pacing back and forth across the room.

Even though the video was truly in a raw state, with the cameraman's zoom going up and down and in and out, and cutting out completely for seconds at a time, it was clear that this was one of the strangest phenomena that mankind had ever witnessed, assuming it was true.

According to what they were looking at and listening to, a man's body in full dive gear, had appeared out of nowhere in the ocean off the coast of the Yucatan Peninsula, very near the Chiczulub crater site in northern Mexico.

"So, what?" Carl blurted out. "A dead body washes up. No big deal."

"Shut up and listen, Carl!" Eric barked at him, as he continued his pacing. "It gets better!"

Becky nearly jumped off her chair at the gruff sound of Eric's voice, but then when she saw Carl's face turn red, and she watched him cower down in his chair, she nearly laughed out loud.

"What a weasel," she thought, feeling quite thankful that she had never met him in person until now, and then she turned her attention back to the television screen.

According to the cameraman, who was narrating the film, sources had already confirmed the identity of the diver. He was a Russian diplomat who had mysteriously disappeared six months ago. His name was Constantine Burdzecki and supposedly, he had been vacationing in the United States with friends and family. Being an avid cave diver, he and two of his brothers were exploring the underground caves at Little River Springs near Branford, Florida.

Ever since new rules had been implemented back in 2010 at all the natural springs parks in the state of Florida, all divers now had to wear identification if they intended to explore the underwater caves. After half a dozen divers had gone missing in one year alone, the governor had mandated that any and all divers who dared risk the dangerous waters below the surface, first had to be cleared by the local police, and then they had to wear their I.D. badges at all times.

The dated Little River Springs sticker on the inside of the man's diving suit, along with dental records and DNA tests that had just been completed, definitely confirmed that the body they just found was indeed that of Constantine Burdzecki.

When the camera lens zoomed in on the body, everyone in the room drew in their breath at the same time.

"Would you look at that?!" Jeremy said, as he leaned in closer to the screen. "His body has been perfectly preserved. He looks as if he just died seconds ago."

"Aww, this is a bunch of horse pucky," Carl scoffed, obviously not convinced there was anything overly strange about the incident. "Who's to say the guy didn't die yesterday? It's a hoax. It's all a stupid hoax."

"I clearly remember when this happened," Mickey piped up. "It was all over the news back then. There was a huge investigation and it almost caused a rift between us and the Russians. If it hadn't been for the fact his two brothers were witnesses, we could have had a major falling out with the Russian government. Thankfully, the story died down after about two months of relentless searching and the Russians finally agreed that he must have gotten stuck inside one of the caves and couldn't get out. I always thought it was odd that they never found his body, though."

"That still doesn't prove anything," Carl kept on. "He could have been trying to defect and after going down for the initial dive, he could have resurfaced someplace else. We all know how easy it is to change your identity in this country. Then, all he had to do was cross the border in Mexico, blend in with the rest of society and live a normal, free life."

"I might have agreed with you earlier," Eric said, looking directly at Carl. "If it wasn't for the rest of the facts, it could very well have been a hoax."

"What other facts?" Jeremy asked.

"Well, it seems that six other bodies have washed up on shore since Mr. Burdzecki's body was discovered yesterday."

"Really?" Jeremy asked.

"I'm afraid so," Eric said. "They were all cave divers who had gone missing in the last four years. One man was diving at Suwannee Springs, two more were at a hot springs in California, another went missing from a hot springs in Montana and the last one was a woman who disappeared from a hot spring in Oregon."

"Where did their bodies wash up?" Becky asked, although she already knew the answer.

"One right after the other, they popped up out of the ocean in the Yucatan Peninsula, all within half a mile of each other. The Mexican authorities have been breathing down our necks for answers ever since eight o'clock this morning."

For a few moments there was complete silence in the room, while everyone digested this information. Becky was furiously scribbling notes, while Mickey had taken Eric's place in the back of the room, pacing back and forth, deep in thought.

"Would you like to hear my theory?" Mickey asked everyone.

"That's why you're here," Eric said, and he took a seat at the table to listen to him, along with the rest of the group.

"When that meteor struck the Yucatan all those sixty-five million years ago, it hit so hard and went so deep into the ground that it created underground cracks in the earth's core. Then, because of the magnitude of the crater opening at the impact site, every time it would rain, water would fall down the huge opening and settle into deep pockets below the surface. After millions of years, there was soon enough water to create a complicated maze of interconnecting rivers deep below the surface," he explained.

After listening to Mickey speak for a few minutes Becky found herself completely intrigued. So much of what he was saying happened to be things that she had seen in her visions ever since she was a little girl. Aside from that, she was also gaining an entirely new respect for the laughing, redneck author.

"Please continue," she said to him, as she sat on the edge of her seat, eager to hear more.

Mickey looked over toward her and he smiled before continuing.

"There are many areas around the globe that are used as exit points for the buildup of steam...or release valves, if you will," he said. "The biggest example, of course, is all the natural springs in the world, especially in northern Florida."

"If I might suggest something here," Becky started, and all eyes shifted onto her. "There had to be something inside that meteor that had gone unnoticed to mankind over the years, because it was so far below the surface."

"I agree," Mickey said.

"Some sort of unknown element," she continued. "I know you're all going to think I'm crazy, but I've been having visions ever since I was a little girl."

That comment drew grunts from everyone except Carl this time. He had firsthand knowledge of her special gifts from all the conversations they had in the past, whether he had truly believed in them or not at the time.

"That's okay," she said, faintly blushing, when she saw the blank stares on everyone's faces. "It's not the first time I've been looked upon as a witch or a freak of nature."

"She really does have extraordinary powers," Carl said, and then he went on to explain his relationship with her over the past twenty years.

"What frightens me is this storm," she said when he finished. "This strange storm that's brewing out in the Gulf of Mexico and doing God knows what beneath the ocean floor. I've been tracking it for weeks, ever since its inception in Morocco."

She had everyone's undivided attention now, so she continued.

"This storm is trying to deliver a message to mankind," she said. "I know you all find it hard to believe that nature can do such a thing, since it's not something we can visually or mentally wrap our heads around, but it's true. This storm is so powerful that it can do things nobody could imagine in their wildest dreams. It can even speak to us."

The mood in the room suddenly went from acute interest to absolute mockery, as everyone tried stifling their laughter. Everyone except Mickey, that is.

"This thing underground has created a vacuum effect by pulling fresh water back through its filtering system at the bottom of the ocean," Mickey interjected. "The divers they just found had vanished long ago, deep within the caverns, and when the currents changed direction, they got sucked through the earth's filtering system.

Eventually they were deposited at the ocean's surface in the direct area of the meteor impact zone."

Becky was about to offer her maps when alarms started sounding throughout the building. Eric rushed out the door to see what was going on and everyone else in the room was right behind him. Once the alarms stopped, the entire command center became deathly quiet, except for the news broadcast on the television that everyone had their eyes glued upon.

Again, it was another raw news video of a bus accident near New Orleans. All the children who were onboard were heading back to a cancer research center after an outing at the beach. The stories these terminally ill children were telling the reporters had everybody in the room spellbound.

CHAPTER 13

Noticeable
Simplistic grandeur
Everyone notices your
Sumptuous beauty
©dp

"**H**ow come we didn't know anything about this storm?" Eric shouted to his entire crew.

"Excuse me, sir, but our computers have been out of commission since yesterday," his assistant, George Myers tried explaining. "In fact, all of our communications equipment is on the fritz."

"Well, I want it fixed now! Get somebody in here to set up some sort of computer system. I don't care how basic it is, but I want it done now!" he continued yelling. "And get it hooked up to a portable generator, too. I don't want any electrical glitches interfering with it."

George just stood there, staring at Eric, as if he thought the man had gone mad.

"What are you waiting for?!" he snapped at George. "Get it done!"

"Yes, sir," George said, and he immediately got on the phone to make some calls.

Meanwhile, the room was abuzz with chatter about what had just happened. It seemed that a powerful hurricane simply appeared from out of nowhere in the Gulf and it came ashore just south of New Orleans.

It had barreled through the Chandeleur Sound, through Lake Borgne, and then it made a sharp left turn straight into the city of New Orleans. Wind speed instruments on ground level had it clocked at 300 miles per hour when it came ashore. The bus driver was still in a state of shock as he tried explaining what he had seen.

"I saw it jump over the levees as if they didn't even exist," he told the reporter. "Then, the clouds split down the middle and all of a sudden we were engulfed in the middle between two storms. The bus started shaking and spinning around and all the kids were screaming at first, especially when the roof of the bus got ripped off."

"At first?" the reporter asked. "What do you mean?"

"Well, we were all lying on the floor of the bus looking up at the sky, and after a while, some of the kids started saying they could see the eye of the storm above them."

"Oh, my goodness, they must have been so frightened," the female reporter said, with her mouth agape.

"That's just it," the bus driver said. "All of the children said it was the most beautiful thing they had ever seen."

The camera then switched over to another reporter, who was interviewing an eighteen-year-old boy who had terminal pancreatic cancer.

"Yeah," he said, still marveling at what had just happened. "All of a sudden, it felt serene and calm as we laid there on the floor staring up at it. There was an aroma, too, but it didn't smell like death or destruction. It smelled like all the flowers in the world rolled into one beautiful scent. Then, all the colors of the rainbow lit up the sky. They were the most brilliant colors I've ever seen. It was like watching a humongous six dimensional, high definition TV screen."

Just then, the camera switched back to the driver of the bus.

"It was the strangest thing," he said. "I don't really know how to explain it, but it seemed as if the children's senses became totally in tune with those powerful forces that were swirling around them. All of them said that it wasn't the howling of the winds that they heard, but it was beautiful symphonic melodies from an ancient culture that they felt somehow connected to on a spiritual level."

"That sounds a little far-fetched, don't you think?" the reporter asked him.

"Far-fetched, crazy, Biblical...call it whatever you want, honey. It had us so awestruck that we couldn't even blink," he said. "And the oddest part about it was that it seemed to last for days, but it was only a matter of minutes. I checked my watch right before it hit and it was five minutes until eight. After the storm vanished, it was exactly eight o'clock on the nose."

"What do you mean when it vanished?" the reporter asked, looking confused.

"I mean just that," he said, snapping his fingers. "One minute it was here and the next it was gone...back out to sea, I suppose, and the oddest thing is the levees are still intact. Heck, look around. There are no damages at all, other than my poor ol' bus."

"Were there any injuries?"

"Injuries? Heck, no! I've never seen these kids so happy before, or so healthy. I mean, look at them," he said, pointing to the group of kids frolicking on the beach. "Little Joey there hasn't been able to walk in three years. Now he's running down the beach like a jackrabbit. It's amazing."

All of a sudden, the lights at the hurricane center flickered on and off about three or four times, until the power finally shut down completely.

"Oh, for crissakes!" Eric shouted. "Somebody get a hold of the power company! This is getting ridiculous!"

There was a flurry of activity in the semi-darkness with people shouting and scurrying about looking for flashlights. Eric then ushered his group of experts back into his office, which thankfully had a window to the outside world, although with it being a moonless night, not much light filtered through the glass panes.

It was clear to everyone that Eric had reached a boiling point, after all that had happened in such a short time, so the mood stayed somber for a few seconds until he spoke.

"Answers," he finally said. "I want some answers. None of this is making any sense to me at all," he added, and then he plopped down in a chair, wringing his hands and shaking his head.

Becky, not one to keep her mouth shut for long when she had intense feelings about something, decided to offer her thoughts.

"Earlier, when the hurricanes went below the surface of the ocean in the Yucatan Peninsula," she started, as she spread out her maps on the table. "They tapped into the crater that was formed millions of years ago by the great comet. The comet then carried and deposited something from the heavens deep into the earth. It was a divine healing dust from the universe and distant galaxies," she said, in an attempt to explain the bus incident in New Orleans.

"Do you really expect us to believe that crap?" Carl asked.

"Will you please shut your trap and let the lady speak?" Eric pummeled him. "Go on, Becky," he said, and then he gave Carl the evil eye.

"As I was saying, this healing dust was buried so deep that it was never detected by man or machine. It has been preserved all these years...until now," she began again. "Mother Nature unearthed its precious cargo; a healing power not seen since the days of the Messiah over 2000 years ago."

From the looks on the faces seated around the table, Becky could tell that all of them, including Eric now, thought she had really gone off her rocker.

"Someone has to be playing a joke on us," Jeremy said. "We really need a working computer right about now, and we need the geekiest experts in the country over here to find and hack into whatever this terrorist group is trying to pull off. We need to know what their next move is."

"I agree," Eric said. "Carl, go find George for me and tell him I need to speak with him immediately."

Carl didn't say a word. He just left to go find George.

Becky thought he looked scared shitless, but then, so was she at the moment.

One thing she didn't agree on was that a terrorist group was behind all of these strange phenomena's. It was the Universe rebelling against the atrocities of mankind. It was Mother Nature herself who was trying to warn mankind of its demise if things didn't change immediately. If nothing else, she knew that was a certainty.

When Carl came back into Eric's office two minutes later, he didn't have George with him. Instead, he had Colonel Madsen on his heels and he looked pissed, even more pissed than Eric.

CHAPTER 14

Desirable
Should our lips ever meet
as our minds have
you would be more than
desirably delicious

If our arms ever met
in a passionate entanglement
you would be much more than
fulfilling

If our bodies ever united
as our hearts have
it would be purely
ubiquitous pleasure
©dp

Over at the immigration center, Wakulla was giving everybody fits. Because he was acting so strange, everyone was afraid to go near him. One minute he would be sitting in the corner of his locked cell quietly chanting in some foreign language, and the next minute he'd be on the floor in a fit of convulsions, yelling and screaming. Four guards tried putting him in a straitjacket at one point, but he was too strong and too powerful, so they eventually gave up.

It was suggested by a local psychologist who had been called in just hours after Wakulla arrived, that he was under some sort of demonic possession. That, of course, went over like a lead balloon, but due to the seriousness of the situation, the authorities allowed a Catholic priest to come in and assess him. He, too, agreed that Wakulla was possessed by the devil.

When they asked the priest to do an exorcism he told them he wasn't qualified to do so. He said the one man who could do the exorcism lived in Italy, but he also told them it could take months to get approval from the Church. Consequently, that idea was scrapped.

The authorities knew Wakulla was Haitian, because of certain pieces of evidence they had found on his boat, but when a Haitian interpreter tried conversing with him, he didn't seem to understand anything she was saying.

That's when Professor Wiggins was called in the previous day, although, he couldn't make head nor tails of any of Wakulla's ramblings, either. Doc had studied many languages himself and he was fairly fluent in Creole, but what he was hearing wasn't the Creole language.

The only word Wakulla spoke that he recognized was the word Dumala, which meant nothing in Creole, as far as he knew. It was an ancient Mayan word, and that's when he knew he needed Mickey's expertise on the language of Mam.

Mickey was one of only four people still alive who had a full understanding of the ancient language. Doc had been trying to reach him for hours, but he wasn't answering his cell phone. So, in total frustration, he left the detention center that night somewhere around midnight to go back home.

Meanwhile, it was now three o'clock in the morning and Mickey and Becky had just arrived back at their hotel.

"I don't know about you, but I'm beat," Becky said, as the two of them were in the elevator heading up to the tenth floor.

"Yeah, it's been a long day," Mickey said. "I have a feeling tomorrow is going to be even longer."

When they got off the elevator, Becky said goodnight and then she went one way, while Mickey went the other. He lingered in the hallway in front of his room for a few moments, pretending he was searching for his room card to unlock the door, but what he was doing was watching Becky walk toward her room.

"Damn, she is one gorgeous woman," he thought. "She has a brain, too, even though some of her theories are a bit 'out there'. Who knows? She could well be right about a lot of it."

Becky had just unlocked her door and before going inside, she glanced down the hallway and saw Mickey staring at her again.

"Is everything okay?" she shouted down the hallway.

"Oh...yeah, everything's fine," he said, and then he yanked the card out of his pocket to show her.

"Okay, I'll see you in the morning," she said, and she went inside and shut the door.

"God, you are such a dork," Mickey mumbled, as he stuck the card in the door. "Have you forgotten how to flirt with a woman, or what? Sheesh!" he said, and then he, too, went inside his room and shut the door.

CHAPTER 15

A Moment of Peace
Arrives just before the dawn
When birdsong is sweet
and flowers are kissed by dew
In earth's early morning calm
©dp

"**M**ickey! Where the hell are you? I thought I told you to stay by the phone?" Doc's voice message blared.

It was seven o'clock in the morning and Mickey had just gotten out of the shower when he realized he had forgotten to take his cell phone with him yesterday. After all, it wasn't as if he was used to carrying it around with him.

The first call came in at nine-thirty last night. There were four more messages after that, all from Professor Wiggins, who was sounding more and more desperate with each call.

Each message was the same. "I need you here at the detention center immediately!"

He also told him to bring Becky Rogers along with him, because he had a lot more questions to ask her.

While Mickey was getting dressed, he realized he was starving for food, since his pizza date with Becky had been cut short last night and he only got to eat one slice of the pepperoni pie. He was thinking about ordering in breakfast when there was a knock at the door.

"Well, good morning, sleepyhead," Becky said when he opened the door.

Mickey was still zipping up his pants when, all of a

sudden, he realized she was staring at his crotch.

"Oops," he said. "As I told you before, you can take me out of Fishbend, but..."

"Yes, yes, I know," she said, cutting him short. "Are you ready to get started?" she asked him.

Last night they had agreed to get together first thing in the morning to review all of Becky's research before doing anything else and she was rarin' to go.

"Aren't you hungry?" he asked her.

"No, I'm not," she said. "I already ate breakfast about an hour ago. Come on, let's go to my room and get started."

"I don't think too well on an empty stomach," he said, rubbing his belly. "Maybe we can drive through a McDonald's before heading down to the detention center," he suggested.

"The what? You want to go to the detention center now? But I thought..."

"Change of plans," he said, as he gathered up his wallet, his room key card and this time, his cell phone, too. "Doc wants both of us down at the detention center to talk to Wakulla."

"Well, what are you stalling for? Let's go!" she said, and she started down the corridor toward the elevator.

Once they were in her car, and once she agreed to stop at the first fast food joint she saw to get him something to eat, Mickey decided to call his father to check on the rising river situation.

"Good grief," she said, when she got a glimpse of his antiquated cell phone. "You really are from the backwoods, aren't you?"

"Hey, don't knock it," he said, when he saw her staring at the phone. "The thing still works," he added quite proudly, and he proceeded to punch in his father's phone number.

"Well, good morning, son," his father said. "I thought you forgot about your old man."

"Now, Dad, you know that is utterly impossible. Nobody could forget you," he said, laughing, which made

Becky snicker, too. "So, what's the river up to?"

"It's the strangest thing," Brent said. "Yesterday me and Joe thought we was gonna get swept out to sea and this morning the river is back to normal again. In fact, the water is down so low that all kinds of debris washed up on the banks, along with a lot of dead fish and a few alligators. Unfortunately, they're still breathing, so me and Joe are keepin' our distance."

"You're kidding!"

"Nope, I'm bein' straight up with you, son. Remember that old shovel I tossed in there about ten years ago that we could never find? Well, I found it this morning stuck in the mud about ten feet away from the barn. Is that somethin', or what?" he asked him, while at the same time nearly laughing his head off.

"Well, I'm glad the river receded. Now, I don't have to worry so much about you," Mickey said, as he breathed a sigh of relief.

"Since when did you ever worry about your old man? I can take quite good care of myself without anybody's help," Brent said.

Mickey knew his father was just being ornery again, so he let that comment slide for the moment.

"I gotta run, Dad. I've got another call coming in," Mickey said, when he heard the beeping in his ear.

"Okay, we'll talk later."

With that, his father hung up, but when Mickey tried to retrieve the other call he got disconnected.

"Damn it," he mumbled.

"Hey, here's a Burger Shack," Becky said, pointing ahead of her. "Should I stop?"

"Well, hell, yeah!" Mickey said, forgetting about the missed phone call for the moment.

Unfortunately, when she pulled in, there was a sign stating that the drive-through was temporarily closed and that people should go inside to place their orders.

"I'm really starving," Mickey said, looking at her with puppy dog eyes.

"Okay, okay," she said, and she pulled into a parking

spot by the door. "Make it snappy," she added, as he got out of the car.

Less than five minutes later, he came back and they were on the highway again heading south, with Mickey in the passenger seat wolfing down a sausage and cheese breakfast muffin. He had ordered two large coffees, too, and he handed one to Becky after he peeled off the hole in the lid for her.

Just then, Mickey's phone beeped at him and he remembered about the call that was trying to come through when he was talking to his father. After he checked the voice message he looked over at Becky.

"What?" she asked.

"That was Eric," he said. "He's ordering us back to the hurricane center."

"He's what? Well, who the hell does he think he is? He can't order us to do anything!"

"Actually, he said it was an order by Colonel Madsen."

"Well, screw him! I don't like that guy. You saw how he treated us yesterday, making us leave as soon as he walked into Eric's office."

"Yeah, he was kind of a jerk, wasn't he?"

"You're being too kind, Mickey," she said. "Geez, he looked like Hitler's double with that stupid moustache and his pants hiked up around his chin," she added.

"Yeah, and if I'm not mistaken, he let one loose when he stepped in the door," Mickey said.

"Oh, come on," she said, rolling her eyes at him. "Did he really?"

"Scout's honor," he said. "You mean you didn't smell it? Phew! He must have had a bowl of bean soup for lunch or something."

"Or maybe he ate some of that stinky fish," she said.

They both had a good laugh and they decided to ignore the bombastic Colonel's orders, until after they had a chance to meet with Wakulla.

During the drive south, Becky started asking Mickey all kinds of questions about his status as a linguistics expert and why he wasn't out in the world making a fortune off his intelligence, instead of living a life of leisure in a one-pony town.

When he answered as best he could, he turned the tables and began asking her why she lived in a remote mountain town. After she explained her humble life and told him she had no college background, he was stunned, but impressed.

"Tell me something," he suddenly blurted out. "Do you have any romantic visions?"

"Excuse me?" she gasped.

"Well, you know...since you seem to have so much insight into natural things like weather and the environment, I was just curious if you ever had visions of your soul-mate."

"How do you know I haven't already found him?" she asked.

"Well, since you're not wearing a wedding band, I assumed you were still single. You are, aren't you?"

"Yeah, I'm single, but I could still have a soul-mate tucked away somewhere back home," she countered.

"Also, since you're here in Miami by yourself, I figured you didn't have a boyfriend or a husband. I mean...if you were my wife, I wouldn't let you out of my sight for a second," he said, grinning.

"I take that to mean you don't have a wife or a soul-mate, either," she said, playing along with his flirtation.

"Nope, I'm still looking. Haven't found her yet," he said with a loud sigh.

"Hmmm..." she said. "While we're at it doing this get-to-know-you stuff, may I ask what your middle name is?"

"My middle name? Why?"

"Oh, I don't know. Sometimes it can tell you a lot about a person," she said, grinning.

"Well, if you must know, it's Brent, after my father," he said. "What's yours?"

"Suzanne," she said.

"Oh, no! Tell me it isn't so! Are you serious?"

"Yes, of course, I'm serious.   What's wrong with Suzanne?"

"Darling, maybe one of these days, when I get to know you better, I might tell you about it."

"It?" she asked.

"Yeah, you heard me.   It," he said.   "End of discussion, okay?"

"Okay," she said, wondering why he got so upset. "Oh, by the way, I was just reading a news story about something going on in Franklin County. Do you know where that is?"

"Yeah, I know where it is," he said, heaving a sigh of relief that they were off the subject of Suzanne. "It's over by Apalachicola Bay, and how did you just read a story? I don't see you with a newspaper."

"I read it on my Droid, silly," she said, as she held up her phone. "Boy, you really need to get with the times."

"A new cell phone is on my to-do list as soon as I get back home," he said, feeling more and more flustered by his technological shortcomings. "So, what's going on in Franklin County?"

"Oysters," she said.   "Or, rather, an abundance of them that just piled up along the entire shoreline."

"You're kidding," he said, recalling the devastation that hit the county back in early 2010.

Huge amounts of human and animal waste had been washed into the bay from overflowing rivers.   It had rained nonstop for weeks and weeks, and the rivers had no place to go, but out to sea, eventually. Ultimately, all that nasty waste contaminated all the oyster beds in the bay area.

"No, I'm not kidding," she said.   "According to this article that came out about thirty minutes ago, there are thousands of people along the beach who are scooping them up in big black garbage bags and five-gallon buckets."

"I hope the Department of Agriculture is out there testing the waters before anyone eats those things. Those oyster beds have been closed for months.   I, for one, wouldn't want to risk it. The bacteria levels in that area of the Gulf have been enormously high for a long time."

"Hmmm..." was all she said, as she concentrated on the traffic ahead of her, which had suddenly tripled with the amount of cars heading south.

"So, tell me about this Droid," he said, which made her crack up with laughter.

By the time they pulled into the parking lot at the immigration building the two of them knew just about all there was to know about each other, for the time being, anyway.

Professor Wiggins was standing outside the front entrance puffing on a cigar when Becky and Mickey walked up the steps. When he spotted them he immediately started reprimanding Mickey, as if he was a five-year-old who had left the refrigerator door open.

"Whoa, slow down, Doc. What's got you so upset?" Mickey asked him.

Doc didn't say anything. He just ushered the two of them inside, past the security desk, and down a long corridor toward the cell where Wakulla was being held.

"He's all yours," Doc said to Mickey. "I'll be waiting right here."

As soon as the guard unlocked the door, Doc literally pushed Mickey inside and then he slammed the door shut behind him.

"What the hell?" Mickey wondered, as he looked out into the corridor through the small window on the door.

Doc was now sitting on a metal chair with his head in his hands, while Becky stood beside him looking confused and dumbfounded. Meanwhile, the guard had his fingers on his gun holster, as he stood with his back to the cell door. Mickey thought he looked as if he was listening for commotion to begin, so he could come back in and fire his weapon.

"Fools," Mickey said, and then he turned around.

Wakulla was sitting on the floor facing the corner of the room and he was chanting in a low, monotone voice. Mickey listened for a while, but it was difficult to hear him because he was talking so low. He did, however, catch a couple of key words. One of them was Dumala and the other one was 'oxe', which was the number three in Mam.

Mam was the major language of ancient Mayans, particularly from the western highlands region of Guatemala, which made Mickey wonder if this guy really was a Haitian.

As far as he knew from his extensive research, there were at least three major dialects within the Mam language, based on the geographical area where it was spoken. The language also varied from village to village, because each village was basically a self-contained unit. Over time, each tribe would formulate their own distinctive slang words, which made interpreting the language even more difficult.

Mam was closely related to the Tektitek language, another nearly obsolete tongue that few people could understand. Wakulla, it seemed was speaking a combination of both.

Throughout the entire world, only about eight hundred people could speak the basic language of Mam, which has twenty-seven consonants and five vowels, along with a glottal stop, which is a voiceless sound one makes when saying words such as Hawai'i or uh-oh. More or less, a glottal stop could be explained as a gap between words.

Mickey recalled someone from his college class stating that language didn't vary because of illiteracy. It varied due to community factors, just like all the different Mayan villages with their distinct dialects.

Even with all the research he had done since he first became intrigued with ancient history, he eventually learned that any and all books on the Mayan language had been destroyed during the Spanish Conquest. Whatever had been written down in the language of Mam centuries ago was lost forever.

All of a sudden, Wakulla shot to his feet and he came charging at Mickey, getting up in his face, yelling the word Dumala over and over again.

Four guards immediately rushed in and pulled him off of Mickey. Then, they yelled at him to get out of the room, which he gladly did.

This time, the guards managed to get Wakulla strapped down to his bed and then they, too, hurried out of the cell, making certain the door was triple-locked behind them.

CHAPTER 16

Rusted
Neglected object
Movement has ceased
Time and elements, victorious
Oxidation
©dp

"Are you okay?" Becky asked Mickey, as they stood in the corridor outside Wakulla's holding cell.

"Yeah, I'm fine. Just a little spooked, that's all. He didn't hurt me and I really don't think he had intentions of doing so," Mickey said, as he straightened the collar on his shirt.

Once he gathered his wits about him, he turned around and peeked through the window at Wakulla, who seemed to have settled down. As he lay shackled to the narrow metal bed, he was back to his quiet chanting again, muttering the same things over and over.

"You know, it's almost as if he's praying to the gods in some sort of ancient ritual," Mickey said, and then he turned back around. "I wish he hadn't lunged at me."

"Me, too," Becky said, looking more frightened than he was at the moment.

"No, that's not what I meant. I was just starting to get a grasp on what he was trying to say. A little bit of it, anyway. You have to remember that I haven't even thought about this kind of stuff for the last fifteen to twenty years."

"You mean translating foreign languages?" Becky asked him.

"Yeah, it's going to take me a while to get back into

the groove."

"I'm afraid we don't have a lot of time," Doc piped up. "The few words that I understood when I tried communicating with him...well, you know as well as I do what Dumala means. With all this crazy weather crap going on, time seems to be of the essence right about now."

Just then, a door opened at the end of the corridor and in walked the most beautiful Hispanic woman Becky had ever seen. The woman's eyes were glued on Mickey's face, and her smile, along with her hourglass perfect figure seemed to have caught his attention, as well.

After a slight nod toward the professor, she stopped right in front of where Mickey was standing. That's when Becky noticed the book she was holding in her hands.

"May I be so bold as to request your autograph?" she asked him, still with a deadly smile on her face that could have slain a dragon.

"Good God, Mickey," Becky thought, as she watched the two of them interact. "Stop drooling. You look like an idiot."

"Well, now," Mickey said, smiling back at the woman, as his face flushed a deep red. "It would be my pleasure."

After she handed him the book and a gold-plated pen, she stepped back to eyeball his body, which Becky had to agree looked most impressive now, since he had dressed in a pair of tight-fitting jeans today, along with a short-sleeved dress shirt that showed off his bulging biceps. He had shed the hunting boots, as well, and now wore bright white tennis shoes instead.

"When the professor told us you'd be visiting us today, I made sure I brought along your book," the gushing woman said. "You wrote some fascinating things in here. I refer to it all the time."

"Ahh, so you're an ancient history buff," Mickey said, as he opened the front cover to begin scrawling his signature.

"Actually, it's the linguistics that I'm interested in. In my line of work I have to be versed in quite a few different languages," she said. "By the way, I'm Elena Rodriguez, the Assistant Director here," she added, and she extended her hand to him.

Becky was quick to notice the huge diamond ring she wore on her left hand, as well as the matching wedding band, but it didn't seem to keep her from batting her long, dark eyelashes at him. It didn't seem to stop Mickey from flirting with her, either.

"Well, I'm happy to make your acquaintance," Mickey said, still acting like a flustered teenager, as he shook her hand.

Doc suddenly grabbed Becky's arm and he pulled her aside, while Mickey and the beautiful Mrs. Rodriguez continued chatting.

"Did you bring your maps with you?" Doc asked Becky.

"Huh? Oh...yeah...umm...yeah, I've got them right...uhh...right here," she said, stuttering like a fool, as she patted the folder tucked underneath her arm.

"May I see them?" Doc asked, looking at her through squinty eyes, while his eyebrows rose up on his forehead.

"Oh...yeah, sure," she said, finding it hard to take her eyes off Mickey and Elena.

There was a small table a few feet away and Doc motioned for her to follow him. Reluctantly, she did as he asked. As he examined the maps, Becky kept stealing glances over at Mickey and she wondered why this scenario with him and Elena was bothering her so much.

"It's not as if I like the guy," she thought. "I have no claims on him, so he can flirt with whomever he damn well pleases."

Just the same, she felt herself growing more and more jealous by the second, especially when she watched Elena hand him her business card.

"We'll stay in touch," she heard Mickey say, as he shoved the card into his shirt pocket.

Elena then turned and walked away, back toward the door at the other end of the long corridor, while Mickey stared at her shapely, toned legs. When she disappeared

behind the closed door, he finally swung around and saw
that both Becky and Doc were staring at him.

"What? Come on, you two," he said. "I'm a celebrity.
What can I say?"

Becky felt like slapping the silly grin off his face, but
again, she realized she had no right to be angry with him
or jealous of his behavior. He was just being a man.

"So, where were we?" he asked Doc, as he wandered
over toward the table, still basking in all the attention
Elena had showered on him. "Ahh, I see you have the
maps all laid out."

"Mickey, keep your thing in your pants," Doc
muttered to him. "We've got an urgent situation here."

That comment seemed to snap Mickey out of his
fantasy world. The smile that had been plastered across
his face immediately turned into a frown, wrinkled brow
and all, which made Becky gloat for a moment.

"I have a suggestion," she said seconds later. "Now
that Wakulla has been restrained, I want to go in there
and show him the maps."

"What! Are you crazy?" Mickey gasped. "No way!
It's too dangerous! You have no idea what he's capable
of!"

"Mickey, you said yourself that you didn't think he
wanted to do you any bodily harm," Becky protested.

"I said I didn't *think* he wanted to. I didn't say that
he couldn't," he said, clarifying his earlier statement.

"Well, I'm not afraid," she kept on. "Doc, would you
go summon the guard to unlock the door, please?"

Doc looked over at Mickey and then back at Becky,
who seemed determined to go in and talk to Wakulla, no
matter how much either one of them tried to stop her.

"I'm going in with you," Mickey said, and then he
looked over at Doc. "Go get the guard," he told him, as if
he was the Colonel himself barking orders.

Becky would never admit it to Mickey or Doc, but she
was scared to death just thinking about what she was
going to attempt. Deep down in her soul, however, she
knew it had to be done and it had to be done by her. She

had seen it in a vision while she slept last night.

Once Doc came back with two of the guards, the door was unlocked and Becky and Mickey cautiously entered the cell. Wakulla immediately stopped his chanting and then he opened his eyes. He didn't move, he didn't blink, he didn't do anything. All he was doing was staring blankly into Becky's eyes.

Bravely, she stepped forward, inching closer to where he lay on the bed. She had unfolded her map and she had it facing toward him as she got closer and closer. Mickey was right on her heels.

All of a sudden, Wakulla's eyes grew large and then he tried lifting his restrained arm to point at the map, while yelling "Dumala! Dumala! Dumala!"

The next thing she knew he was pointing to the pen she was holding in her left hand.

"He wants the pen, Becky. Give it to him," Mickey urged her.

When she held it out to him he snatched it from her, and with his other hand he reached for the map, but his arms were too restrained to grab it from her.

"You want the map?" she asked him.

Both she and Mickey were amazed when he nodded his head. He seemed suddenly quiet and subdued, as he traced a line on the map from Morocco down across the continent to the coastline of Mozambique, and then west across the Indian Ocean to the western coast of Australia. Then he made three huge circles in the waters of the Gulf of Mexico.

"Oxe," he said to Mickey. "Oxe," he repeated, and then he went into convulsions, screaming the word Dumala again and again, until the guards came rushing through the door.

"You two need to get out of here now!" one of them screamed. "Now!"

Becky snatched the map from Wakulla's grip, tearing off a small corner piece in the process, and then she and Mickey went back out into the corridor. Doc was standing there with his eyes bugged out and his face an ungodly white. Becky thought he looked on the verge of having a coronary.

"We're okay, Doc," she said. "We're both okay."

"Why don't we go outside and get some fresh air," Mickey suggested, and Doc managed to nod an affirmative.

As soon as they made it outside, Professor Wiggins suddenly fell in a heap onto the pavement, gasping for air.

"He's in trouble, Becky!   Go get help!" Mickey screamed at her, and she rushed back inside the building.

Within minutes, a rescue truck arrived.   One of the paramedics told them that Doc had just experienced a minor heart attack and that they would be transporting him to the hospital.

"Is he going to be all right?" Becky asked him.

"I think we got to him in time.   We'll know more after we get him to the hospital," the paramedic said.

After the ambulance left, Mickey looked over at Becky, who seemed to still be in a state of shock herself.

"I think I know what Wakulla is trying to tell us," he said with a deadpan look on his face.   "In fact, I'm almost sure of it."

CHAPTER 17

Tears
River of tears cried
With time the water all dried
Sweet salt of the earth
©dp

"Where are we going?" Becky asked Mickey, as they walked back to her car. "Back to the hurricane center?" she asked, struggling to keep up with him because he was walking so fast.

"It's too late for that, I'm afraid. It's time to go speak to the storm," he said, as he opened the passenger side door and slid in.

"Cool!" she said, and then she went around and got behind the wheel.

While Mickey was engrossed in Becky's map, which now had Wakulla's lines and circles added to it, she was beaming with excitement. The last thing she wanted to do right now was put up with Colonel Madsen's obnoxious behavior. Just as she turned the key in the ignition, both hers and Mickey's cell phones started ringing.

"It's Jeremy," she said, as she looked at the LCD showing the Caller I.D.

"I've got Eric here," Mickey said, as he held up his phone to show her.

"What do we do?" she asked, as both phones continued ringing; Mickey's with his Star Wars theme and hers with an old Blood, Sweat & Tears tune.

"Start heading north," he said.

Becky smiled even bigger and then together, they

both turned off their phones.

Since Mickey was a Florida boy and knew his way around the state, he gave her directions to hop onto Interstate-75 and just keep driving north until they made it to Tallahassee.

"Do you have a road map?" he asked her.

"I think there's one in the glove box," she told him, as she eased out onto the highway.

"Great," he said. "I know how to get to Tallahassee, but I'm not quite sure which road we take to get to Wakulla Springs State Park."

"Did you say Wakulla? There's a park by that name?" she asked.

"Yep, and I can't believe I never made the connection before now. Heck, even my father tried getting through to me," he said, shaking his head. "Our little friend back there at the immigration center told me this is the place we need to be, in order to speak directly to the storm."

"Elena told you that?" she asked, looking thoroughly confused.

"Huh? Oh, heck, no. Wakulla told me, silly."

"Ohhh..." she said, nodding her head. "She's married, you know."

"Huh? Who?" he asked, looking more confused than her.

"Elena," she said. "You mean to tell me you didn't see that big rock on her finger?"

"Uhhh...actually, no, I didn't notice her hands," he said, grinning.

"Yeah, I know. You were too busy looking at her boobs and her ass."

"Ha! Do I detect a note of jealousy in your voice?" he asked, still with a shit-eating grin on his face.

"Jealous? Me? Now, why on earth would I be jealous of a beautiful *married* woman?" she asked, stressing the word married, as she looked at him.

"Eh...I don't know," he said. "Maybe you're starting to like me just a little bit," he said, only this time he didn't look her in the eyes.

"Hrmph," was all she could think to say at the moment.

"How's the gas situation?" he asked her.

"We've got about a quarter of a tank," she said, as she looked down at the gauge.

"There's a Citgo up ahead," he said, pointing to a gas station about two hundred yards ahead of them. "We should probably gas up now. If we're lucky we might be able to drive straight through without having to fill up again."

"Okay, sure. By the way, would you like to drive?"

"I thought you'd never ask," he said, smiling. "Do you mind if we put the top down? It's a beautiful day."

"Sounds like a winning plan to me," she said, since she didn't care much for driving in the first place, especially in a strange town.

She was also wondering why she hadn't lowered the top already. After all, she thought, why rent a convertible if you're not going to make use of the removable roof?

Once they gassed up and bought a few snack items and drinks, they got back on the highway with Mickey behind the wheel. He was mildly exceeding the speed limit, in order to keep up with the flow of traffic on the Interstate, and it made her feel thankful that she suggested he take the wheel instead of her.

"People drive crazy down here, don't they?" she asked him, as she watched dozens of cars zoom past them doing at least eighty or ninety miles an hour.

"Oh, yeah," he said. "That's one reason why I live in Fishbend Creek. There's no traffic...period."

Becky leaned back in her seat to let the sun beat down on her face, briefly closing her eyes to bask in the warmth. When she opened her eyes again she spotted something in the sky just above them and she started shaking her head.

"Let me ask you something," she said, looking over at Mickey's handsome profile.

"I'm all ears," he said. "Ask away."

"What is your theory behind these chemtrails?" she

asked, as she pointed to the big white X in the sky overhead.

Mickey started laughing.

"You sound just like me," he said, still laughing. "I used to ask my father questions all the time about the universe. I still do," he said. "And, according to my dad, this chemtrail conspiracy is a real and imminent danger to society."

"Well, I happen to agree with him," she said.

"Remind me to introduce you to the old man once this mess is behind us," he said, and he glanced over at her with a cocky grin on his face.

"If you think your father is crazy, then maybe you need to read my research papers on the subject," she said, wondering if he was making fun of her. "Of course, that will be later on...after this other mess is behind us," she added. "Besides, I left all that paperwork at home."

"Hey, I never said I thought it was all a hoax. On the contrary," he said. "And I'll bet you a big shiny nickel our Colonel Madsen has intimate knowledge of the government cover-up by the EPA, the FAA, NASA, NOAA and the Air Force."

"So, you agree that they've been up to no good all these years, huh?"

"Definitely," Mickey said. "There's been too much discussion about the contrail/chemtrail issue over the years for there not to be something shady going on. Whether they're poisoning people or messing with the weather or God knows what...I definitely have a lot of unanswered questions."

"It seems like whenever the skies are devoid of clouds over a particular area...you know, when it's just blue, blue gorgeous sky as far as the eye can see...well, that's when all those high flying jets are up there drawing their humongous X's and cluttering things up," she said.

"Yes, I've noticed that, too, especially where I live, but, as you said, we'll have to discuss it in further detail later."

With that, he smiled at her, and all of a sudden, her

heart skipped a beat. She really did think he was quite the handsome devil, although, if she ever caught him flirting with a married woman again, she knew she would have to set him straight.

"Maybe that kind of stuff can fly in Fishbend, but it ain't flyin' with me," she thought, smiling back at him.

The two of them had a long eight-hour drive ahead of them, and the way things were going so far, it seemed to Becky that they had a lot to talk about. As the hours went by, she was discovering that they shared a lot of common interests, not only about weather and the environment, but they also had the same tastes in music and art.

During a lull in their conversation, Mickey turned on the car stereo. A loud rap song started booming through the speakers and he immediately switched to another station.

"You listen to that crap?" he asked her.

"Heck, no! I didn't put that station on. In fact, I haven't even turned the damn thing on since I got the car from the rental agency."

"Yeah, sure," he said, joking with her, as he searched for another station. "Ahh, that's much better," he said, once he heard a country music song begin to play.

"Yes," she agreed. "Much, much better."

MEANWHILE, SINCE EARLY THAT morning, thousands of people had been lining up along the shorelines from Key West to the Big Bend, and all around the Gulf States to Texas and down into Mexico. Even the people in Cuba had their eyes on the storm.

Becky and Mickey had been listening to news reports in between songs and the closer they got to Tallahassee, the more anxious and excited they were both becoming.

It was closing in on seven o'clock in the evening when they crossed over into the city limits of Leon County. That's when Mickey asked Becky to get the road map out and give him directions on which road to take into Wakulla Springs State Park.

Once they passed through the entrance gate of the park, Becky noticed the sun was getting close to setting for the evening, as it hovered just above the horizon, but oddly, it was still quite bright out and extremely warm all of a sudden.   There was a distinct aroma of sweet magnolia mixed with the tart smell of orange blossoms in the air, giving the evening an eerie, yet expectant feel. At least, that's how Becky described it to Mickey, who replied that he couldn't smell anything except diesel fumes from the 18-wheeler he'd been behind for the last five miles.

"Typical man," Becky said, laughing. "You guys just have no sense of smell."

"I may not be able to smell the fragrances of fruits or flowers, but I can certainly detect the odor of burning marshlands," he said, and then he pointed to Becky's right, where a small brush fire was smoldering in the woods.

"Hey, you're good," she said. "I didn't notice that smell."

"Of course not," he said. "You're a girl."

Just then, they both heard a loud roar and then voices in the distance that sounded like panicked chaos.

They were just a few yards away from the coastline now, after weaving through the entire park and then onto a dirt road that led them toward a remote beach area. Suddenly, it became eerily quiet. After Mickey parked the car, they both got out and walked over toward the beach. As soon as their feet touched the water, another loud scream bellowed from the depths of the bay.

"Holy crap!" Becky said. "It sounds like it's crying, doesn't it?"

"Yeah," Mickey said. "Something like that."

As they stood looking out across the bay, the water began swirling, going faster and faster around in circles in three separate spots, until upside-down, tornado shaped balls of dark black clouds formed just above the surface.

Again, loud, piercing screams bellowed out from the

sea, only there were three distinct tones now. Mickey looked dumbstruck, as Becky ventured out closer to the water's edge, as if she was in a trance.

"Becky! Get back here!" he shouted. "Becky!" he screamed again, but she acted as if she didn't hear him.

She just kept walking farther and farther out into the water. Mickey wasted no time in running in after her and dragging her back onto the beach.

"What happened?" she asked, looking at him with glazed over eyes.

"I'm not sure," he said. "I'm not sure."

CHAPTER 18

Water
Peaceful serenity
Submerged in calm
Body and mind relaxed
Floating
©dp

"Are you positive you're okay?" Mickey asked Becky for the umpteenth time, as he held her close to him.

"Yes, I'm fine," she said, as she pried her body away from his. "I could sure use a dry pair of shoes, though," she added, as she looked down at her feet and her sopping wet jeans.

"You and me both," he said. "These are brand new sneakers, you know."

"Put it on my tab," she told him, trying to make light of the situation.

Suddenly, out of nowhere, a ten-foot wave approached the beach, and when they both looked up it was clear that they didn't have time to get out of the way. Mickey just grabbed onto Becky and he threw them both down onto the ground.

As they waited and waited, nothing was happening. When Mickey finally looked up he was stunned to see a big mountain of water suspended in mid-air just three feet out from the shoreline.

"Would you look at that!? Holy Mother of God!" he said in awe. "What the hell are we dealing with, Becky?"

When she lifted her head up from the sand, she, too, was astounded at the sight before her.

"I believe it's playing a game of *Truth or Dare*," she

said. "The storm is teasing us, Mickey."

Just then, a park ranger pulled up beside them in a four-wheel drive jeep. He, too, was staring at the bizarre sight in the surf.

"You two need to get out of here!" he yelled over at them. "The park is closing in a few minutes!"

Mickey and Becky were looking at the guy as if they couldn't believe he was acting so unaffected and calm.

"Do you not see that?" Becky asked him, as she pointed out toward the massive, stationary wave hanging over them.

"Yeah, I see it," he said. "It's been doing that all day. Come on, now. Both of you get back in your car and get the hell out of here before you get locked in for the night."

Suddenly, there was another loud roar from the sea and the wave reversed direction, swooshing back out to the middle of the Gulf before disappearing underwater.

As the ranger was getting out of his jeep to physically force them to leave, a resounding crack echoed through the forest, and then a huge, twelve-foot long pine tree limb crashed to the ground, missing the front end of his vehicle by mere inches.

"Okay, that does it for me," he said. "You two can stay here if you want, but I'm getting the hell out of here!" he shouted, and he hopped back in his jeep and sped away, kicking up dust and stones in the process.

"Well, now, that was freaky, wasn't it?" Mickey said to Becky.

"No more freaky than that," Becky said, pointing to another wave that was aimed straight for them.

This time they didn't fall to the ground to take cover. They stood there, feet firmly planted in the sand to face this thing head-on. As it got closer, Becky reached for Mickey's hand and she held on tight, expecting the worst, yet not feeling nearly as frightened as the first time.

In the distance, she could hear laughter from a group of people standing along the shoreline about four-hundred yards around the curve of the beach off to their right, as if they were amused by this strange phenomena.

The laughter came to an abrupt halt when a thirty foot wave came up out of nowhere and pounced over top of them. Many of them were sucked out into the water hundreds of yards when the wave suddenly reversed direction. Mass panic ensued, as all those people struggled to swim back to shore. Those who were left on the beach were screaming and shouting. Soon, they began scrambling back to their cars, and one by one, they all sped away leaving their friends and family members to fare for themselves out in the middle of the Gulf.

As Becky and Mickey stood watching them, the other wave kept its course on the two of them, getting closer by the second. Again, when it got to within three feet of the beach it suddenly stopped, suspended in mid-air just like before.

This time, it was Mickey who started walking toward it, with Becky reluctantly following alongside him. The storm began talking to Mickey in a language Becky wasn't familiar with at all. It sounded a bit like some of Wakulla's rantings, but it was mixed with something else.

When Mickey started talking back to it, she let go of his hand and she started to panic, not believing what she was seeing. Now, it was he, who seemed to be in a trance. When their conversation ended, Mickey fell to his knees, staring out at the wave, as it eased backward, until it disappeared below the surface again.

Then, like magic, the waters in the Gulf slowly transformed into a smooth glass-like surface and it became eerily quiet again. All those people who had been washed out to sea had made it safely back to shore and within minutes they, too, fled on foot away from the angry storm.

Mickey eased himself up to a standing position again and then he walked back to where Becky was.

"Would you mind explaining what just happened?" she asked him, with a look of pure terror on her face.

"The storm wants Wakulla here now, or else," he said, with his eyes as big as saucers.

"What are we going to do? They've got him locked up

in that damned cell miles away from here," she said.

"You think I don't know that?" he asked her, sounding irritated with her pessimism, although he still looked scared out of his wits.

"I'm sorry," she said, and she went over to hug him.

After they held each other for a while, they started back toward the convertible, both of them deep in thought.

"I suppose it's time to put this thing to use," he finally said, and he pulled Elena's business card out of his shirt pocket.

CHAPTER 19

Passionate Lust
On the edge of an
adrenaline rush
Smooth kind of cocktail
Makes amorous nights
go down easy
©dp

"Uhh, Becky, would you mind if I used your phone?" Mickey asked her, as they sat in the car, watching the still calm bay waters gently lap at the shore.

"What's wrong? Did that old dinosaur poop out on you?" she asked him, not doing a good job of hiding her giggles.

"I can't get a signal," he said. "Either that or the battery died."

"Did you charge it last night?"

"Huh? Oh, uh...I guess I forgot," he said, with a sheepish look on his face.

"What's the number?" she asked. "I'll punch it in for you."

While Mickey rattled off the number, Becky was hitting the buttons one at a time. When the call connected and started ringing on the other end, she handed the phone to Mickey.

"Where do you talk on this thing? And where do you listen?" he asked, as he fumbled with the device.

"You're a trip, Mister Author," she said, still giggling at him. "Just hold the thing up to your ear. Trust me...you'll hear when someone answers."

After the operator put him through to Elena, he

briefly explained what had just happened.

"I was just watching it on T.V.," she said. "Not what happened to you, but what happened to all those people who got sucked out into the ocean. It was frightening."

"Well, it's going to get even more frightening if you don't do as I ask...or rather, what the storm asked."

He then proceeded to tell her word for word what the storm demanded had to be done now, or else dire consequences would ensue.

"You want me to do what?" she shrieked when Mickey told her to make arrangements to have Wakulla brought to the state park immediately, if not sooner. "I don't have the authority," she told him. "And the director isn't here at the moment. Only he could authorize such an outlandish request."

"Elena, you're not listening to me. This is a life or death situation, and I don't mean just mine," Mickey said, raising his voice about two octaves. "The entire civilization of Planet Earth is in danger!" he stressed again. "If you don't believe me, ask Professor Wiggins."

"I'd love to, but as you well know, he's in the hospital in a coma."

"He's what? Oh, my God!" he shrieked. "Becky, Doc is in a coma now!" he said, as he held his hand over the phone.

"Oh, no," was all she could say.

"Elena, I didn't want to bring this up and scare you..." Mickey started.

"Scare me? What are you kidding? I'm scared out of my mind just watching the news about all of this," she said.

"The storm told me the exact coordinates of its first target," he went on. "It's a coal-powered electricity facility in Biloxi, Mississippi. It told me that if Wakulla wasn't brought here immediately, it would have no choice but to strike the target," he said.

That comment made Becky sit up straighter and glare at him through unbelieving eyes.

"Holy Mother of God," Elena gasped, and then there

was silence on her end.

"Elena! Are you there? Elena! What's going on?"

"It just happened, Mickey," she said.

"What just happened?"

"The coal plant," she said, as she stared at the television screen. "It's been demolished...completely destroyed by...by what, I don't know, but it's gone! It's just gone!"

After a few more minutes of pleading, Elena finally relented and she said she would have one of their search helicopters bring Wakulla to the park immediately.

"Thank you, Elena," he said, breathing a sigh of relief. "I owe you one."

"You two just stay safe and stay in touch with me!" she ordered him, and she hung up.

"Why didn't you tell me?" Becky shouted at him when he handed her back the phone. "Why didn't you tell me that part?"

"Because I knew you'd freak out, just like you're doing now," he said.

Becky's eyes swelled with tears and she reached for Mickey. Before she realized what was happening, he was embracing her and then smoothing the hair away from her face.

When he leaned in to kiss her, she let him. It was a long and passionate kiss. One like she had never experienced before and she didn't want it to end.

CHAPTER 20

Scorched
Kindled coals of passion
Bursting into flames
Scorching careless hearts
©dp

"**H**as anybody heard from those two idiots yet?" Colonel Madsen yelled, as soon as he walked into Eric's crowded office.

He had just returned from having dinner at a nearby restaurant in the area, and judging from the stains on his shirt and the residue on his chin, he certainly enjoyed his barbecued ribs.

"No, Colonel, according to the hotel manager, both their rooms are empty and neither one of them are answering their cell phones," Eric said, referring to Becky and Mickey. "I think between me and Jeremy, we've left both of them about thirty voice messages each. If I didn't know better I'd say they turned the damned things off."

"It's just as well. All those two would do is get in my way," Madsen said. "So, what's the latest on this storm?" he asked, looking around the conference table at sixteen pairs of weary eyes that looked as if they needed a few hours of sleep.

"Take a look for yourself," Eric said, and he turned up the volume on the television.

Every news channel in the country had been airing nonstop coverage of the freak Gulf disturbance since early that morning. Eric preferred CNN, but right now he had the TV tuned in to the Weather Channel. All twelve of the correspondents were stationed at different points along the beaches throughout the Gulf basin, from the

Keys to the Mexican border.

As the network switched from one correspondent to the next, scenes were being aired showing the massive waves that seemed to be teasing all the people gathered along the shores. The waves would swoop in to within feet of land and then they'd rush backward out to sea, only to do it over and over again. Many of the people were laughing it up and a lot of them had set up chairs and tents on the beach to sit and watch the strange phenomenon. A few of them had even set up portable picnic tables and cranked up their barbecue grills, as if they were simply having a fun family outing.

One reporter, who was transmitting from a news helicopter, said that he spotted three separate stormy areas out in the middle of the Gulf.

"They look like gigantic boiling cauldrons," he said, which made Madsen laugh out loud.

"They're just tsunami waves...little ones, at that," he explained to Eric. "Didn't we just have a small earthquake over in Chile the other day?"

"The quake struck Sweden, sir," Eric corrected him. "And it was a 10.5 on the Richter scale. I'd hardly say it was a small event."

"Aahh! Whatever!" Madsen said, brushing Eric off with a wave of his hand, and letting him know he didn't appreciate being corrected by him or anyone else.

So far, there had been no reports of injuries or deaths other than the two men from the coal plant in Biloxi who were still unaccounted for. It was assumed that they were out somewhere eating dinner, as no one wanted to believe they may have been washed out to sea.

Even though the entire plant had been leveled, somehow, everyone managed to escape. A few of the guys looked fairly shaken up, but no one was hurt, other than a few minor scrapes and bruises.

After watching the TV for a few minutes, Madsen took a seat at the head of the table.

"I've got some of my men coming in," he said, sounding like a barking dog, and then he glanced at his watch. "They should be here in about ten minutes."

"Would you mind explaining what you're going to do?" Eric asked him.

"Well, since you boys can't seem to get your computers up and running, I've called in my experts. They'll have this place humming in no time," he said, gloating.

Eric was beginning to despise the arrogant Colonel Madsen. Ever since he had arrived at the hurricane headquarters he had been treating the entire staff as if they were bumbling idiots, even insulting one of Eric's top forecasters, who walked out after a heated argument with him earlier in the day. No one had seen or heard from him since.

The electric company had restored service about thirty minutes ago and Eric's top two I.T. guys had been trying since then to get all the communications equipment back on line. Unfortunately, they weren't having much success. In one sense, Eric could understand Madsen's frustrations, but in another, he didn't think the guy had any class whatsoever with the way he treated people, himself included.

What really irked him was when Madsen basically stripped him of his power and stature, and proclaimed that he was taking over operations at the hurricane center, until the storm either let up or was obliterated by one of his secret weapons.

Eric had an idea about what some of those secret weapons might be and he hoped it didn't come down to using any of them as a last resort. He knew they were capable of doing more harm than good.

Just then, the door opened and Eric's secretary, Julie, announced that the Air Force had arrived. As Madsen got up to go greet them, Julie looked over at Eric and she rolled her eyes, as if to say, "Sheesh, this Madsen is a real jerk." Eric couldn't agree more, as he nodded back at her.

Suddenly, it was all business out in the main command center with a small troop of uniformed men not-so-politely asking everyone to step aside. Madsen's so-called government computer geniuses immediately went to work to, as he stated before, "Get this place humming."

CHAPTER 21

Decompress
Eliminating stress
Breathing out toxicity
Comfortable surroundings exuding peace
Home
©dp

It had been nearly three hours since Mickey had gotten off the phone with Elena and during that time, Becky had come to the realization she was quite attracted to the laughing author.

Of course, due to the seriousness of the present storm situation, they only shared that one kiss, after which she thought he looked truly embarrassed, or perhaps, he was just too interested in watching the raging sea.

It really was spooky, she had to admit, especially when the storm wouldn't quit ranting and raving out in the Gulf. The off-and-on ten-foot waves that kept rolling in and out every fifteen minutes was keeping both of them on alert. Mickey had even suggested they put the top up on the convertible, just in case the storm became impatient again.

While the two of them awaited Wakulla's arrival, she agreed with him that they needed to concentrate on the issue at hand; the angry storm out at sea and what it really wanted. By doing so, it helped keep her mind off the escalating passion she was feeling for him. She had a funny feeling he was going through the same agony.

As they studied her map and compared it to the one from the hotel restaurant that she had taken a picture of and printed out, similarities were becoming more and more apparent. When Mickey told her that the artist who painted the picture was a descendent of the ancient Mayans, she nearly flipped out.

"How do you know that?" she asked him.

"Umm...well, I studied the ancient Mayans for three years while I was in college. I even spent two summer vacations over there working with a group of archaeologists. Plus, I believe I have read every book ever published about the subject. This painter's name immediately jumped out at me the first time you showed the picture to me. His lineage goes back centuries."

"Why didn't you say something sooner?" she asked him.

"I guess because it took me this long to put all the puzzle pieces together."

"Hmmm...do you think that's the reason this storm chose you?"

"Nah," he said. "It chose me to fall in love with you. And besides, you needed someone with big, strong arms to keep you in line. I still can't believe you started walking out into the ocean. Can you imagine what would have happened if I wasn't there to drag you back?" he asked her, grinning.

"All righty, then," she said, diverting her gaze from his piercing blue eyes. "As I was saying...about this map," she added, but then she couldn't help herself and she laughed out loud.

Mickey soon joined her, after which he snuck in a quick peck on her cheek. Now, she was embarrassed, so she quickly got both of them back to the business at hand, and she spread the map out on the dashboard. With the additional lines that Wakulla had drawn on her map, the outline of the image seemed to draw Mickey in like a magnet. Soon, his eyes lit up with excitement.

"This storm, if Wakulla is correct, actually originated in Australia before weaving its way across the ocean to South America," he started. "Then it went upward to Morocco, which is where you began tracking it."

"How do you know that?" she asked him.

"I told you, I studied ancient Mayan history," he

reminded her. "Pay attention, will you?" he asked her with a straight face, although she knew he was only joking.

"Okay, then," she said. "From there it crossed the North Atlantic to its entry point in New Jersey and then down through the rivers in the Southeast sector of the United States, where it eventually spilled out into the Gulf of Mexico," Becky added.

"Yep, that's the way it looks, assuming all your research is accurate," he said, evidently still trying to rattle her cage. "If you look at the map from a distance, the lines clearly resemble the symbol of the World Triad," he told her.

"The World Triad? What is that?" she asked.

"Well, it's a symbol that has oriental origins, which were eventually adopted by Western society. According to what I have read and researched, the symbol forms a threefold nature of reality that many civilizations in years past associated with fate, or the yin-yang representation of eternity, depending on one's beliefs."

"It all makes sense now," she told him, as they sat together in the front seat of the rented convertible."

"Yes, I agree," he said, smiling at her again.

"The earth is alive," she said, as she formed a huge circle with her arms. "That's what this storm is trying to tell mankind. All forms of nature have joined together to fight back. Earth, wind, fire and water are communicating with each other and they're trying to get a message to all us idiots on Planet Earth to wise up," she added.

"I wish this storm hadn't picked such an ancient and nearly extinct language to get its message across," Mickey said. "It's been a real challenge trying to decipher everything, but you know what? It seems to be getting easier as I go along. That's strange, don't you think?"

"Not as strange as why it picked you and me to figure this thing out," she said, rolling her eyes. "Why, out of all the billions of people on this planet, did this thing choose me?"

"Aww, come on, Becky," he said. "After all the environmental movements you've been involved in recently, as well as your genuine love of mankind and the natural elements, well...if I was the storm I'd have picked you, too!"

"Be serious, Mickey," she said, slapping his arm and suddenly feeling like a universal celebrity, no matter how nutty other people thought she was.

"I'm being quite serious. You are the perfect environmental icon to get the undivided attention of modern man," he said. "Your mission, should you choose to accept it, is..." he added with a chuckle. "To tell the world that even with all our technological advances, we are still at the mercy of Planet Earth. And besides that, you're absolutely the most beautiful woman I have ever laid eyes on."

He was smiling at her as if she was the goddess of love herself and all those lustful feelings came back like gangbusters. As she was leaning over to plant a wet, juicy kiss on his lips, she heard noises up above the trees.

"Here they come!" she shouted, when she saw the AS350 float-equipped helicopter hovering about fifty-feet above sea level straight out in front of them about twenty yards.

"Just my luck," Mickey said, but she was so excited that she didn't hear him.

With all the pine trees crowding the beach area where she and Mickey were located, along with the heavily forested trail leading into the park, the helicopter pilot had no choice but to do a sea-drop, in order to bring Wakulla to them. Within seconds, a rubber raft was dropped into the water and, one by one, Elena, two armed guards and Wakulla were lowered into the boat.

When they got closer to shore, Mickey and Becky walked out into the surf to help them disembark. As soon as Wakulla's eyes met Mickey's, they started conversing in their strange Mayan-mix language. Becky thought Wakulla seemed irritable and on edge, and he kept nodding toward the shackles around his ankles and wrists.

"Elena, the restraints have to come off," Mickey told her once they were on land. "They have to come off, or this won't work."

Elena looked at one of the guards and caught his gaze, and then she looked at the other one. Both of them gave her a negative shake of the head with fear pouring out from their eyes.

"Elena, come on," Mickey urged her. "We don't have much time."

Meanwhile, the helicopter was still hovering overhead. When Becky looked up she saw two uniformed men aiming laser rifles at Wakulla's head. The red dots on his forehead were unmistakable and she suddenly felt a wave of compassion for this poor man standing in front of her.

Elena looked at Mickey, holding his gaze for a good ten seconds and, all of a sudden, she extended her arm toward the guard standing to Wakulla's left. Reluctantly, the guy reached into his pocket and then he handed her a key.

"I want you to wait until we're back onboard the helicopter," Elena said to Mickey, and then she motioned for the two guards to release their grips on Wakulla's arms. "Then, you can do as you wish, but I can't be held responsible for whatever happens," she added, and she placed the key into the palm of his hand.

"I understand," Mickey said, sensing that she, along with everyone else who didn't understand what was truly going on, was scared to death of Wakulla.

It took Elena and the two guards less than three minutes to get back into the rubber raft and out far enough to begin their ascent back up to the waiting chopper. During all of this, the sea was extremely calm and the in-and-out wave action had seemed to cease, at least for the moment.

All of that calmness changed as soon as all three of them were safely onboard the aircraft. As they were raising the raft, a fifty-foot wave emerged from the sea about seventy-five yards away from the chopper. As quick as lightning, it began to barrel toward the hovering helicopter. The pilot soon spotted it and he yelled for someone to cut the line to the boat. Two seconds later, the chopper took off, accelerating speed and height to get away from the advancing wave of water. Then, exactly like all the times before, the wave reversed direction and sank back below the surface, leaving the waters slick as glass again. The rubber raft then drifted towards shore.

Once the helicopter was out of sight, Mickey proceeded to unlock the shackles from Wakulla's swollen wrists and ankles. Becky watched in amazement as Wakulla dropped to his knees and bowed before Mickey. It was as if he thought Mickey was a pagan god or a high priest, or someone worthy of worship. Mickey just stood there dumbfounded, as if not knowing what he should do next.

Out of nowhere, a flock of about three hundred black crows began circling them. Their wingspans stretched at least ten-feet wide from tip to tip and all their beaks were aimed downward at the three of them, as if circling for prey.

Wakulla then turned toward the sea, still on his knees and still bowing up and down with his hands clasped together. He was chanting the same words over and over, just like he was doing back at the immigration center, only this time he didn't seem to be in agony. He was actually smiling from ear to ear.

Becky reached for Mickey's hand and together they watched as the sea roared its head again, only this time it rose to unbelievable heights as it rushed toward them. Soon, they were completely engulfed in a dark, foggy cloud of mist.

"I can smell it now," Mickey said. "I can smell the sweet magnolias and the orange blossoms. It's awesome," he said, as his face lit up into a huge smile.

Moments later, the wave receded and all was calm again.

BACK AT THE HURRICANE CENTER, everyone was cheering, as all the computers came to life. Suddenly, everything was working normally again. All the communications equipment began purring like well-oiled machinery, in perfect synch with the intricate programming systems on the master computer's mainframe.

One of Madsen's men, Corporal Daniel Evans, immediately hacked into what he thought was the terrorist's network that was commandeering the strange weather patterns over the Gulf of Mexico.

"Ha!" Daniel yelled. "I gotcha!"

CHAPTER 22

Mellow
The sun mellows to
an orange~yellow puddle
drenching the heavens
with splendid colors and hues
sadly in minutes so few
©dp

As evening dusk moved in across the southeastern region of the United States, the sun was laid to rest in the western sky, while the moon slid behind a cluster of grey rain clouds toward the east. Darkness had settled in and the sea, it seemed, had taken its cue and settled down for the night.

All of the television networks had ceased coverage of the storm, as well, and they had resumed the regular night's programming, as if the storm was old news already.

Many of the gawkers along the shoreline of the Big Bend area had also left and gone back home, evidently bored with the non-catastrophic events going on out at sea.

Becky and Mickey could only see one small group of rowdy partiers who decided to hang around for a while. They had been in the same spot along the beach at Port St. Joe since morning, and they didn't seem to have any intentions of leaving anytime soon.

Wakulla hadn't moved from the beach since he arrived, still on his knees, and still chanting and praying. Mickey convinced Becky to just let him alone for the time being, and they went back to the car to wait and see what would happen next.

Hours later, just seconds after the strike of midnight, the sky above where Wakulla was kneeling suddenly lit up in glorious blue and gold rainbow colors. Then, another gigantic wall of water rolled toward shore and stopped within a few feet of the white sandy beach.

"Becky, look," Mickey said, nudging her awake from where she had fallen asleep, snuggled up against his left shoulder.

"Holy crap," she muttered, as she wiped the sleep from her eyes.

"Come on," Mickey said. "This is it."

As the two of them approached Wakulla, a light rain began to fall. Soon, a spooky mist surrounded them, which Becky thought felt like velvet against her skin. Even more amazing was that all three of their minds were now somehow connected, as if they were one human being with only one voice and one set of ears.

As they stood behind Wakulla, he began speaking to the storm in that same ancient language, only this time Becky could understand every word he was saying.

"I am here," Wakulla said, sounding prayerful and obedient.

"That is good," the storm replied, and again, Becky clearly understood every word the storm was saying.

All of a sudden, the wave shifted to the left and a purple shroud of dust fell onto Mickey's body.

"Mickey, you have only been on Earth for forty-two years," the storm said. "I have been here for one-hundred million years. The time has come for all of mankind's destructive ways to end."

As tears streamed down Mickey's face, he began trembling and then he fell to his knees.

"My God!" he cried, looking up at the huge wave. "You know my name!"

"Yes, I know your name and I can tell you that your father is safe for the time being."

Mickey's eyes grew wide and he shot back to his feet, as the purple shroud lifted and fell onto Becky's shoulders.

"Changes must be made immediately to reverse the damaging effects of pollution, environmental waste and destruction, corporate greed and the despicable treatment of the elderly," it commanded her. "These changes must be written into law within seventy-two hours. You, my child, know exactly what needs to be done."

Then, as quickly as the mist had arrived, it suddenly vanished, and the huge wave slithered back into the depths of the sea.

Unbeknown to Mickey and Becky, a television crew had been filming the entire scene just a few hundred yards behind them. Their van was hidden behind a cluster of trees, but the photographer had been out in the open catching everything on film. As he was gathering up his equipment, he realized he'd been spotted.

"Wow! Can you believe that?" he shouted to Becky and Mickey, as they approached him. "It was awesome!"

"What did you see? What did you hear?" Becky nervously asked the guy.

"What did I see?" he asked her, looking at her as if he thought she was crazy. "I saw this gigantic wave hanging over top of you guys. Then all these purple lights. As for what I heard...shoot, lady, I heard the same things you heard. A bunch of gibberish," he said.

Becky looked up at Mickey and for the first time since all of this storm craziness had started, she felt a sense of dread and helplessness. Deep down in her soul she knew it wasn't going to be an easy task trying to convince the people of the world that the storm was serious and that it had spoken to them in comprehensible English.

Meanwhile, the reporter was inside the van trying to get his satellite feed to work, so he could transmit the film back to the television station.

"What do we do?" she asked Mickey.

"We tell our side of the story," he said. "Wait here...and don't move. On second thought, go get those maps out of the car and hurry back here."

While Becky ran to get the maps, Mickey walked over to the open door on the side of the van to speak to the reporter, who was still struggling with the satellite equipment. Then, as she was rushing back to where the cameraman was, she heard loud voices, which sounded like Mickey arguing with the reporter. Seconds later, the two of them emerged from the van and they walked over toward her and the photographer.

"Joey, get that camera set up again," Dave, the reporter told him.

"What? I just got it all broken down," he tried arguing with him.

"Just do as I said!" Dave ordered him, and then he jerked his head toward Mickey, who was standing directly behind him. "Now!" he repeated, as his eyes grew wider.

"Okay, okay," Joey said, looking at both Mickey and Dave, as if he thought they were as crazy as Becky.

"Becky, get ready," Mickey said. "I want you to talk to the camera and be specific. Tell them everything."

Once Joey had Becky on live transmission, she spoke in intricate detail, describing the demands of the storm, before explaining the apocalyptic symbol on the map she was holding. She ended by stressing that these changes had to be written into law within seventy-two hours, or else more devastation would occur.

"It will be much worse than the destruction of the coal plant," she said, suddenly astounded by all the words that had come out of her mouth, as if it wasn't her who was speaking, but the storm itself.

When she finished, Mickey told Dave to go back inside the van and air the segment showing the wave that had made the demands. Within seconds, scenes of what had just happened on the beach were transmitted, as Mickey and Becky watched from outside the van's door. Just like the photographer had said, the storm merely sounded like a bunch of gibberish, yet there was the crazy Becky Rogers telling them she understood what it was saying.

When the tape finished Mickey told Dave that he and

Joey were free to leave. It only took a minute or two before the two of them got all their equipment packed up, and then they jumped into the cab of the van. As Becky and Mickey stood back, they watched as the van shot out of there like a bat out of hell.

"Do you think anyone will believe me?" Becky asked Mickey.

"I hope so, but it might take a little more convincing before any action is taken," he said. "You did a good job, girl. Now, let's hope that jerk Madsen doesn't do something stupid."

"How did you get that reporter to do as you asked? He looked scared to death."

Mickey grinned and then he lifted up his shirttail to show her the pistol he had shoved into the waistband of his pants.

"I guess that explains it," she said. "Dang, you're just full of surprises, aren't you?"

"Oh, you ain't seen nothin' yet," he said, still grinning. "Come on, let's go round up Wakulla."

As she and Mickey walked back toward the beach, they rehashed the entire scene that had just played out. The rain clouds that had been threatening to let loose all night had grown even thicker above them, blocking out the light from the moon and the stars, so the beach was pitch black darkness. All they could hear was the gentle lapping of the waves caressing the shoreline.

"Hey! Where did Wakulla go?" she asked Mickey, as her eyes scanned up and down the dark beach.

"Shit! I don't know!" Mickey shouted. "We need to find him, though! That's for damned sure!"

CHAPTER 23

Thorns
As love grows deeper
Like thorns in my fragile heart
You show no mercy
©dp

"It's a hoax!" Madsen yelled. "Can't you people tell it's all a hoax? Look at that crazy troublemaking woman! I had her thoroughly checked out and she's been causing havoc for years with all her wild environmental schemes!"

As the reporter was narrating his story on national television, he was showing the scenes of what had just happened on the beach. After that, Becky's face filled the screen with her interpretations of the storm's demands. All the top officials who had gathered at the hurricane center were speechless, all except for Colonel Madsen, that is.

"I'm not so sure about all of that," Eric snapped back at the colonel.

"What are you, off your rocker? You actually believe a body of water can talk?" Madsen continued, directing his angry tirade at Eric. "It's trick photography is all it is."

"I saw the same thing you just saw, Colonel. Something is out there causing all these strange weather disturbances. I don't know what it is, but it seems to be bigger than any of us," Eric said, looking around at all the other faces in the room, but getting no reaction other than stunned looks.

"Eric, you surprise me. You're a scientist for godsakes. Act like one," Madsen said, much more sedately now, and then he reached over to turn off the television.

"I'm trying to, Colonel, but I've never seen anything like this before. None of my staff has been able to figure out what's causing all this mayhem out in the Gulf. We still have no answers on the reverse river currents, either, or all the flooding that was there one day and gone the next. None of it makes any logical sense."

"Well, perhaps, it's time to let more experienced people take over," Madsen said, sounding calm as a cucumber under the circumstances.

"Like who!? You!?" Eric yelled, as he slammed his fist down on the table.

"That's exactly right, Eric," Madsen said, still not raising his voice or acting the least bit upset. "I want you out of here now. This is officially a military operation from this point forward."

Madsen immediately ordered two of his men to remove Eric from the room and he went kicking and screaming, yelling at Madsen not to do anything stupid.

"Damned idiot," Madsen mumbled, and then he turned to his assistant. "I want you to let all those reporters in here now," he ordered him.

"Yes, sir," the young soldier said, and he stepped out of the room.

Ever since the storm had raised its ugly head out in the Gulf, there had been reporters from every news station across the country milling about out in the parking lot, waiting to speak to someone in authority. Now, though, there were only two diehard journalists left behind, and they were immediately summoned into the command center. Minutes later, Colonel Madsen was being broadcast on live TV.

"I will not be ordered to comply with these idiotic demands by some overgrown wind bag and two insane environmentalists!" he shouted, and then he went on and on with his own theories that made absolutely no sense, except to him and the blind people who were following his orders.

For the next several hours, Madsen's men were busy deciphering all the computer codes they had found on the Internet, including Corporal Daniel Evans, who had sworn earlier that he had hacked into the terrorist's network. In the mean time, the colonel excused himself and he left the building, saying he'd be back first thing tomorrow.

MEANWHILE, BECKY AND MICKEY were frantically searching for Wakulla along the beach. With the low cloud cover and the steadily falling rain it was difficult to see anything.

"Do you think he ran away?" Becky asked him, as she shielded her eyes from the stinging raindrops.

"I certainly hope not," Mickey said. "Without him to interpret the storm we're lost. You realize that, don't you?"

"Do we still need him for that?"

"What? Are you kidding? Do you really think that just because *you* got on national television and warned people to follow orders from a force of nature that people are going to comply? Let's face it, all anyone else could hear was gibberish, just like those two reporters told us," he said. "Trust me, Becky. They all think you're a nutcase, especially Madsen."

"Is that what you think?" she asked, on the defensive now.

"Of course not! Look, honey, I'm in this with you all the way," he said. "I witnessed the same things you did earlier. I heard the demands just like you did. Do I think it's preposterous that a big ol' wave of water or an entire body of seawater can speak? Hell, yeah! But it happened, Becky."

"Yes, I know it happened," she said, looking at him with tears in her eyes.

"It happened and it will continue to happen until the world's inhabitants do something to reverse all the damage they've caused for centuries. They're not going to do it without a fight, though. This storm has only just begun. Things are going to get a lot worse before they get better, and without Wakulla we're up shit's creek without a damned paddle."

"Look! Over there!" she suddenly shouted. "It's that raft from the helicopter. Do you think Wakulla is in it?"

About sixty yards south of them was the bright orange rubber raft that the helicopter pilot had left behind. It was sitting in the surf bobbing back and forth in the oncoming waves against the shoreline.

"There's only one way to find out," Mickey said, and the two of them started running toward it.

When they got to within three feet of it, however, it was clear there was no one inside of it.

"Damn!" Mickey shouted. "Where the hell is he?"

Becky stood with her feet buried in the sand, looking out across the sea, but seeing nothing other than a steady roll of gentle waves rushing in and out.

"There's no way he would have swam out to sea. I mean...that would be just plain dumb," she said.

"Do you have your phone with you?" Mickey asked.

"No, I left it in the car," she said.

"Why don't we head back there, and as much as I hate to call Elena again, I don't think we have any other choice," he said. "Maybe they can bring that helicopter back with a search light and help us find him."

"Yeah, maybe," she said, although she doubted the pilot would make a return trip after what happened earlier.

When they made it back to the car, Becky opened the driver's side door to retrieve her cell phone that she had left on the dashboard. She was about to shut the door when she heard a noise in the backseat.

"What the...?" she started. "Well, I'll be damned. Would you lookie there?"

"Hurry up, Becky," Mickey shouted, as he stood near the shoreline, still searching the beach for Wakulla.

Quietly, she closed the car door and she calmly walked over toward Mickey, broadly smiling. When he turned around and saw her face, he looked at her as if she'd gone mad.

"I found him," she whispered.

"Huh? What do you mean you found him?"

"He's asleep in the backseat of the car," she said. "He looks so peaceful, too."

"Well, I'll be a son-of-a-gun," Mickey said, shaking his head.

He, too, was smiling now and then, all of a sudden, he scooped Becky up in his arms and he kissed her.

"I wasn't the least bit worried," he said, as he held her in his arms. "I knew he wouldn't leave us high and dry."

"Yeah, right," she said, laughing. "You were as scared as I was."

"Well, maybe just a little," he said, and then he kissed her again.

This time it was a deep, passionate kiss that went on and on and on.

CHAPTER 24

Memory
Humid images
Thick, annoying, clinging
Leaves me sadly wilted
Recollections
©dp

When Colonel Madsen returned to the hurricane center at eight o'clock the next morning, he asked for an update on the storm, and then he took his place behind Eric's desk. Moments later, as he sipped on his coffee, Corporal Evans walked into the room.

"Well, what did you find?" Madsen asked him.

"I'm afraid we weren't able to find anything unusual," he said, looking embarrassed and humiliated.

"Do you mean to tell me that the greatest computer minds in the military can't find anything? I thought you were the best, boy. What happened? Did you lose your touch, or what?"

Just then, there was a knock at the door and Jeremy stuck his head in.

"Excuse me, Colonel, but you might want to come out here and see this," he said, looking anxious and nervous.

"See what? More foolishness?" Madsen barked, but he followed Jeremy out into the command center, anyway, with Corporal Evans on his heels.

All four computer monitors along one wall of the command center were alive with satellite and radar pictures of the waters out in the Gulf of Mexico.

"What the hell?" Madsen gasped, but everyone remained silent as they watched the screens. "Somebody better speak up!" he then shouted.

"Sir, there are three separate hurricanes out there in the Gulf and they are all bigger than anything we've ever seen before," Jeremy told him. "The disturbing part is that they're all stationary. They're not moving and we can't tell which way they might go."

"The wind speed according to some of the buoys out in that area are clocking these things at three-hundred miles per hour, not only at the cores, but around all three storms for miles," another of Madsen's men piped up. "They're very compact and very powerful."

Meanwhile, the news stations all around the Gulf coastline area were being swamped with callers who were watching the three storms. Soon, all the network channels were back to continuous coverage of the strange phenomena. Eyewitness reports were coming in that the seas were groaning again with foreign words being repeated over and over. One of the words that everyone said was clearly distinct was the word Dumala.

Webcams at various beach locations all around the Gulf were showing thousands and thousands of people lined up along the shorelines, watching and listening. This time, however, no one was laughing.

Just then, Captain Jake Richards from the Miami Beach Coast Guard walked into the command center wearing his starched-white uniform and reeking of cologne.

"Who are you?" Madsen growled at him.

After Jake explained who he was and why he was there, Madsen's face lit up, as if he was happy to see another arm of the military getting involved.

"Well, now, Captain, let's hear what the Coast Guard has to say about all this nonsense," Madsen urged him.

"First of all, I have to say, that with all my twenty-five years in the Coast Guard and with all the hurricanes I've experienced in my lifetime, this thing out there, whatever it is, is damn monstrous. Not only can't our boats get close enough to see anything, but we can't get our helicopters or aircraft any lower than thirty-thousand feet above it," Jake told him, and it was clear from the look on his face that he was completely baffled. "Nothing is showing up on our sonar or radar, either."

"Okay," Madsen said, sounding impatient. "And what is the second thing you're going to tell me? You don't know how to battle it? You don't know how to prepare the people? What?"

"With all due respect, sir, we're doing all we can to try and figure this thing out," Jake said.

"Well, I know exactly what to do," Madsen said. "As for you, feel free to leave anytime. I don't need you," he said, and he went back into Eric's office and slammed the door shut.

Jake took his cue and he turned to leave, slamming the main entrance door shut behind him in an angry huff.

Corporal Evans, who had been sitting in front of a computer screen in the corner of the command center, suddenly spewed out a string of curse words, yelling at the monitor and swearing at the storms as if they were human.

Seconds later, everybody in the room heard the angry response from the storm, as it blasted through the loudspeakers.

"Dumala!" it shouted. "Dumala! Dumala!"

The sounds were so loud that everyone had to cover their ears.

"Where did that come from?" Corporal Evans shouted, as he looked around the command center.

All those who had clearance to be inside the hurricane center were standing in the command center. There was no one else in the building. As Evans looked around the room, glaring into each person's eyes one at a time, nobody had an answer. There was absolutely no explanation as to how those sounds got into the loudspeaker system. Even Madsen, who had stepped out of Eric's office when he heard the sounds, looked freaked out, but then he went back inside, slamming the door shut again.

He immediately got on the phone to Air Force

headquarters in Washington D.C. Within seconds he was patched into the commander's office.

After taking the heat for a good five minutes from the commander-in-chief of the Air Force for not handling the situation, Madsen admitted that he was at a loss as to what to do. After a few more minutes of being ridiculed and humiliated, he suggested they resort to Operation WB77X, which was a top secret, untested weather bomb to disperse of this "trivial troublemaking storm", as he so eloquently stated it.

The commander finally agreed and after they hung up Madsen immediately flew into action. Seconds later, he was on the phone with the captain on duty at an Air Force base on the east coast of Florida. In no uncertain terms, and after citing a direct order from the commander, he told the captain to proceed with Operation WB77X. He then put his assistant on the phone to give the guy all the particulars.

"Now we're getting somewhere," Madsen said with a wicked grin, and then he left Eric's office to head for the men's room.

CHAPTER 25

Hands
A stroke of a hand
The desire burns within
Wantonly waiting
©dp

"Do you remember the Kyoto Protocol?" Becky asked Mickey, as they strolled down the beach early the next morning.

After an uncomfortable night trying to sleep in the front seat of the convertible they both needed to get out and stretch the kinks out of their bodies. Wakulla was still in the backseat of the car, although he was awake now. He was munching on potato chips and sipping on a warm soft drink, as his eyes focused on the troubled sea out in front of him. Becky thought he seemed content to just sit and watch.

"Yes, I remember," Mickey said. "The United States has stubbornly refused to actively participate in that protocol ever since the United Nations first adopted it back in December of 1997. Al Gore may have signed the agreement, but as far as I know, it was never ratified in Congress."

"No, it wasn't," she said. "To this day I simply don't understand their reasoning. After all, the objective was simple enough; reduce greenhouse emissions over a set period of time. All they were trying to do was fight global warming."

"True," Mickey said. "But you have to remember that not everyone believes there is a problem. One administration after the next since that time has pretty much ignored the Protocol. Plus, now that the end of the agreement is about to come to a close, the general consensus, I'm sure, is, 'Why sign it now?'"

"By the way," Becky started, and then she looked into Mickey's eyes. "Why are we still here? Why didn't we leave last night and go find a hotel room or something, instead of sleeping in the car?"

"Hmmm...that's a good question. I wish I had an answer," he said, scratching his chin. "Maybe the storm put some sort of subliminal message into our brains last night."

"You mean like y'all better hang around because I'm not finished yet?" she asked, laughing.

"Yeah, I guess...something like that," he said, laughing along with her. "Or maybe it wants us to think long and hard before we pounce on each other on a bed of white linens and start making babies."

"Ohh...yeah, that could be," she said, sounding serious and reflective, yet wondering what he really meant. "After all, overpopulation has been the major factor behind all of Earth's problems from the very beginning," she added, trying her best to keep things on a serious note.

"Yep, it certainly has," Mickey said. "I imagine that's why there have been so many devastating earthquakes, hurricanes, tornadoes, tsunamis and other natural disasters wiping out people by the thousands. The Universe is trying to save itself from overpopulation."

"You know, you're very cute when you talk so sensitively and intelligently," she said, tossing seriousness into the wind and suddenly realizing that she was totally infatuated with Mickey DeRosa, the laughing author.

"You're pretty darned cute yourself, Ms. Becky Rogers," he said, which made her blush.

"I have another question," she said, feeling uncomfortable again in the presence of such a handsome, intelligent man, even if he was bald as an eagle.

"What's that?" he asked.

"Why did the storm choose this area to show its face?

I mean...if overpopulation is the real issue behind all of this craziness, then, why didn't the storm terrorize Japan or China?   Haven't they been the worst offenders throughout history?"

"Perhaps," he said. "If you want my opinion, though, I think this area of the ocean was chosen because it has so many dead zones...probably the worst in the world. All that excess nitrogen from farm over-fertilization that flows down the Mississippi River from the Midwest, along with all the sewage, vehicle and factory emissions, not only from the Mississippi, but from the Suwannee River...well, it all lands right out here in the Gulf of Mexico."

Just then, a loud, ear-piercing roar bellowed up from the depths of the sea.

"Dumala!" it shouted. "Dumala! Dumala!"

"Holy crap," Becky gasped, barely able to find her voice. "I think it heard you. You must have hit the nail on the head."

"I told you it was going to get worse," Mickey said, and then they both saw the swirling winds out in the middle of the bay, growing higher and higher into the sky.

CHAPTER 26

Seasons
Light, shadow then darkness
Leaves whisked away by the wind
Seasons turn around
©dp

"**H**ey, boys! Come on in here and watch this!" Madsen shouted to Jeremy and Carl, who were sitting together out in the command center.

"What's going on?" Jeremy asked, as he stepped into Eric's office with Carl on his heels like a trained puppy.

Ever since Madsen had tossed Eric out on his ear, he had literally taken over use of his office. Late last night, he had his men set up a mini-command center on the conference table, which nearly duplicated all the equipment out in the real command center, although on a much smaller scale.

Madsen was a cigar smoker and it truly stunk in Eric's office now. Even though smoking indoors had been outlawed years ago, Madsen didn't seem to think the law applied to him, so he just smoked away, oblivious to all the grunts and groans from everyone around him.

"You are about to witness history in the making," Madsen said, as Jeremy and Carl stood near the doorway. "In just a few hours the Gulf of Mexico will be back to normal again. We're going to rip those storms to shreds," he added, gloating, as he leaned back in Eric's oversized leather chair.

His trained monkey assistant, young Sergeant Wally Emerson, was busy getting all the computer programs up and running and it was clear from the way he was acting that he thought Madsen was God himself.

Just then, the phone rang and Madsen answered it, soon grinning from ear to ear. After listening to someone on the other end talk for a good three minutes, he said, "Thank you, sir," and he hung up. "Okay, boys, this is it," he said to Jeremy and Carl. "Hang onto your hats!"

Jeremy and Carl took a seat at the table and then Madsen nodded to Wally. Two seconds later, the voice of a jetfighter pilot could be heard on the computer's speakers, as he conversed back and forth with the control tower. The aircraft was already in the air and halfway between the east and west coasts of Florida, somewhere above the Orlando area.

"Sergeant, would you bring us some more coffee?" Madsen asked, talking down to Wally as if he was his personal slave.

"Yes, sir," Wally said, and he zipped out the door to do as he was asked.

By the time he returned with three more Styrofoam cups of hot coffee, the atmosphere inside Eric's office had changed from jubilant victory into panicked confusion.

"I don't know what's wrong, Colonel! I seem to have lost control of all my instruments!" the pilot shouted, with his voice cracking in obvious disbelief.

"What the hell are you talking about?" Madsen yelled into the microphone, but all he got back was static on the other end.

Then he told Wally to get the military base on the phone and he was immediately patched through to the control tower.

"We needed our best pilot on this mission!" he shouted to the captain on duty. "Why did you let some young punk up there who doesn't know how to fly a damn airplane?"

"He's our best pilot, sir. He's flown three hundred missions during his career and he's never had an incident," the captain told him.

Just then, the pilot's voice came back through the speakers loud and clear again.

"This is crazy! Somebody has set new coordinates! The plane is turning and heading north-northwest now! I can't stop it!" he continued yelling.

After he rattled off the coordinates to the control tower there was silence for about two minutes before the captain spoke again.

"Colonel," he calmly said. "The aircraft is on a direct heading toward a federal penitentiary in Kansas. There's nothing else around there for miles. What the hell is going on?"

"That's what I'd like to know!" Madsen screamed and then he slammed down the phone.

IT WAS A TYPICAL MORNING inside the heavily guarded federal prison located in an isolated area in the vast plains of rural Kansas. It was a day just like any other day for the most violent criminals in the United States. The worst of the worst were housed in this facility. Hundreds of murderers, pedophiles, rapists, kidnappers, and cold-blooded killers topped the list of offenders, who had been in and out of this facility for years.

As the inmates sat in the cafeteria eating lunch, there was conversation and laughter among one group of men, who were boasting about their crimes as if they were truly proud of them.

They spoke of rape and torture, and senseless murders of children. Not one of them showed any remorse for what they had done. Many of these men were repeat offenders, who had beat the court system time and time again, continually being released, striking again, and then being re-incarcerated.

One man joked about how he had raped and tortured a little girl.

"Yeah, that little thing, she cried and she bled, and then she called out for her mommy and daddy," he said, laughing. "That's when I put my hands around her tiny little neck and I choked her to death."

Everybody sitting at the table laughed and then it was

one-upmanship, as each of them took turns relating their own gruesome stories.

"Come on, you turkeys! Eat up! This food is damn good!" one of them finally said.

"Yeah, can you believe we get three healthy meals a day?" another one piped up.

"Yes-siree!" the first guy shouted.   "All those mommies and daddies, aunts and uncles, and brothers and sisters of those little girls we raped, tortured and killed are paying their taxes so that we can eat high on the hog!"

"Don't forget the dentists and doctors who take such good care of us! And hell, we get to watch TV, work out in the gym, make arts and crafts, and all the while they're out their working their asses off to foot our bill!" another one added.

Many of these men had been on death row for decades, continually avoiding their fate by hiring the best lawyers in the country to file one appeal after the next. Working the system had become an art to these men. Oftentimes, the worst case scenario, especially for the pedophiles, was that they'd get locked up for a while, which only meant that they didn't have to worry about finding a job. The only thing they were concerned about now was where they could score their next cigarette.

 In the meantime, the military was scrambling to get the airplane under control, when suddenly, the pilot was ejected somewhere over Little Rock, Arkansas.   He landed safely in a patch of trees, although he dangled there in the high branches for two hours before help arrived.

The unmanned airplane kept on a steady course toward its target. Soon, a computerized voice inside the aircraft radioed back to the control tower in Florida. It demanded that a warning be sent to the prison warden that he had twelve minutes to get his guards and administrative staff out of harm's way.

Mass chaos ensued when the Air Force Commander phoned the warden to advise him of the situation and to tell him that they were powerless to stop the approaching fighter jet and its deadly cargo.

One of the secretaries, who had worked at the prison for the last twenty years, heard the conversation on the warden's speakerphone and she immediately prepared to flee the premises. On her way out the door, she paused for a moment in the doorway of the warden's office.

"What took them so long to kill these bastards?" she asked him.

COLONEL MADSEN, WHO HAD already viewed himself as a hero for initiating the weather bomb plan, was now completely embarrassed and humiliated. When the same computerized voice from the aircraft began resounding through the speakers of Madsen's computer, he nearly fell out of his chair. It was a vivid warning that made the hair on the back of his neck stand on end.

"You should take council for a second opinion and not listen to the words of one who is so quick to judge," the voice said. "Throughout history, man has attempted to destroy what he does not understand, and more often than not it has devastating results."

Everyone inside the hurricane center heard the voice because it was playing over the loudspeakers. They also knew that it was directing its comments toward Madsen, who looked as if he had reached his boiling point. It was clear to everyone in Eric's office that he was infuriated for being singled out and embarrassed by an inanimate object.

Madsen began yelling and cursing, using words that many had never heard before. He was standing in the middle of the command center now with his forehead drenched in sweat. His fists were balled up so tight that his hands were beet red, matching the color of his face.

"I *will* have victory and I *will* draw first blood!" he shouted, and then there was silence, as the power went off and the computer screens went black.

CHAPTER 27

Hurricane
Destruction untamed
Nature's anger released
Affecting countless lives sorrowfully
Devastation
©dp

As the three hurricanes continued to swirl out in the Gulf of Mexico in a basically stationary mode, people in the Gulf coast cities began gradually falling into panic mode, especially when the media played up the danger as possibly being the end of the world, and even more so when news of the airstrike at the prison went public.

Religious experts, philosophers and scientists were being interviewed one after the other, and they were all saying the same thing. The end is near.

Becky's face had been plastered across the nation's television screens as she sent out her warnings and the demands of the storm. Of course, everybody wanted to know who this Becky Rogers was and why she was on national TV scaring the crap out of everyone. Those who had seen her before knew she had been shot down by the experts time and time again over the years. They also knew she had been labeled as an environmental troublemaker.

It didn't take but a few hours, though, before some of the more diligent weather experts began compiling all the recent strange weather events and putting them together, finally realizing that they were all somehow connected. All the wild stories about river currents reversing direction, bodies washing up on the shores, old ships floating to the surface of the oceans, massive and devastating earthquakes, violent volcanic eruptions, and all the extreme weather events of the past several winter seasons were finally being lumped together as one monumental problem that mankind was up against.

Soon, as more and more people were made aware of the situation, thousands of them embarked on a mass chaotic exodus, trying to get as far away from the storms as possible. Of course, the naysayers had their time in the spotlight, as well, scoffing at all the supposed experts and laughing in their faces.

As dark storm clouds eased closer and closer to the shorelines, those who chose to stay behind had their eyes glued to their TV sets, as they watched the odd events unfold on national television. The same question was on everyone's mind. "What is going on?"

Nobody in authority seemed to have an answer, though; not the government, not the weather experts, not the military, and not even the President seemed to have the slightest clue what this thing was or how to deal with it. For now, it was a watch and wait scenario.

Major highways were suddenly jammed with a wall-to-wall procession of vehicles heading either north or northwest. As the hours went by, the police and fire rescue couldn't keep up with the rash of accidents along the major southern arteries, and hospital emergency rooms were nearing full capacity with injured motorists steadily coming in.

Airplanes at all the major airports were filled to capacity with folks leaving the country and going to places as far away as Europe and Asia, thinking no place in the United States was safe from the wrath of these three powerful storms.

Warnings to just stay put that were being sent over the airwaves by mayors, governors, the police and the President were being ignored. It was total and mass hysteria, surpassing the level of fear that was created by the 9/11 attacks on the World Trade Center.

The Mexican people were also heading southwestward, due to the proximity of the hurricane to their eastern coastline. Over the course of the day, mass pandemonium had definitely set in and it wasn't a pretty sight.

There were many people, however, especially those who lived far away from any affected coastal areas, who simply ignored the strange events and they continued going about their daily lives without a care in the world. There were also just as many people in high government offices who thought the whole thing was just a stunt by some environmental activists to draw attention to their causes.

The government of the United States was split on their assessment of the situation, just like the horrific divisions between the Democrats and the Republicans in Congress; they just couldn't agree on anything and so they did nothing.

CHAPTER 28

Storm
The strength of a storm
is never predictable
until, it's over.
©dp

Wakulla had gone out to the edge of the surf and again, he was on his knees, absorbed in his chanting ritual when Becky and Mickey returned to where the car was parked.

"Oh, no," Becky said, as she watched him. "Do you think the storm is about to speak to us again?" she asked Mickey.

"I'd say there was about a ninety-five percent chance of us about to see another wave come ashore," he said, as he gazed out across the bay. "Hmmm...make that a hundred percent," he added, as he watched a thirty-foot wall of dark blue water come rushing toward them.

The same flock of huge black crows that had circled overhead yesterday was back, only this time they had doubled in number. A light misty rain began to fall and with it came the fragrance of sweet magnolias and orange blossoms surrounding them in a purple haze of brilliant color.

"Oh, God, I'm scared," Becky said.

"Don't be," Mickey told her, and then he reached for her hand, as they walked toward Wakulla.

"Dumala! Dumala! Dumala!" the storm shouted, and then, just as before, all three of their minds linked together as the wave hovered over their heads.

"We are here," Wakulla said, lifting his head toward

the sky.

"I can see that," it said. "Your leaders, however, don't seem to understand the gravity of the situation. Instead of honoring my demands, they are attempting to destroy me. You must urge them to act swiftly or I shall be forced to counter-attack with an even more devastating blow to your infrastructure. The federal prison was a joy to demolish and I am certain the American people are looking upon it as a blessing, but the next event will make them take me seriously."

"We have tried to warn them," Becky said. "What else can we do?"

"You must hurry back to your fearless, incompetent leaders. You must contact the media and implore the world to change their destructive ways. They will listen to you, Becky, but you must hurry," the storm ordered her.

"But what if they won't listen? What will you do?" she asked.

"Do not worry, my child. By the time you and Mickey return to the hurricane center, I will have already set in motion my next acts of persuasive arguments. They will be ready to listen to you."

Just then, the sky parted, the purple shroud lifted and the wave rushed back to the sea.

"Dumala! Dumala! Dumala!" they heard in the distance, and then the waters returned to a flat, motionless sea of eerie calm.

"Damn! I wish I had thought to bring my computer with me," Becky said, as she stood there in amazement and wonder. "I feel so cut off from what's going on with this storm. I need my mapping program."

"Now, how in the heck would you be able to get Internet access out here in the boonies?" Mickey asked her, laughing.

"It's called a wireless Internet card," she said, rolling her eyes at him.

"Oh," he said. "But how would you get power for your laptop?"

"Boy, you really need to get with the program. It's very simple to hook up a computer to a car battery...you know...with one of those cigarette lighter adapters," she explained.

"Oh, yeah, sure," he said, but she could tell he didn't understand at all.

"We must go now," Wakulla said in perfect English, and he started walking back to the car.

"Wow, did you hear that?" Becky whispered to Mickey, as she stared after Wakulla.

"Yeah, I heard it all right," Mickey said. "Well, we'd best be getting a move on. There's no telling what this storm is going to do next."

"You drive," Becky said, and she tossed Mickey the keys. "I'm too freaked out to even think at the moment."

"And I'm okay? Sheesh, girl, you must think I'm a fearless lion or something. This crap has me scared out of my wits, too," he said, shaking his head.

"Yeah, but you're a guy," she said, and she smiled at him, as she slid into the front passenger's seat. "And besides that, you're the one who told me not to be afraid."

"That was merely a statement of self-preservation," he said. "I've got the same dark streaks on my underwear as you do right now," he added, which made her giggle.

Wakulla was already in the backseat, sitting with his back to the right of the car behind Becky with his legs stretched out across the leather seat. His eyes were clamped shut and he seemed to have fallen asleep.

Minutes later, they were back on the highway heading south with the convertible top down. It was a beautiful day with the sun beating down on them, brightening their mood for the time being.

"I'm going to have to stop for gas soon. We've got less than a quarter of a tank," Mickey said, as he looked down at the gauge.

"Yeah, and I need a bathroom," Becky piped up. "That peeing in the woods crap is for the animals and the critters of the world."

"And the men," Mickey said, laughing at her.

"I'll bet you pee off your front porch when you're at home," she came back at him.

"Nope...the back porch," he said, and then they both had a good laugh, which was sorely needed after what they had just been through.

Once they gassed up, bought more snacks to eat, and everyone took their turn in the restroom, the three of them were back on I-75 speeding southward.

"I suppose I should call my mother," Becky said. "She's probably out of her mind with worry."

"Good idea," Mickey said. "Maybe she can clue us in to what's happening out here in lala-land. I'm anxious to hear about what the storm did to that prison."

"Oh, that's right," she said. "I almost forgot about that."

Once Becky's mother got done chewing her out for not calling sooner, she calmed down enough to tell her what was happening on the television. Halfway through the story about the prison, however, Becky's cell phone shut off.

"Oh, shoot," she said. "My battery died."

"Don't look at me," Mickey said. "Mine went kaput yesterday."

"Don't you have a car charger?" she asked him.

"I might," he said. "But if I do, it's back home still in the box. By the way, this is your rental car. How come you didn't bring a charger with you?"

"I wasn't exactly planning on traveling the entire state of Florida and spending the night in the forest," she said, rolling her eyes at him again.

"Neither was I," he said. "So, what did your mom say?"

"Well, it seems our friend, the storm, hijacked a jet fighter airplane, and after it ejected the pilot over Arkansas, it dumped itself and some sort of bomb right on top of a federal prison, leveling the entire facility and killing all the inmates."

"No shit? Damn!" he said, as his eyes grew wide.

"No shit," she said. "If it can do that, I can only

imagine what else it has up its sleeve."

"Yep...we can only imagine," Mickey said with a heavy sigh.

CHAPTER 29

Hello?
The ring of the phone
So many different tones
Who could be calling?
©dp

"Excuse me, Colonel," Sergeant Emerson said, as he stood in the doorway of Eric's office. "The Vice President is on the phone."

"Vice President of what?" Madsen barked at him, acting as if he couldn't care less if the Pope himself was on the phone.

"The United States, sir," Emerson told him.

"Oh...well, in that case, I'd better not keep the man waiting," he said, changing his tune. "Shut the door on your way out."

The power in the building had only been back up for a few hours, after mysteriously shutting down right after the failed air drop. None of the telephones had been working, either, but once the power was restored they hadn't stopped ringing.

Once Emerson left, Madsen picked up the receiver. Five minutes later, after receiving orders from the second in command of the United States, Madsen was patched through to a conference call with Admiral Stephens of the U.S. Navy. They were both ordered to work together to put an end to this storm that was terrorizing the nation.

Within the hour, a Navy ballistic missile submarine was dispatched toward the Gulf of Mexico. Its cargo was three torpedoes that were carrying the secret weather bomb. Since Madsen couldn't seem to get anywhere with all his high-tech air power, this underwater attack seemed the next logical choice. At least, that's what the Vice President told him.

At twelve noon, the first torpedo was launched. Ten seconds later, the second one hit its target and then the third was released into the center of the last of the three storms swirling in the Gulf.

Inside the command center it was deathly quiet as all eyes were glued to the radar screens. Everyone was holding their breath, as they watched the storms slowly dissipate one right after the next. Even Colonel Madsen had stopped puffing on his nasty smelling cigar, as he stood watching from the middle of the room.

"Mission accomplished, sir," the submarine captain calmly announced over the radio that had been patched into the command center.

While Madsen gloated, everyone was shouting and laughing and high-fiving their cohorts. It sounded like a Fourth of July celebration inside the room. All that was missing was the popping of champagne corks.

"Didn't I tell you I could whip that storm?" Madsen said to both Carl and Jeremy.

"Yes, you did," Jeremy said, and he shook the colonel's hand.

"Okay, people!" Madsen shouted. "Let's get this place dismantled and go home!"

Again, there was more jubilant shouting, as all of Madsen's men prepared to break down their equipment and call it a day. Halfway through that process, as Madsen sat behind Eric's desk talking to the Vice President on the phone, Sergeant Emerson knocked on the door.

"I'm sorry, sir," Emerson started, but Madsen waved him off. "Sir, we have a problem," he kept on. "We have a real problem."

Madsen seemed totally unaffected by Emerson's frantic tone and he merely continued his phone conversation, until he finally hung up thirty seconds later.

"Emerson, I could send you back to boot camp! You know that, don't you? How dare you interrupt me when

I'm talking to the Vice President?!" he screamed at him, as he pounded his fist against the desk.

"I'm sorry, sir, but we have reports coming in about massive floods up the Mississippi River."

"What? Emerson, I don't give a rat's ass about river floods. I came here to disperse a few hurricanes and I did my job. Now, I'm going home to my wife."

"But, sir, it's bad. It's not just water that has overflowed the river," he said. "It's massive amounts of sewage and bacteria. It's flooding thousands of homes from New Orleans on up to Minnesota with tons of dark black sludge."

The Mississippi River, being the largest river system in the United States, had always been a source of flooding over the years, but what was happening now was beyond what anyone could have ever fathomed. From its origin at Lake Itasca, Minnesota, down to where it exited into the Gulf of Mexico near New Orleans, all the rivers and streams had surpassed the highest flood stages ever recorded.

Not only had the river reversed currents, but it was backwashing all the bacteria and sewage that had been dumped into the Gulf for hundreds of years and sending it back and over the banks of all the connecting rivers and streams in ten different states. The entire midsection of the country was in a panic and a few minutes later scenes of the destruction were being aired on every news channel on TV.

Madsen rushed back out to the command center and looked at the radar and satellite screens. He was mildly shocked to see that the Gulf of Mexico looked like a pristine, unspoiled pool of sparkling blue water, as if the entire bay area had just been washed down with massive amounts of chlorine.

Feeling defeated again, as he continued watching the scenes of devastation from the Mississippi flooding, he plopped down onto a chair, holding his head in his hands. Meanwhile, the phones were ringing off the hook throughout the building. Then, for the next two hours, he and everyone else in the room watched one news report after another. In some areas along the river entire homes had been completely demolished and washed upstream. Acres and acres of farmland were completely underwater. It was dark and ugly water, though, filled with all sorts of bacteria, oil slicks, and human and animal waste.

Thousands of people were stranded on top of their vehicles on flooded roads, and others were huddling atop roofs waiting to be rescued from the poisonous waters that continued rushing over the banks of all the rivers and streams.

"Colonel," Sergeant Emerson said. "Take a look at the radar screen."

"Holy mother of God," he gasped, as he watched the three storms regroup back out into the Gulf, only now they were even bigger than before.

Just then, the door opened and in walked Mickey, Becky and Wakulla.

CHAPTER 30

Cigars
Aromatically stinky
Causing some nausea
Pleasurable to some others
Controversial inhalation
©dp

"What the hell is all this?" Madsen shouted, clearly taken aback at the sight before him. "What are you people doing here? And why isn't that man in custody?" he asked, as he pointed an angry finger at Wakulla.

It was just about to strike five o'clock in the afternoon when Mickey and Becky arrived at the hurricane center, bringing a reluctant Wakulla inside the building with them. They had made excellent time on the highway because the Interstate was virtually devoid of traffic in the southbound lane. On the opposite side, however, it was bumper to bumper traffic with one long procession of cars, trucks, motorcycles and RV's heading north. People were still in a panic trying to flee the area.

During the last hour of their trip, Becky had been arguing with Mickey about whether or not to risk bringing Wakulla in to confront the colonel. Mickey was insistent, though, telling her that without Wakulla there to serve as interpreter, he'd be hard-pressed to understand the language of the storm. Then, he reminded her about the triangular meeting of the minds with all three of them clearly hearing English when the storm spoke. She finally relented, but she warned him that Madsen would probably do something asinine.

Before she realized what was happening, six of Madsen's men tackled Wakulla to the floor and then they handcuffed his legs and arms together, as he helplessly struggled to fight them off. Once they had him under their control, they dragged him down the corridor and into a small office, shutting the door behind them.

Becky was dumbfounded watching this scene play out before her eyes. When she looked at Mickey it seemed he was even more stunned than she was. Seconds later, both she and Mickey were being physically escorted into Eric's office with Madsen leading the way.

After everyone, including Jeremy and Carl, was seated at the conference table, Madsen glared back and forth at Mickey and Becky.

"One of you better start talking," he said, as he lit up another cigar.

Soon, the room was filled with a smoky haze and an awful stench as he puffed away. Becky thought he looked like a human chimney...a big fat one, no less, and she glared back at him with a look that clearly showed her disdain for the man.

Mickey was sitting beside her and he reached for her hand, giving it a gentle squeeze, as he winked at her. That one little act of affection seemed to comfort her and give her a sense of safety just having him beside her for support.

"Colonel, we heard the reports on the radio on the drive back down here," Becky started. "The storm told us it was going to do something when we spoke to it earlier this morning."

"That's right, sir," Mickey said, corroborating her story. "We just didn't know it was going to be something this drastic."

For about thirty seconds there was complete silence in the room, while Madsen sat staring at the two of them, still puffing on his cigar, as if it helped him to think.

"Do you two really expect me to believe that a storm or a wave or a body of water can actually talk? That it has a brain?" he asked them, raising his voice about ten octaves. "Do you realize how preposterous that sounds?"

Madsen's cheeks were flaming red now and his face

was dripping with perspiration, as were his armpits. Then his eyes turned into tiny slits as he continued glaring at them. Becky thought he was going to have a stroke. She looked over at Mickey and he shrugged his shoulders, as if he didn't know how to respond in order to make the colonel believe their story.

Becky was about to say something when the room went dark. It was only a few minutes past five now, but when she looked outside through the big pane glass window behind where Madsen was sitting, it was dark as night. Shivers traveled up her spine as the air inside the room turned cold as ice.

"What in the name of God...?" Madsen gasped.

Just then, Sergeant Emerson burst through the door and his face was white as a sheet.

"Colonel!" he shouted. "The sun just went out! It disappeared!" he continued, as he stood in the doorway shivering like a naked man in the Swiss Alps.

"Dumala! Dumala! Dumala!" the storm resounded through the loudspeakers.

Becky leaned into Mickey, wrapping her arms around his waist, trying to warm her body, but it wasn't helping. She just couldn't stop shaking.

"Don't worry, honey," he said, as he pulled her closer. "It will be all right."

Madsen jumped up from his seat and he went to look out the window at the pitch black darkness. Then, he swung around and he pointed his finger at Becky.

"What does it want? What the hell does this thing want?" he screamed at her.

"Show him the map, Becky," Mickey whispered to her. "Just show him the map and the words will follow."

Becky's hands were shaking and her teeth were chattering, but she managed to reach into her purse and pull out the map she had made. She went on to explain that the dark black lines were drawing the route of the storm from its inception to the here and now.

"This last line in red is the final piece to the puzzle," she said, and with her finger she traced it from the Gulf of

Mexico, up the Mississippi River to Canada and then over toward Alaska. "After that, it will travel across the Bering Sea to Europe and Asia before weaving its way back home to its origin in Australia."

"The completed lines, assuming it ever gets that far, will draw the symbol of the world triad," Mickey explained.

"The United States must make the first moves toward meeting the storm's demands," Becky said directly to Madsen. "Then the rest of the world will follow. That's the price we have to pay for being the world's foremost leader in economics, technology and military power."

Then, again, "Dumala! Dumala! Dumala!" they all heard.

"Tell that thing to shut up!" Madsen shouted.

"Colonel, we need Wakulla with us to communicate with the storm," Mickey told him. "Without him it's pointless."

"That man is a terrorist! He and his tribe of savages are behind all of this! I don't want him anywhere near me!" Madsen screamed, as he stood cowering next to the window.

His entire body was shaking and his face, which had been boiling red just a few minutes ago, had turned an ungodly shade of blue.

Mickey was about to protest when suddenly the room lit up again. As if a magic wand had just been passed over them, the room warmed up within seconds. Then, everyone's jaw dropped when Professor Wiggins walked into the room.

"Doc! What are you doing here?" Mickey gasped.

"I came back from the dead," he said, proudly smiling, as if he really had been reincarnated. "I do believe you two need some help here convincing the colonel that if he doesn't meet the demands of the storm, then he may as well get his rosary beads out and start praying to whatever God he believes in."

If there had been a basement in the building, that's where all those dropped jaws would have been when the next three people walked into the room. First, the President of the United States stepped inside, followed by the Pope, and then Wakulla.

Once everyone was seated, Professor Wiggins asked Becky to repeat everything she had told the reporter yesterday morning. With Mickey standing next to her holding her hand, she reiterated word for word the exact same message, again wondering how her brain was remembering all the details.

"This is the Universe making these demands," she stressed when she finished. "The Universe, God or whatever higher being you believe in...it is not a human terrorist group behind all these horrific events."

"Here is the list of demands, Mr. President," Professor Wiggins said, and he passed out copies to everyone seated around the table. "We have less than forty-eight hours to get these things written into law, otherwise more destruction will follow and it will be worse than anything you could ever conjure up in your minds," he added, as he looked around at all the faces in the room.

CHAPTER 31

Ruin
Ruin the earth
Ruin the next generation's future
©dp

There were only three items on the list, however, Professor Wiggins informed everyone that this was only the beginning of a long series of changes that needed to be made. The three items were as follows:

1) Implement a government mandated alternative energy source plan for conversion to solar and/or wind power, in order to reduce the burning of fossil fuels. It would apply not only to businesses, but also to residential consumers.

2) Require all landfills to be properly fitted, using cutting edge technology that could convert landfill waste into cleaner burning energy. Since the technology already existed and was being tested, this demand would be the easiest to institute.

3) Fix the Medicare system to ensure all senior citizens have access to the finest healthcare, and double their social security payments, so that they no longer had to live in poverty.

"We, Mr. President," Doc started, looking directly into his eyes. "We, the United States of America, have to be the ones to initiate these changes, because we are the ones who have instituted all the harmful environmental practices that are destroying our planet. If other countries see that the United States is finally serious about these issues, then they will follow in due time."

"I see," the President said, as he skimmed down the

list again.

"All of these protocols must be written into law in forty-eight hours or those three storms out in the Gulf will advance onshore and begin destroying everything in their path," the professor urged him.

"Uhh, Doc?" Mickey piped up. "I do believe we're down to forty-seven hours now."

"And I do believe you are correct, Mickey," he said with a nod toward the clock that was ticking away on the wall.

"May I say something?" Becky asked.

"Please do," the President said, seeming totally overwhelmed at the moment.

"The major factor behind all of mankind's current environmental issues is overpopulation," she stressed. "That, in turn, has forced man to deplete the oceans by over-fishing. He has destroyed the rain forests by chopping down too many trees for wood-based products. He has caused over-farming of the land and destroyed our natural soil by over-fertilization."

"With too many people on Earth, there are too many cars on our roadways that are emitting poisonous gases into the atmosphere," Mickey added. "Too much unnecessary technology has depleted the Earth's core of vital elements by exploiting its natural resources. Too much land development to build houses and factories for all these humans has forced mammals into extinction by taking away their natural habitats. Then, there are all those manmade plastics that don't breakdown, which have created too many toxic landfills."

"We should feel lucky that the storm didn't demand that we tear down all the dams in the country," Becky added, in an attempt to lessen the difficulty of the three demands.

"Why would it ask us to do that?" Carl wanted to know.

"Because they're interfering with the natural flow of rivers and their sediments," Mickey told him. "The dam reservoirs are altering the natural temperature of Earth's water, and as a result, it is impacting plant and animal life as it flows down our rivers and streams. It's one of the major factors behind global warming."

"These dams are also generating methane gas, thus contributing to the pollution problems in the atmosphere," Becky said.

"Why did it choose the Gulf of Mexico to present itself?" Jeremy asked.

"The Gulf has the most ocean dead zones in the world. They're caused by excess nitrogen from farm fertilization that flows down the Mississippi River from the Midwest," Becky told him. "Add to that all the raw sewage and factory emissions that get dumped into our waterways and you have one big fat ugly mess."

"Ahh, so the Gulf of Mexico is the perfect site to bring this message to the people," the President said, nodding his head in agreement.

"I believe there is also an underlying message in all of this, warning mankind to use common sense when procreating. Of course, it knows that all it can do is make the suggestion. Mankind has to make the wise decision not to overpopulate the world," Becky said.

"That is one reason why there have been so many devastating earthquakes, hurricanes, tornadoes, tsunamis and other natural disasters wiping out people by the thousands," Doc said. "The Universe is trying to save itself from overpopulation."

"We're getting way off course here," the President interjected. "I realize you three have an extensive list of complaints about the environment," he said, as he glanced over at Becky, Mickey and Doc. "Right now, the main issue is the three demands of this storm. Let's stick to that for the moment."

After a bit more discussion, the President called a recess, saying he needed to contact his advisors back in Washington. Once he left the room, Madsen cornered Carl and Jeremy and the three of them stood by the window, talking in hushed, yet frantic conversation. Meanwhile, Mickey and Becky pulled Doc aside.

"How in the hell did you pull this off?" Mickey asked him.

"I wish I could answer that," Doc said. "All I know is that one minute I was lying in a hospital bed in a coma and the next I was watching Becky on TV telling the world to shape up or ship out. I called my friend in Washington, who shall remain nameless for the time being, and I asked for this meeting today."

"How did you know we would be here? How did you get these lists printed up so fast?" Becky asked him. "And how did you get the Pope here?"

"Ahh, my sweet child," Doc said, as he put his arm around her shoulder. "One must never question the powers of the Universe. Sometimes it is best not to know everything."

Meanwhile, all the people who had fled the Gulf coast states to head to the Midwest and points beyond were now trapped on the flooded highways. The entire country was in a panic and nobody seemed to know which way to go to be safe.

CHAPTER 32

Red Velvet Sunset
Black satin sky
Evening has fallen
Moon rises high
Night birds serenading
Worries slowly fading
Calmness overtakes me
Peaceful is the night
©dp

"I could sure use a shower," Becky said to Mickey, as she scrunched up her nose. "I just know I'm reeking and my body feels so sticky from all that salty seawater."

"Yeah, me, too," he said, laughing as he sniffed his underarms. "I could use a big fat juicy steak and a bottle of ice-cold beer, while I'm at it expressing my wishes," he added.

"Do you think they'll let us leave? I really need to change out of these clothes," she kept on, as they stood in the corner of Eric's office.

"I'd like to help you," he said, and he kissed her lightly on the cheek.

"I'll bet you would," she said, grinning with embarrassment at his sudden overtures, especially with the Pope in the room.

"Come on. It can't hurt to ask," he said. "I have a feeling all these hotshots in the room are going to need a bit of time to make some decisions."

"Yeah, so, what's new?" she asked him, rolling her eyes, and knowing just how true his statement was.

Everyone else in the room was huddled around the conference table debating the demands of the storm, with

Madsen being the loudest and most obnoxious, and still trying to convince the others that it was all a terrorist act. Earlier, the Pope had politely requested that the boisterous colonel snub out his putrid smelling cigar, which he reluctantly did after another four angry puffs. The odor, however, was still hanging in the air like a dirty gym sock.

Meanwhile, Wakulla was sitting lopsided in a chair at the end of the table and he was sound asleep. Unfortunately, Madsen had insisted that he be chained up, until he made absolutely certain he wasn't part of some large-scale terrorist organization. The others, not wanting to butt heads with the loudmouth, overbearing colonel, eventually agreed to it just to shut him up.

"I don't think we should ask them," Becky whispered to Mickey. "Maybe if we just quietly walk out of the room, no one will notice we're missing."

"It's worth a shot," he said, and three seconds later, they slipped out of the room undetected by anyone.

Just outside Eric's office, the command center was abuzz with activity. Most everyone's eyes and attention were on the radar screens, watching the three storms swirling out in the Gulf. It was standing room only, too, with so many security personnel milling about. Between the president's bodyguards, all the homeland security people, and the Pope's entourage of guards, along with his medical team, it was a chore just getting through the crowd. Oddly, though, no one seemed the least bit suspicious of them, as they meandered down a long corridor toward the back of the building.

"We did it!" Becky squealed, once they made it outside by sneaking through a temporarily unguarded side door. "Let's hurry before someone comes after us."

"I'm right behind you," Mickey said, smiling from ear to ear.

They had to dodge a few reporters as they ran through the parking lot, but thankfully, the majority of the newshounds were hanging around the front entrance. Becky thought they all looked like predators, as they stood around with their camera lenses aimed at the door. Of course, she knew every one of them wanted that exclusive shot of the President, or at the very least, a photograph of the Pope, who had been fighting a terminal illness for the last few months.

"Vultures," she thought, as she sneered over at them.

She had absolutely no respect for any members of the media, especially after all the hell they had put her through over the years, labeling her an environmental troublemaker, among other things.

It wasn't until after Mickey pulled the car out onto the freeway and amid all the other traffic that she was able to breathe a sigh of relief. She did, however, keep one eye on the cars behind them to make sure they weren't being followed. For the moment, it seemed they were in the clear.

"Hey, that was pretty slick, wasn't it?" she asked him with a wide grin on her face.

"Dang right, it was," he said, and he reached for her hand. "We make a good team, you and I."

"Yeah," she said, still smiling and feeling a surge of emotion rise to her throat. "We do work quite well together."

Once they made it back to the hotel, Mickey pulled up to the front entrance. After he tossed the keys to the valet, he and Becky rushed through the lobby and over toward the elevators. On the way up, he attempted to give her an innocent hug, but she backed away from him.

"I feel too skuzzy right now," she said. "I know I must stink to high heaven."

"Aww, come on, Becky, you smell like sweet magnolias and orange blossoms," he said, and he winked at her.

"More like sour pickles and rotted fruit," she said, with her nose scrunched up again.

When they reached the tenth floor, the elevator doors opened and they stepped out into an empty corridor.

"Ummm...your room or mine?" Mickey timidly asked her.

"Well, I don't know about you, but I'm going to my room," she said. "I'll leave the door unlocked," she added with a wicked grin, and seconds later she disappeared inside room 1020.

"Well, I'll be darned," Mickey said, as he stood in the hallway shaking his head. "Does she want me to join her, or what?"

After standing there for a good thirty seconds, debating whether or not to follow her into her room, he finally decided he'd better not push his luck or seem too eager, otherwise he might blow his chances with her.

In the mean time, Becky was dealing with her own crisis. The first thing she noticed when she entered her room was that the fishy smell had returned with a vengeance. The bulk of it was coming from the bathroom, and when she peeked inside, the stench was so strong that she had to slam the door shut before the fumes made her pass out.

"That's impossible!" she yelled. "That's utterly impossible! I flushed that damn thing!"

Mickey had just unlocked his door and he was about to go inside his room when he heard her screaming.

"What the hell?" he wondered, and he sprinted down the hallway to see what was going on.

He didn't even bother knocking. He just rushed inside, thinking someone was hurting her. Becky was standing in the middle of the room, gagging and coughing with her hands covering her mouth, and she had the most dumbfounded look on her face.

"Don't open that door!" she yelled to him, pointing toward the bathroom.

Mickey, unfortunately, couldn't resist and he flung open the door, only to have the most hideous smell bellow out of the room and up into his nostrils. Soon, he was gagging, too, so he slammed the door shut again.

"Good God! Let's get out of here!" he said, and he grabbed her hand and pulled her out into the corridor.

"I can't believe that stupid fish smell is back!" she said. "I flushed that thing down the toilet! It couldn't have come back up the pipes, could it?"

"Hey, we've seen stranger things happen, don't you think? Nothing would surprise me at this stage of the game."

"What do I do now?" she asked him, clearly shaken up. "Do I call management? Hell, they'll think I'm the one who stunk up the room. I'd feel so embarrassed."

Mickey put his arm around her and he started walking back toward his room.

"You're welcome to stay in my room," he said, doing a fairly good job of hiding the excitement in his voice. "Besides, we don't have time to deal with management right now."

Becky looked up at him, not certain she heard him correctly.

"All my stuff is in that stinky room," she said. "Oh, no! Everything will be ruined! I'll never get that smell out of my clothes!" she shrieked, and then she pulled a big lock of her hair around and she smelled it. "Yuck!"

Mickey had already opened the door to his room and before he realized what was happening, she rushed past him, stripping off her clothes, while aiming straight for the bathroom.

"I have this tremendous urge to take a hot shower right now!" she yelled.

Just as she entered the bathroom, Mickey caught a glimpse of the prettiest bare rear end that he had ever seen.

"Put my clothes out in the hall!" she yelled to him.

"It would be my pleasure!" he shouted back to her.

There was a plastic garment bag hanging in the closet, so he grabbed it, stuffed all her smelly clothes, as well as her shoes inside, and then he hurried out into the corridor.

"God help whoever picks this up," he said, as he dropped the bag to the floor, but then he changed his mind. "Aww, geez, I can't leave this here. What will people think?"

Pinching his nostrils together with one hand, he

reached for the bag with the other and he ran down to Becky's room. Thankfully, the door was still unlocked, so he threw the bag inside, shut the door, and then he ran back to his room, still holding his breath.

"Phew!" he said, once he was safely inside and away from the putrid fishy odor that was still lingering out in the hallway.

As much as he wanted to join her in the shower, he restrained himself and went to the sink instead to wash his hands and face. Once he heard the shower turn off, he went and tapped on the bathroom door.

"I've got some extra clothes you can wear," he said, as he was drying his hands. "That way, you won't have to go back to your stinky room."

"Oh, thank goodness," she said. "Just hang them on the doorknob, please."

With that, he flipped open his suitcase and he started rooting around through his clothes, looking for just the right outfit.

"Hmmm...I wonder if this will fit her," he said, as he pulled out a T-shirt from his suitcase and held it up. "Yep, this should do just fine."

The T-shirt was brand new and never worn. He had ordered it online from his favorite clothing store, Bass Pro Shops. It was one of those redneck creed shirts that said, *Always up a creek, but never without a paddle.* He felt it was quite fitting under the circumstances. As for pants, all he had that might fit her was a pair of blue cotton boxer shorts.

"All she needs is a belt to hold them up," he said, although he didn't bring one with him. "I guess we'll have to improvise," he added with a chuckle.

Still laughing to himself, he went over and hung the clothes on the doorknob as she had asked. Ten minutes later, she emerged from the bathroom.

"This thing looks like a dress on me," she said, referring to the extra-large T-shirt she was wearing that came down to her knees.

She was holding the shorts in her hand and seconds

later she was looking at him, shaking her head, as if she thought he was crazy to think she would wear them.

"Hey, that's fantastic! Now I don't have to go buy a belt for those shorts."

"You're a real hoot, Mickey," she said, tossing the shorts at him, while she went over to grab her purse off the bed to look for her brush. "Do you really expect me to walk around with no underwear?"

"I hear it's the latest fad," he said, laughing.

"Oh, good grief, look at this mop," she said, ignoring his comment, as she stood in front of the mirror on the outside of the bathroom door.

"Yeah, it seems that riding around in a convertible can play havoc with one's hair. Here, let me help," he said, and he came up behind her and snatched the brush from her hand.

As he slowly drew the brush through her beautiful chestnut hair, he wondered how he could prolong this detangling event. Ever so slowly, he gently pulled the bristles down and through small sections of her long locks, trying not to pull too hard, but mainly wanting to make the moment last as long as possible.

"Do you mind if I sit down?" she asked after a while.

"No, not at all," he said, and he followed her over to the edge of the bed.

Becky had her eyes closed as she sat there chatting away about the strange fish incident in her room, but all Mickey could focus on was how beautiful she was. How intoxicating her scent was, especially with the sweet smell of conditioner lingering in her hair. Her voice, her laugh, everything about her was perfect. He was smiling behind her, as he looked down at the gorgeous, sweet, intelligent woman, who was wearing his shirt.

"This is too good to be true," he thought. "I am definitely dreaming!"

After he finished combing through her hair, he softly caressed her shoulders.

"Would you like a massage to ease the tension in your neck? You're awfully stiff. So is your upper back and your shoulders," he added, as he continued caressing her.

"Yeesss...I would love that," she said in a strangely sultry tone that momentarily threw him for a loop. "I haven't had a massage in so long," she added.

Mickey felt himself beginning to melt, as he ran his strong hands over her beautifully tanned shoulders. He was savoring every moment, knowing that this would probably be the only time in his life that he would ever be this close to the beautiful Becky Rogers.

As she began to ooh and ahh, and move her body in rhythm with his deep penetrating squeezes, Mickey found himself becoming tremendously aroused. From behind her, he kept watching her body move in the semi-darkness. Her breathing had become heavier and her body was pushing against his hands. He was beginning to wonder if he could control himself.

With his eyes closed, he envisioned his hands moving slowly down to the small of her back and then to her shapely hips. The temptation to slide his hands down even farther was unbearable.

"What will she think?" he wondered. "Will I ruin this moment if I go too far?"

When she turned her head to the side, he could see the profile of her beautiful, unblemished face. He heard her sigh and then he felt her warm breath on his shoulder. There was a look of passion in her eyes and he found himself riveted to her, as she drew him in like a moth to a flame.

"You can move your hands a little lower to explore back there," she softly whispered, in that same seductive, sultry voice, which made a shiver run up his spine. "I'll let you know when to stop."

It was as if she could sense that he was in turmoil and he wondered if she was feeling the same strong emotions. He finally leaned into her and said, "Thank God! My fingers were beginning to cramp!"

They both burst out laughing and then Mickey buried his face into her still damp hair. She reached up behind her and pulled his face even closer to hers. Soon, they were both laughing so hard that it could only have come from deep within their souls.

After laughing like two hyenas for several moments, Becky turned around and she looked at him with a mischievous grin on her face.

"Now it's your turn," she said, pointing to the bathroom.

"Yeah, I really should get in there now," he said, knowing that an ice cold shower was definitely in order.

It had been years since he had been intimate with a woman. One thing he knew for certain was that if he continued to massage and caress her gorgeous curves, then his uncontrolled, pent-up passion would release itself just from the feel of her velvety skin. He didn't want to totally embarrass and humiliate himself, and he didn't want to disappoint her, either. As stunning as she was, and as worked up as he was at the moment, however, he wondered if a cold shower would even do the trick. It seemed, though, to be the only course of action to take.

Without further ado, he got up from the bed and he started toward the bathroom. Suddenly, he felt her presence behind him and he turned around. Without saying a word, she reached up and slowly unbuttoned the top button of his shirt. He froze as he watched her fingers move down to the next button and the next. Then, she partially opened his shirt, revealing just a small swath of his chest hair. She was in complete control and he knew it. He was putty in her hands and she seemed to instinctively know that he was burning up with desire, even as hard as he had tried concealing it.

Meanwhile, Becky's mind had drifted off into some otherworldly place and she lost control of her actions. The mere thought of the handsome, intelligent Mickey DeRosa wanting her, made her crave him even more. She couldn't remember the last time she had felt so aroused.

She continued to slowly unbutton his shirt, all the while trying to keep from drooling at the sight of his bare chest. When she glanced up at his striking facial features, somewhere in the back of her mind, she thought to herself, "This man would make beautiful children."

Quickly, she dismissed that thought, due to the fact that two different doctors had told her she would never have children. With his shirt completely unbuttoned now, she could see his prominent abdominal muscles. It was shocking that a man his age still had such amazing six-pack abs; the kind that could make a woman succumb to lustful yearning.

She was almost purring now and Mickey, it seemed, could sense her approval, so he gently placed her hands on his chest. When he looked into her eyes, though, he felt that same incredible urge to burst out laughing again. Evidently, so did she, and for the next few minutes they laughed like two high school kids who had just discovered the opposite sex for the first time.

The passion didn't seem to want to end, though, as they both struggled to regain their composure. Soon, Becky's soft hands were sliding across his chest and he closed his eyes to relish in her touch. He breathed deeply, and then a slight shiver shook his entire body from head to toe. She was taking her time exploring every inch of his well-built torso and every time her hands moved across his chest, he could feel his nipples getting harder.

Becky was having the same sensations and she soon realized that he wouldn't last much longer at this rate, nor would she.

"I really must get into that shower right now, Becky," he finally said.

"Umm, yes, let's get you into that shower," she said, agreeing with him, or so it seemed.

When she reached down to unzip his pants, he thought he was going to explode. Then his eyes widened, as her hands inadvertently touched his growing erection. When he twitched, she looked at him and she smiled. His groin was aching so much that he wanted to just throw her on the bed and be done with it, but he controlled his urges. As she fumbled with his zipper, it seemed as though it was stuck and she couldn't get it to go down any further. He tried to take over, but she insisted that she had it under control.

To get a better grip on it, she knelt down in front of him, obviously acutely aware that it would arouse him even more. All the while she was tugging on his zipper she was looking up at him with a mischievous grin on her face. Mickey, however, wasn't looking at her. His eyes were tightly shut. She started giggling and then she said, "Open your eyes and look at me."

Mickey complied, but then he said, "If you're trying to torture me, it's working."

That comment made both of them start laughing again. They were both completely consumed by this overwhelming passion between them and it seemed neither one of them knew how to stop it. Yes, there was nervous laughter and uncertainty, but the foreplay was more intense than a Mount Vesuvius eruption.

While Becky was still kneeling in front of him, she suddenly remembered that she wasn't wearing any panties, only a long T-shirt borrowed from Mickey. Still struggling with the stuck zipper, she repositioned herself to get a better angle on it. That's when she felt something wet between her legs.

"Wow," she thought. "That hasn't happened lately. Maybe I didn't dry off completely."

Mickey finally came to his senses and he reached down to pull her up to him. Deep inside his soul he knew that now was not the time, nor was it the place to consummate this relationship. Not in a cheap hotel room. As much as he wanted her, and as much as he felt she wanted him too, it just didn't feel right. Something was missing.

"It seems there's a reason that zipper doesn't want to come down," he said to her. "Besides, it's getting late and I really do need a shower."

"Yeah, I suppose you're right," she said, and she stood up, looking quite sheepish.

"Don't worry," he said. "We'll have lots of time for amore once this storm stuff is behind us."

"Well, then, get in the shower, you dodo-brain. You stink," she said, which made both of them laugh hysterically again.

Ten minutes later, when Mickey emerged from the bathroom, Becky was sitting on the edge of the bed reading the room service menu.

"I don't know about you, but I'm starving," he said, when he saw what she was doing.

"Yeah, me, too," she said. "But there's nothing good on this stupid menu. Can I borrow your flip-flops?" she asked, as she pointed to the blue and white thongs lying on the floor beside the bed.

"Of course," he said, laughing again. "I can't wait to see you walk in those size twelve's."

"Not a problem," she said. "Watch me."

After she slid them on her feet, she started over toward the door, nearly tripping about three times before she made it. After another round of hilarious laughter, she tried it again and she didn't trip but once.

"What do you say we eat downstairs in order to save some time trying to decide on another restaurant nearby, since neither one of us is familiar with this area," Mickey suggested. "Besides, you're not exactly dressed properly to be seen out in public."

"Do you really think I give a hoot what people think?" she asked him.

"Oh, that's right," he said. "You're Becky Rogers."

"You got that right," she said. "Okay, we'll eat downstairs, but just remember, don't eat the fish."

"Don't worry, hon," he said. "I'm a steak and potatoes kind of guy."

"Well, we'd better hurry because I do believe the restaurant closes at eleven," she said.

"Wow! It's that late already?" Mickey asked, as he glanced at his watch.

"Time flies when you're having fun," she said, grinning at him.

An hour and a half later, after feasting on a fabulous steak dinner, along with a bottle of wine rather than beer, a familiar face walked into the restaurant.

"Well, Doc," Mickey said, as the professor approached their table. "What took you so long?"

"Hrmphh," Doc said, as he sat down across from the two of them. "If I had come any sooner I'm afraid I would have interrupted something very important."

"Ahh, you are a smart man, professor. A very smart man, indeed," Mickey said, and then he proudly slipped his arm around Becky's shoulder and kissed her cheek.

CHAPTER 33

Trust
Release control
Faithful confidence evolves
A mutual understanding gained
Bonded
©dp

"You're being awfully accommodating, Doc," Mickey said, as he and Becky walked alongside him toward the elevators. "What's up with that? Did you fall in love, too?"

"Me? Heck, no," he said. "I gave up on women ten years ago, after my wife died."

"Oh, well, that's a shame. It's a good feeling. You have no idea what you're missing," Mickey said, and then all three of them stepped inside the elevator.

"Maybe so, but right now, we have more important matters to think about," he said, reverting back to the old stuffed shirt professor again.

"Oh, my goodness. Did I just hear Mickey say he was in love?" Becky wondered, and it made her smile. "Yes, I know that's what I heard."

Once they exited on the tenth floor, Becky pointed to the right and Doc and Mickey followed her. Going back into the smelly room wasn't something she was looking forward to, but there was something she needed to get before heading back to the hurricane center.

"Here's my room," she said when she got to her door. "I just need to grab my cell phone and then we can be on our way."

When she opened the door she was astonished to find

that the smell had dissipated. There was absolutely no fish odor at all.

"Oh, this is fantastic," she thought. "Now, I can put my own clothes on, assuming they don't stink."

Amazingly, when she opened her suitcase, she didn't detect any strange odors other than the lilac fabric softener she had used on them.

"I need you to bring your laptop with you and all of your research papers," Doc said, as he waited in the doorway.

"What? Why?" she yelled from the bathroom, as she hurriedly changed clothes. "I've told you everything already! There's not much more to explain!"

"It's at the request of the President, Becky," he flatly told her. "He just wants to explore all his options before doing anything drastic."

When Becky came back out, she looked over at Mickey, but all he did was shrug his shoulders.

"Well, I suppose if the President asked for it, then I don't have much choice," she said, heaving an irritated sigh. "But I want it all back. I have months and months of hard work here," she said, as she packed up her laptop and gathered all her paperwork together.

Doc just nodded his head and then he walked out into the corridor, as if he was in a hurry to leave. Becky was suddenly agreeing with what Mickey had said earlier about him being overly accommodating. It gave her a sick feeling in the pit of her stomach, making her wonder what was really going on.

"Eh, I'm just being paranoid," she finally admitted to herself. "After all that has happened in the last few days, is it any wonder?"

Once she snatched her cell phone off the charger and shoved it into her purse, she went back to her suitcase, which was still lying on top of the bed unpacked, and she grabbed her car charger.

"Just in case," she thought. "Just in case."

Mickey had been standing in the doorway watching her, and when she joined him he was looking at her with pursed lips while shaking his head back and forth.

"What?" she asked him.

"Oh, nothing," he said. "It's just that I forgot to charge my phone earlier."

"You dodo," she said, and she smacked his arm. "It looks like somebody needs a woman around to remind him to do things."

"I thought I had one," he said, laughing. "By the way, did you notice the smell was gone?"

"Well, yeah," she said, keeping her voice low so that Doc couldn't hear her.

"Are you two ready to go?" Doc asked, not seeming amused at all with their back and forth banter. "It's almost two o'clock in the morning. I'm running out of patience."

"Yep, we're ready," Becky said. "Let's go, dodo," she said to Mickey, who merely looked at her and chuckled.

"Is there anything you need from your room?" Doc asked Mickey, as they were walking back to the elevator.

"Nope, I've got everything I need right here," he said, and he patted Becky's behind, which drew another smack on the arm from her.

As they were descending in the elevator, Doc told them his car was waiting out in front of the hotel and that all three of them would be riding together. The way he stated it, he made it sound as if there better not be any rebuttal from either one of them, so they both kept quiet and did as he said.

"Good grief, Professor!" Becky gasped when she saw his onyx black Lincoln Navigator SUV parked just outside the front entrance. "I can't believe that you, of all people, would choose to drive such a gas hog vehicle."

"It wasn't my first choice," he said. "All I wanted was a little two-seater, but the college administrator insisted that this was the only car they had available, and that if I didn't take it, then I'd have to pay for my own transportation. What can I say? They didn't pay me enough back then to go out and buy a car, so I took it."

"I can understand their reasoning, Doc," Mickey said,

as he slid into the backseat. "With all the cross-country traveling they forced you to do and all the literature you had to lug along with you, it wouldn't have made much sense to drive a sports car. Heck, you would have needed to haul a trailer behind you to hold all that crap."

"Or you could have tried flying," Becky suggested.

"I haven't been on an airplane since 9/11, Becky," Doc told her, and that was the end of that conversation.

No sooner did they walk through the doors of the National Hurricane Center twenty minutes later, than Becky felt that same stabbing pain in her gut.

"Something's wrong," she thought. "I can feel it."

It was oddly quiet inside the command center, even considering the late hour, but with the magnitude of the situation at hand, Becky assumed the place would be crawling with people trying to figure out how to stop the storm from doing any further damage. Instead, there were only a handful of people milling about. The door to Eric's office was closed, but just as Doc was about to knock, it swung open and out walked the President.

"Well, I see you two made it back here," he said, smiling at Becky and Mickey, as if he thought they had been up to no good.

"Yes, sir, I'm sorry," Becky said, as her face flushed beet red. "I needed to go back to my hotel room and get cleaned up. We both did," she clarified, pointing to Mickey as she spoke.

"That's quite all right," he said, still smiling. "Now, why don't you all go inside and have a seat?"

Madsen had been standing behind the President during all of this and he had the most evil, wicked look on his face, as if he'd just committed a heinous crime and gotten away with it.

While he continued sucking up to the President, yapping away at him as they stood in the doorway, Becky, Mickey and Doc went in to sit down. The first thing Becky noticed inside Eric's office was that Wakulla was gone. Again, she looked at Mickey, but he seemed confused, too.

"Is the President leaving?" she asked Doc.

"It certainly looks that way," he said, and then he pulled out a chair for her to sit down.

Mickey sat down in the chair to the left of her and then Doc sat down on her right.

"Do you know if they did anything yet? Did they agree to the storm's demands?" she asked Doc, but he just shrugged his shoulders.

It seemed to her that nobody knew what was going on. Even Carl and Jeremy were sitting quietly, as if they were afraid to look at her. Just then, the door shut and Madsen calmly walked over to where the others were sitting and he plopped his big behind down at the head of the conference table.

"Well, well," Madsen said, as he looked up at Becky and Mickey, and then over to Doc. "I see you found our little escape artists, Professor Wiggins."

"Yes, sir," Doc said. "They were right where I told you they'd be, at their hotel."

"By the way, how did you two manage to sneak out of here with all the security personnel posted throughout the building?" Madsen asked them.

"It was quite simple, Colonel," Becky flatly said. "We walked out the door."

From the tone of her voice, it was clear to everyone in the room, including Madsen, that she didn't feel the least bit intimidated by him.

"Hrmphh," was all the response Madsen gave her.

"Where is Wakulla?" she boldly asked him.

"Ahh, yes, I was wondering when that question would come up," he said. "Your friend, the illegal Haitian immigrant, is on his way to a maximum security prison in our lovely city of Miami."

Now, it was Mickey's turn to go ballistic and he jumped up from his seat, waving his fists.

"Are you crazy, Colonel?" he shouted. "Don't you realize that without him we're unable to communicate with the storm?"

"Mr. DeRosa, please sit down or I'll have you thrown

out of here," Madsen said, again in such a calm tone of voice that it was spooky.

Once Mickey sat back down, the colonel continued.

"By a unanimous vote, it has been decided that your friend, Wakulla, is, as I have stated from the beginning, a part of the Al-Qaeda terrorist network, and they, my dear, Mr. DeRosa, are the masterminds behind all of these strange weather phenomena's we've been experiencing."

It wasn't a question, it wasn't a supposition, it was simply a statement of fact and Madsen didn't want to hear any arguments from anyone. Becky and Mickey weren't deterred, however. After several minutes of screaming and shouting obscenities, the two of them finally had to be physically restrained by some of Madsen's men and ordered to sit quietly or go to jail.

"Nobody in their right mind could possibly believe that the *Universe* is behind all this bullshit," Madsen said, stressing the word universe as if it was difficult for him to say it without laughing. "There is no logical sense behind any of your findings, Ms. Rogers," he added quite emphatically.

"But you're wrong, Colonel," Becky said, trying not to raise her voice.

"Maybe in your eyes, Ms. Rogers, but not in the President's," he said, gloating like a wolf who had just singlehandedly slain a dragon.

Madsen, proud, gloating ass that he was, then revealed his newest counterattack plan. He was going to detonate a nuclear bomb in the middle of the Gulf of Mexico to obliterate the three storms in one fell swoop.

"Of course, there will most likely be some collateral damage, if people don't heed my warning to evacuate, but it's the only way to disperse of this menace."

"Colonel, you're crazy!" Becky shouted at him. "You are so, so wrong about all of this!"

"Gentlemen, please remove all three of these intruders immediately!" he snapped at his henchmen, while waving his pointed little finger at Doc, Becky and Mickey. "I want all of you to get the hell out of my sight and go back to the woods where you came from!"

It was no easy task dragging all three of them out of the room, especially Becky, who was kicking and screaming and demanding that Madsen give her back her laptop and her research papers.

"I need these for evidence!" he shot back at her. "Now get out of here! All of you!"

As they were being escorted out the main door, Becky could hear Madsen in the background barking more orders to his blind followers.

"Start the mandatory evacuations immediately! Anyone within a two-hundred mile radius anywhere along the Gulf of Mexico must leave within the next twenty-four hours or risk a horrible death!" he shouted.

"Yes, sir!" three of his men said, as they saluted him.

"The rest of you!" he continued shouting. "Start dismantling everything now! We'll be moving everything down to our bomb shelter in South Miami!"

CHAPTER 34

Nightbird
A lone night bird sings
me awake at three a.m.
Slumber now broken
to four a.m...worrying
Still, the sound was sweet
©dp

"**M**ickey, this is outrageous! Why are they doing this to us? Don't they know that they need us?" Becky kept spouting off, as Madsen's men stood guard in the parking lot, waiting for all three of them to vacate the premises.

Doc was behind the wheel and Mickey was sitting up front in the passenger seat because Becky refused to sit "next to a traitor", as she so eloquently lambasted him.

"They're all a bunch of idiots, Becky. We knew that already," Mickey said, trying to calm her down, and then he looked over at the professor. "And you, Doc!" he shouted. "Why exactly did you turn on us? I thought you were our ally!"

Doc seemed to have lockjaw because he wasn't saying a word to either one of them. All he was doing was trying to maneuver his huge SUV around the cars in the lot, so that he could be on his way.

"Mickey, they've got my laptop! They've got all my hard work! All my papers! And the maps!" she screamed from the backseat, as Doc pulled out onto the highway and hit the accelerator.

"You have backups, don't you? At least you told me you did," he said.

"Yeah, at home," she told him. "But those maps were

the originals."

"It's okay, honey, we don't need them anymore. As for the laptop, don't worry about that, either. When all of this is over I'll buy you a newer, better one. We'll go shopping together and you can tell me which one you want and which one will work best for me. It's time I got with the program," he said, reiterating her statement from the other day and trying to ease her mind.

After Doc drove about a mile down the road, he suddenly pulled off onto the shoulder and stopped the car.

"I had absolutely no idea that Madsen was going to pull that stunt," he said through clenched teeth, as he stared straight ahead. "You have to believe me."

"Give me one good reason why!" Becky shouted.

Doc turned around in his seat and he looked directly into Becky's dragon-flaming eyes.

"I believe in you, Becky. I believe in everything you and Mickey have told me," he said, as a tear trickled down his cheek. "I've had visions, too, just like you've been having. I truly believe that is why the three of us have been brought together."

For a few moments there was complete silence, as the two of them stared each other down.

"Really?" she finally gasped, when she realized he was telling the truth. Then she glanced over at Mickey, who looked stunned, as well. "Oh, my God! Doc, I'm sorry...I'm so sorry," she said, softening her tone, as she reached up to place her hand on his shoulder.

"Now is not the time for apologies," he said, as he wiped his eyes. "We must find a way to stop this madness. We must find a way to keep Madsen from destroying the world."

"Let me ask you something, Doc" Mickey interrupted them. "How did you magically come out of that coma?"

"It must have been divine intervention, is all I can figure," he said. "When I woke up I felt fine, and when the doctors finished doing all their high-dollar tests, the results all came back the same. There was nothing wrong with me. I can't explain it," he said, shaking his head.

"So, you have no permanent damage to your heart?" Mickey asked.

"Nope, in fact, the doctors all said that I had the heart of a twenty-year-old, not a seventy-year-old."

"So, what do we do now, Mickey?" Becky asked.

"Well, the first thing we do is pat ol' Doc here on the back for gaining another fifty years of life," he said, grinning. "Then, I suppose our next order of business is figuring out how to rescue our friend, Wakulla. After all, without him we're powerless to interpret the storm's language."

"But we have so little time," Becky said. "How are we going to get close enough to him to even attempt a rescue?"

Mickey just smiled and then he reached into his shirt pocket and pulled out a business card.

"What are you crazy?" Becky shrieked. "Elena is probably sitting in a jail cell for authorizing Wakulla's release the first time!"

"I'd like to give it a shot, anyway," Mickey said, sounding much too confident.

"You just want to see her boobs and ass again," Becky said, only half-joking.

"I've got all the boobs and ass I can handle for the moment," he said, and he winked at her, which made her smile. "Uhhh...could I borrow your phone?" he meekly asked her.

"Yeah, sure, dodo-brain," she said, and she handed it to him.

Mickey's face was as red as the faceplate on Becky's phone, as he punched in Elena's number. After two rings she picked up.

"Elena, hi, this is Mickey De..." he started, but she cut him off.

"Oh, thank goodness you finally called," she said. "Hold on one second."

"Yeah, sure, I'll hold," he said, and he glanced back at Becky.

"Wow, I can't believe she's there at four o'clock in the morning," Becky said, shaking her head.

Mickey could hear a door shut in the background and then seconds later Elena picked up the phone again.

"I'm sorry about that. I had to make sure no one could overhear this conversation," she said.

"That's quite all right," he told her. "I know it's late...well, actually, you could say it's early morning. Anyway, I'm glad you're there and I'm sure you know why I'm calling."

"Yes, I know, and I will do everything in my power to help you," she said. "This fool, Colonel Madsen, needs to be stopped."

"Oh, so, you know what he's planning to do?"

"Yes, he wants us to send Wakulla up to the state penitentiary in Starke. Madsen lied to you that he would be housed in Miami, since there are no facilities here. Mr. DeRosa, I just cannot do that to Wakulla. He is not a terrorist. I know that for a fact," she said.

"Oh? And what makes you so certain?"

"Are you a religious man, Mr. DeRosa?" she asked him.

"I consider myself to be more of a spiritual man, actually, but yes, I believe in God," he said.

"Good, then, perhaps, you will understand when I tell you that God spoke to me in a vision last night."

"Really? Dang! It seems everyone is having visions except me," he said, trying not to laugh, but not succeeding.

"It is no laughing matter," she sternly said. "This is not the first time He has spoken to me in such a way."

"I'm sorry," he said. "I guess I'm just jealous because I haven't had one of those visions yet."

"Oh, but you have," she said. "It was just presented to you in a different way."

"Okay," he said, scratching his chin as he tried to understand. "Now that we've got that straight, I'm not quite sure how you can help us, but something told me to call you, so maybe that was my vision after all."

Becky was chomping at the bit, squirming in her seat and trying to urge Mickey to get to the point.

"Yes, I believe it was," Elena said. "By the way, no one knows that it was me who let Wakulla out of here the other day."

"You're kidding! How did you manage that?"

"The helicopter that was used to deliver Wakulla to you last time belongs to a close friend of mine in Cuba who owed me a favor. The mix-up over Wakulla's immigration status, which allowed him to avoid being in lockdown, was blamed on one of my staff. That, in turn, got me off the hook with just a mild slap on the wrist."

"That's fantastic!" he said. "Not for your staff member, but for us, that is."

"Yes, I agree."

"Is Wakulla there now?" Mickey asked her.

"Yes, he is being processed as we speak."

"Well, we have less than twenty-four hours to stop Madsen from detonating that nuclear bomb, so we need to work fast."

"A nuclear bomb?" she shrieked.

"Yes, I thought you knew. He's going to drop it into the Gulf to try dispersing the three hurricanes."

"No! I had no idea!" she gasped in horror. "The man is insane!"

"Yes, he is," Mickey agreed.

"If I told you what he did to me five years ago you would..." she started, but she got so choked up she couldn't continue.

"Elena, can you help us?" Mickey finally asked her.

"I will do whatever it takes. Just tell me what needs to be done."

"I need you to free Wakulla and bring him to us," Mickey said, although he didn't know where the words were coming from. "Same place as before," he added. "We have less than twenty-four hours to stop Madsen, so time is of the essence, Elena."

"Are you there now?" she asked.

"No, but we'll be there in about eight hours, so that

should give you enough time to handle things on your end."

"He will be there," she said. "Now, you must hurry."

The line went dead and Mickey wasn't sure if she hung up or the call was dropped. When he handed the phone back to Becky, he could see the fear in her eyes.

"It's going to be okay, honey," he said. "Trust me."

CHAPTER 35

Aromatic
walk in the forest
sensual, aromatic
like-scent of your skin
©dp

"Would you mind if I drove, Doc?" Mickey asked the professor.

"Be my guest," he said. "I'll take the backseat, if you don't mind."

After all three of them swapped places, Mickey swung the car around and he headed north toward the Interstate.

"Are you sure you want to come with us, Doc?" Mickey asked, as he watched him from the rearview mirror trying to get comfortable in the backseat. "I could head over to the hotel, and then me and Becky could take her rental car instead."

"Are you kidding me? I wouldn't miss this for the world!" Doc shouted.

"Okay, but let me give you fair warning. It could get quite hairy."

"Good! I like hairy!" he shouted. "Hey, Mickey, maybe we can convince that storm to give you some hair, too," he added, laughing like a hyena on steroids.

"Everybody's a comedian," Mickey said, shaking his head, and then he glanced over at Becky.

"Hey, did I say anything?" she asked him with a stunned look on her face. "As a matter of fact, I happen to like your little cue ball head."

"Okay, that does it," he said. "As soon as all this is

over with, I'm growing it out again.

"Hey, it's your head," Becky said, and that was the end of that.

About two hours into their trip north, Mickey started complaining that he was hungry again.

"Why don't we stop somewhere and order a huge buffet feast of food to take with us?" he suggested. "After all, this could be our last meal," he added with a chuckle.

"Gee, thanks, Mickey," Becky said. "That makes me feel a whole lot better."

"Aww, come on, I was only kidding," he said. "How about you, Doc?   You hungry?" he asked over his shoulder.

"He's sound asleep, Mickey," Becky said, as she glanced behind her.   "By the way, how's the gas situation?"

"We've got a full tank," he said, as he looked down at the gauge. "Heck, with the size of the gas tank on this baby we could drive straight through to Canada."

"That's not a bad idea," she said.

"What are you, turning chicken on me?" he asked her. "Look, you know as well as I do that no place on this planet will be safe if we don't stop Madsen."

"Yes, I know, but it doesn't make me any braver thinking about confronting this storm again."

"We have to keep the faith, baby," he said. "That's all we've got working for us."

Becky was silent for a few minutes, as she stared out the window watching the trees flash by in a blur of greenery.

"Ohh! Look! Stop, Mickey! Stop here!" she said when she spotted a roadside vegetable stand up ahead of them.

"What? Aww, come on, honey. There's got to be a McDonald's up ahead somewhere."

"Mickey, please...pull over, will you?" she begged him.

"Okay," he said, as he slowed the car down. "But I ain't happy about this."

Once he pulled off onto the shoulder, Becky opened the door.

"Well, come on," she said, grinning. "Let's go pick out our last meal."

The roadside stand turned out to be more like a mini-farmer's market. Edgar, the old man selling all the fruits and vegetables, told them that everything was homegrown in his own forty-acre farm just a couple miles east. Becky was in pure heaven as she filled three large brown bags full of blueberries, blackberries, strawberries, grapes, oranges, grapefruits and kumquats. She put Mickey on vegetable duty, giving him his own three bags that he filled with cucumbers, onions, tomatoes, broccoli, pole beans, carrots, peppers, squash and lettuce.

"I don't use any pesticides on my crops," the old man assured them, as they were checking out and paying for their purchases fifteen minutes later. "Everything you see here is clean, fresh and healthy for you."

"I'm sure it is," Becky said. "Keep up the good work, Edgar."

"Yes, please," Mickey said, as he shoved a wad of bills into his hand. "The world needs more folks like you."

"Thank you. Oh, here," Edgar said, and he handed Mickey a large glass bottle and a stack of paper cups. "Since you folks were so generous, the least I can do is let you have some of this homemade lemonade. My wife made it this morning."

"Aww, that's so sweet of you," Becky said. "Thank you so much."

"Thank you," Edgar said, broadly smiling, and then he waved goodbye as they were walking back to the car. "Come back again!"

"We will!" she yelled back to him, but then she turned and looked up at Mickey. "At least, I hope we can come back," she whispered to him.

"You worry too much," he said. "Come on, we've got a bomb to stop."

"Oh, yeah, like that statement is going to make me not worry, you goofball."

Once they loaded everything into the back end of the SUV they were on their way again. Becky went to work peeling the rind off an orange, while Mickey kept his eyes trained on the road ahead of him.

"Dang! That smells fantastic!" he said, as she continued peeling off the rind.

"It does, doesn't it? Ummm..." she said, as she popped a slice of orange into her mouth. "This is awesome."

Mickey didn't say anything. He just kept driving. After a few more minutes, though, he couldn't stand it anymore.

"Would you mind sharing?" he asked her.

"Huh? Oh, you mean you'd like a piece?" she teased him.

"Uhh, yeah," he said, rolling his eyes.

"Wouldn't you rather have a big ol' greasy hamburger?"

"No, thanks. You talked me out of it about fifty miles ago," he said.

"Cool," she said. "Here you go. Open wide," she told him, smiling as she slid a juicy orange slice onto his tongue.

"Wow, this is good," he said, once he swallowed it. "Got any more?"

"Sure thing," she said, and she proceeded to feed him slice after slice of the organically grown fruit.

"Hey, what's that I smell?" Doc suddenly said from the backseat.

"Fresh oranges," Becky said. "Go ahead. Grab one. There's a whole bag of them right behind you."

"Don't mind if I do," Doc said.

"Toss me another one while you're at it," Becky said. "I think I made a convert out of Mr. Meat and Potatoes Mickey here."

Soon, the entire car smelled like an orange grove. The only thing missing was the aroma of sweet magnolias.

CHAPTER 36

Crisp Scent
A late summer breeze
carried autumn's crisp fragrance
The scent of dry leaves
©dp

"If today was the last day of your life, what would you do?" Becky asked Mickey out of the blue, as they continued their journey north.

"Excuse me?" he asked her, and then he stretched his head from side to side to loosen his stiff neck muscles.

"You heard me," she said. "If you knew you were going to die tomorrow, what would you do today?"

After only one bathroom break just north of Gainesville, the three storm chasers were now less than three hours away from the entrance to Wakulla State Park. Doc was still in the backseat, sprawled out and snoring, while catching another quick catnap, which he'd been doing on and off since they left Miami.

"Hmmm...what would I do?" Mickey asked himself, as he pondered her question for a few moments. "Well, if I had been asked that question last week I would have said that I'd fill a large cooler with a case of ice cold beer, then I'd grab my fishing pole and hop in my bass boat to spend the day on the river," he said with a satisfied grin.

"And what would you say today?" she pressed him.

"Well, today I would fill an extra-large cooler with two cases of beer, grab two fishing poles, hop in my bass boat, and spend the day on the river," he said, and then he glanced over at her. "With you," he added, and he leaned over to kiss her.

"Awww, what a sweet man," she said, blushing. "But

seriously, what would you do?"

"I just told you, sweetheart," he said. "One thing you need to know about me is that I'm really a simple man who enjoys simple pleasures."

"If it was me, I'd be in bed with a gorgeous woman, making love until the lights went out," Doc said behind them.

"Why, Professor Wiggins!" Becky gasped. "You surprise me!"

"Hey, I may be an old man, but I still enjoy the pleasures of a good woman," he said. "Perhaps you'd like to join me in this fantasy," he added, and he winked at her.

"Sorry, Doc," Mickey said. "She's taken. Go find your own woman."

"Aw, y'all are no fun," he scoffed at them. "Anybody want some strawberries?" he asked, as he rooted around in the bags.

"Only if you've got some whipped crème to go along with them," Mickey said.

"Boy, oh, boy," Becky said, shaking her head. "Typical men...both of you."

Soon, they were all laughing, while Doc kept passing strawberries up to Becky and Mickey. It was a welcome relief to all of them to just let go for a while. It kept their minds off the task ahead of them, which was saving the world from monumental destruction.

As they got closer to the park, however, Becky was dealing with her own worries about being in the direct line of fire if and when Madsen detonated the bomb. After a while, though, she figured if he did go through with it, then she wouldn't want to be alive, anyway. It would truly be hell on earth if thousands of people died, due to an American attack on American soil by an American Colonel, backed by the American President, no less.

MEANWHILE, MADSEN AND HIS men were gearing up for the countdown. All of their equipment had been moved into the bomb shelter and Madsen had been on the phone for hours talking to all sorts of high government officials.

He was under strict orders not to make any mention to the media that a nuclear bomb was about to be dropped on American soil. The plan was to increase the hype that the three storms were about to move from their stationary position and begin coming onshore. He was urged to warn residents that the storm surge would bring massive flooding and that anyone who stayed behind would face certain death.

The mandatory evacuation order had been in place since five o'clock that morning, but the majority of the residents in the affected area didn't get the notice until nearly mid-morning.

By twelve noon, it was mass chaos on the highways again and all the news stations were airing segments about the three hurricanes that continued to swirl in the Gulf. Oddly, the storms hadn't moved from their original locations since they were first spotted, but they seemed to be growing stronger and more powerful, which only helped Madsen's scheme seem more believable.

"Where the hell did those two turkeys run off to?" Madsen asked Sergeant Emerson, referring to Carl and Jeremy.

"I'm not sure, sir. They left the hurricane center about two hours before we did. They should be here somewhere."

"Well, find them!" Madsen ordered him. "I don't need any screw-ups from those two idiots!"

"Yes, sir," Emerson said.

"Find those other three whackos while you're at it! If they start talking to reporters about this bomb, we're going to have one big mess on our hands!" he added, obviously regretting letting them in on his secret plan of attack.

"Yes, sir, I'm on it," Emerson said and he rushed out of the room.

CHAPTER 37

Naked Exposure
Delightful experience
Most of the time
©dp

"Well, here we are," Mickey announced, as he pulled up to the park entrance.

"Oh, no," Becky said, as she looked ahead of her. "The gate is locked. What are we going to do?"

"Ram it!" Doc shouted from the backseat. "Hell, we've come this far! Besides, that's why I have insurance!"

Mickey just laughed and shook his head, and then he put the car in park and opened his door.

"Where are you going?" Becky asked him.

"I've got it covered," he said, and he winked at her. "Trust me."

"You've been saying that a lot lately," she told him.

"Yep, and I've been meaning it a lot, too," he said with a grin.

With that, he got out and started walking over toward the locked gate, while he reached underneath his shirt to grab his pistol.

"Bang!" went a gunshot that immediately echoed throughout the woods.

Mickey then swung the gate open and he calmly walked back toward the car.

"See?" he gloated, as he slid back behind the wheel. "Didn't I tell you to trust me?"

"Uhh...yeah," she said, not knowing whether to laugh out loud or scold him. "By the way, how did you get past that X-ray scanner at the hurricane center with that thing?"

"I shoved it under the front seat of the car before we went inside."

"How did you know to do that?"

"I don't know. It must be a male thing."

"Yeah, or something," she said, rolling her eyes at him.

"Hey, you're the keeper of the phone and I'm the keeper of the fire power. See? We both have our roles in this unfolding drama," he told her.

"What's mine?" Doc asked him.

"Yours, Professor Wiggins, is to keep us entertained with your astonishing wit and your enigmatic intelligence," he said.

"I can do that," Doc said, nodding his head up and down.

Becky couldn't stop marveling at the transformation that had taken place with the professor's behavior over the last several hours. When she first met him he was all business and totally professional, barely breaking a smile. Now, he was cheerful, funny and a pure delight to be around. She wondered if the storm had anything to do with it.

Then, there was Mickey, who didn't seem to have a frightened bone in his body. He was taking all of these incredible, science fiction-like events in stride, as if he was Superman himself and could conquer the world with a pistol and a fishing pole.

"So, why am I so scared?" she wondered. "Why can't I muster up the same blind faith as these two guys?"

"Look up ahead, Becky," Mickey whispered to her. "I think we have company."

"Boy, do we ever?" she gasped, as she stared through the windshield.

The tree limbs were loaded with birds of every color, size and species, from tiny finches, to mocking birds and cardinals, to gigantic bald eagles way up high in the trees. Alongside the roadway there were hundreds of foxes, raccoons, armadillos, possums and even a stray deer every now and then, as Mickey slowly eased the car westward through the park. All the wildlife around them wasn't road-kill, either. They were all very much alive, frisky, and extremely chatty.

"This is amazing," Doc said, as he stared out the side window.

"Isn't it?" Mickey agreed with him. "Gee, I wonder if we should start building an ark. Do you think we have time, Becky?"

"Not in this lifetime, I don't think," she said, still in awe at the sights around her.

Just then, the skies above them turned dark, as a huge flock of black crows circled the forest, blocking out the mid-day sun. Mickey even had to turn on his headlights, so he could see the road ahead of him.

"Are you freaked out yet, Doc?" Mickey asked.

"Not yet," he said. "But I'm getting there."

"Well, the best is yet to come, so prepare yourself, okay?"

"Yeah, sure," he said. "Is there a bathroom nearby?"

Mickey laughed, knowing exactly what he meant.

"There's one up ahead a little ways. I'll stop so we can all take care of business."

"You mean there's a bathroom here?!" Becky screeched.

"Well, yeah," he said. "It is a state park, you know."

"Why, you little turkey!" she yelled. "Why didn't you tell me the last time we were here?" she asked him.

"It was more fun watching you squat in the bushes," he said, laughing, which prompted a slap on the arm from her.

"Well, in that case, I guess I don't need this roll of toilet paper I shoved into my purse back at the hotel," she said.

"You didn't!" Mickey snorted.

"I certainly did," she said, and she showed it to him.

"Ahh, my little backwoods girl," he said, and he leaned over to kiss her.

"Keep your eyes on the road, silly," she said, feeling

embarrassed at his overtures with the professor in the backseat watching them.

"Ahh, yes," he said, grinning at her. "We must be discreet."

Once he drove past the boardwalk that surrounded the natural spring, and then past the lodge area, he turned off to the left where the public restrooms were located and he parked the car.

"Okay, Doc," he said. "This is your last shot to use the john. Once we get out by the beach we'll have to beg Becky for a few strips of her sacred toilet tissue if the need arises."

"Yeah, and it's gonna cost you, too," Becky said with a cocky grin on her face.

Ten minutes later, after all three of them used the facilities, they were back inside the car to continue their journey toward the coastline. The crows, in the mean time, had disappeared, and all the birds and critters they had seen earlier had vanished into the deep woods.

"What time is it getting to be?" Mickey asked.

"It's almost two o'clock," Becky said, after a quick glance at her watch.

"Hmmm...that leaves us about what? Another fifteen hours before D.T.M. time?"

"D.T.M.?" Becky asked, wondering what he meant.

"Yeah, death to Madsen time," he said.

"Oh, I wish I had your confidence," she said. "Let's just hope Elena comes through for us. I don't think I'll be able to relax until I see Wakulla standing next to me."

"Don't worry, hon. He'll be here," Mickey said.

"Yeah, I know. Trust you," she said, rolling her eyes.

"Hey, you catch on quick," he said, grinning.

Minutes later, he was pulling up to the same exact spot as the last time he and Becky were here. The tire tracks from her convertible were still visible in the hardened sand. Once they all got out of the car, Becky walked over toward the gently breaking surf, while Mickey and Doc lagged behind, trying to stretch the kinks out of their bodies.

"Are you as certain about all of this as you make yourself sound?" Doc asked Mickey.

"What are you, kidding? I'm scared shitless," he said.

"Then, why are you telling Becky all of this crap?"

"Doc, if I don't ease her mind by sounding positive and upbeat, then we'll have a crazy woman on our hands to deal with, along with this freaky storm and that asshole Madsen. It's just a survival technique," he explained.

"Ahh, I see," Doc said. "It makes perfect sense."

"Come on," Mickey said. "Let's hurry and catch up to her before she decides to go in for a swim."

"I'm right behind you," Doc said.

When Becky heard them approaching, she turned around and she had a huge smile on her face.

"Look what I just found," she said, pointing to something bobbing in the water about twenty yards out.

"Holy crap!" Mickey said. "That looks like my bass boat!"

"What?" she shrieked. "Are you serious? You can't be serious."

"I'll let you know in a few minutes," Mickey said.

With that, he stripped down to his shorts and he dove into the surf.

"Woo-hoo!" she heard him shout when he reached the boat. "It's mine! Hot dam! It's my boat!"

When he got back to shore he was all smiles. Then, he explained that he knew it was his boat because of the registration sticker.

"FL7707ZW," he said. "This is definitely my bass boat. If you'll look in that little cubbyhole, I'll bet you a big bear hug that there's four empty Miller cans in there," he said to Becky. "Go on and look for yourself."

"Wrong!" she said, after she looked inside the boat. "There's five!"

"So call me a liar for one lousy can of beer," Mickey said, laughing.

"I'll give you a big bear hug, anyway," Becky said, and she did.

"So, how the heck did your bass boat wind up here?"

Doc asked, as he scratched his head, deep in thought.

"It must be an omen, is all I can think," Mickey said. "When Jockey Joe told me it floated away that day when the river rose so high, I figured it was lost forever."

"Do you think the motor still works?" Becky asked.

"There's only one way to find out," Mickey said, and he hopped into the boat.

When the engine roared a few seconds later, her question was answered.

"This is just so cool," Mickey said, clearly flabbergasted. "Anyone want to go for a little boat ride?"

"Maybe later, kid," Doc said. "Right now, I'm hungry for some more of them delicious strawberries."

"Me, too," Becky said, and the three of them walked back to the car.

ABOUT TWO MILES BEHIND THE trio of adventurers was an unmarked NASA vehicle. Inside were Jeremy, Carl and Eric, who had been on the road northward since they left the hurricane center.

Carl had been staying in touch with Eric ever since Madsen had booted him out of his office. Carl, even though he outwardly agreed with everything Madsen was saying and proposing, underneath it all he truly despised the man, especially after the way he treated his best friend in the business, Eric Donley.

As soon as he and Jeremy left the hurricane center earlier that morning, Carl called Eric on his cell phone and asked him if he wanted to tag along. He was all for it. He lived only a few blocks away, so they picked him up and started heading north toward the state park on a hunch that Carl had.

"I certainly hope you're right about this girl, Carl," Jeremy said. "If she's all you say she is, then we've either got salvation to look forward to or utter obliteration."

"I know what I'm doing, Jeremy. It's all here on her laptop," Carl said, as he patted the computer case that was wedged between his legs on the floorboard. "She's had me intrigued and spellbound with her forecasts ever since that first time she called me when she was thirteen years old."

"Do you think Madsen figured out yet that we left his abominable company?" Jeremy asked, as he stared at the road ahead of him.

"Madsen? That freakin' idiot could care less about us. All he's worried about now is not making a complete fool of himself in front of the damned President of the United States."

"He is quite the ass, isn't he?" Jeremy rhetorically asked, as he shook his head back and forth.

"Look! Up ahead," Carl said, when he spotted a car parked in front of a roadside fruit stand. "Slow down a second. I do believe that's the professor's car."

"What should I do?" Jeremy asked him. "I don't want to scare them off."

"I'm not sure. Maybe we should just hang back for a bit," Carl suggested.

"Good idea," Jeremy said, and he pulled off to the side of the road next to a dense area of scrub brush.

"Now, we just sit and wait," Carl said.

A few minutes later, when he spotted Mickey and Becky getting into the car, he breathed a sigh of relief that his hunch had been correct after all. Now, it would be a breeze to follow them to wherever they were headed, which Carl was quite certain was Wakulla State Park.

CHAPTER 38

Uncomfortable
Restless sleep
Makes bad days
Grumpy attitudes are displayed
Insomnia
©dp

"What time is it now?" Mickey asked Becky.

"About ten minutes later than the last time you asked me," she said, not even bothering to look at her watch.

"Sorry," he said, and he reached for her hand. "I guess I'm starting to feel a bit anxious."

"Yeah, me, too," she said with a heavy sigh.

Becky had the pant legs of her jeans rolled up past her knees and she had taken off her long-sleeved shirt, leaving her in just a thin, white tank top. With her bare feet in the sand and her eyes closed, she was trying to imagine herself on a remote tropical island without a care in the world. Mickey, however, kept putting a damper on her fantasy by constantly interrupting her to ask what time it was.

He was still in just his boxer shorts, trying to dry out from his dip in the ocean to retrieve his bass boat, or so he told her. The rest of his clothes were draped across a lone scrub palm about two feet behind where they were sitting. She figured he was just getting a kick out of being half naked as he sat beside her, and to be honest, she was enjoying stealing glances at his lean, muscular body every once in a while.

The two of them had been lounging on the beach for the last couple of hours, for lack of anything better to do, while they waited on Wakulla's arrival.   Basking in the warmth of the sun and engaging in mindless chitchat about their lives back home kept them occupied for a while. Of course, it wound up being a fruitless effort in the end, because their conversations kept reverting back to the reality of the situation they were facing.

Meanwhile, Doc had worn himself out after a long walk up and down the beach and he was back in the car taking another nap.

"More lemonade?" Becky asked Mickey.

"Yeah, sure," he said, so she poured him another cupful. "All we need is some vodka and some Jimmy Buffett music and we could actually pretend we were on vacation."

"Yeah, right," she said, laughing. "Actually, aside from those three dark, angry looking storms out there in the ocean, today has been absolutely gorgeous."

"It sure has," he said. "And the best part is the fact there's been no wave action yet. No fifty-foot, scary waves coming ashore to speak to us."

"Wakulla's not here yet," she reminded him.

"Oh, that's right. I guess this is the proverbial calm before the storm, as they say."

"Shhh," she suddenly said. "Do you hear that?"

"What?" he asked, and then both of them looked up in the sky.

"It sounds like a helicopter to me," she said.

"Yep, it sure does," he said, and then he spotted it off to his left. "Uh-oh, it's not the one we're looking for, though. Come on," he shouted. "We have to hide!"

With that, he grabbed her hand and they shot to their feet and ran back toward the trees to take cover.

"It's one of Madsen's," Mickey said. "Do you see the Air Force insignia on the side?"

"Yeah," she said. "What do you think it's doing here?"

"Looking to make sure there's no collateral damage hanging around the beach, I'm sure. I hope they don't spot our car."

Then, as quickly as the helicopter had arrived, it did an about face and zipped off, heading back south again.

"Phew! That was close," Becky said. "Now, all we need is to see Elena's helicopter and we'll be all set."

"Yeah," Mickey said. "We'll be all set."

This time, however, Becky noticed his voice clearly lacked that note of confidence that had kept her sane all day and it gave her the shivers.

"What time is it?" he asked her again.

"It's almost seven o'clock," she told him, only this time his question didn't irritate her.

"I guess I should get dressed before our company arrives," he said.

"Yeah, we wouldn't want Elena seeing you in your underwear, now would we?"

Mickey merely laughed, and then he went to grab his clothes from the palm tree, while Becky stood and watched.

"You're enjoying this, aren't you?" he asked her, laughing.

"Oh, maybe just a little," she said.

"Hey, Mickey, are you trying out for the Chippendale's or what?" Doc shouted, as he stood next to the car stretching his arms.

"Ha! More like Alvin and the Chipmunks!" he shouted back. "Sheesh! So many comedians today," he added, shaking his head and laughing, as he zipped up his pants.

By the time the sun was getting ready to set for the night, all three of them looked weary, even Doc, who had been napping for the majority of the day. As hard as Mickey had been trying to keep an upbeat and positive attitude all day, Becky could tell he was beginning to wear down. With a wrinkled brow and his lips pursed together, he had been staring aimlessly out across the bay for the last half hour, saying nothing for the longest time.

As the three of them sat on the beach watching the sunset, a light misty rain began to fall, but it didn't seem to bother any of them. They just stayed put and sipped on lemonade. Becky, for one, was actually enjoying the feel of the cool raindrops falling on her sunburned face and arms.

"Are you guys going to stay here all night?" a familiar voice asked from behind where they were sitting, which made all three of them jump to attention.

"What the hell?!" Mickey shouted, and then he shot to his feet. "How long have you guys been here?"

"Oh, since about two o'clock," Carl said, grinning, as he stood flanked on either side by Eric and Jeremy. "You three have been driving us crazy for hours. I wish we had thought to bring along some food and water."

"Are you here as friend or foe?" Becky wanted to know, as she glared at him through suspicious eyes.

"You know how I feel about you, Becky. I'm with you...we're all with you, all the way," Carl said, as he nodded toward both Jeremy and Eric.

"I could really use something to drink," Jeremy said.

"Me, too," Eric piped up.

"Hrmphh...do we have any lemonade left?" Becky asked Mickey.

"Maybe just a little," he said. "Perhaps you boys would like to join us for dinner, too."

"Yeah!" Carl said, as he patted his stomach. "What's on the menu?"

"We've got a royal feast for you," Mickey said. "I do believe we have enough to serve to these three fine gentlemen, huh, Becky?"

"Oh, yes, we've got plenty to go around," she said, giggling. "Come on, Doc, help me set the table."

"Yes, ma'am," Doc said, and he followed her back to the car.

Ten minutes later, Becky couldn't stop laughing as she watched everyone standing around the back end of Doc's SUV nibbling on all the raw, fresh vegetables they had bought earlier in the day.

"It's not steak or lobster, but it's darned good," Mickey said.

"And good for you," Becky added, still laughing

hysterically.

While they were eating, Becky and Mickey filled the three newcomers in on what they envisioned would be the next steps, as far as the storm was concerned. As they were finishing up with a dessert of blackberries, orange slices and kumquats, Becky thought she heard something in the distance.

"Shhh...listen," she said, as she cocked her ear toward the sky. "It sounds like another helicopter."

"It better be Wakulla this time," Mickey said, and then he told her he heard it, too.

Sure enough, it was the same helicopter that had brought Wakulla to them the first time. This time, however, only one person was lowered into the water. There was no bright orange raft to bring Wakulla to shore, and thankfully, there were no high-powered rifles aimed at his head, either. Once the drop was completed and the line was hoisted back up into the chopper, Elena stuck her head out.

"Good luck!" she shouted to them.

Mickey saluted her and then the helicopter turned around and headed southeast, vanishing into the darkness seconds later. Meanwhile, Wakulla was swimming to shore, using long, swift arm movements, with his face buried in the water, as he paddled with both feet.

No sooner did he step foot on land and struggle to his feet, than a huge wave of water appeared out of the depths of the sea.

"Dumala! Dumala! Dumala!" the storm shouted to the heavens.

The wave rose higher and higher, reaching a height of more than fifty feet in the air before beginning its journey toward shore. Wakulla immediately turned around and he fell to his knees. He started chanting again in the same foreign tongue, just like before.

"Holy crap!" Carl gasped, nearly choking on his phlegm, as he stood frozen to the ground.

"Don't be afraid," Becky said, and she squeezed his

hand, although she wondered where this sudden spurt of courage sprang from, since she was standing there shaking from head to toe.

As all six of them stood side by side behind Wakulla, the wave rushed in at warp speed. Then, exactly as before, a swirl of purple haze engulfed them, as the fragrance of orange blossoms and magnolias filled the air.

"We are here," Wakulla said, as he bowed before the storm.

"Ahh, I see you have brought more of my children with you," the storm said to Wakulla, and then the bright purple lights lifted from his face and rested on Becky's shoulders. "You have done a good job, my child."

"Not good enough, I'm afraid," she replied, as she squeezed both Mickey's and Carl's hands.

"There is no need to be afraid, my child. I am well aware of what your leaders are about to embark on. They will not succeed," it said. "You must not flee from this spot. None of you. That is all I ask of you now. Soon, all of you will have ringside seats to witness the power of the Universe, as it protects itself from ignorant, misinformed and greedy leadership."

Then, in the blink of an eye, the wave rushed back out to sea, taking the purple haze and the glorious fragrance along with it.

"Dumala! Dumala! Dumala!" it shouted, and then the wave disappeared below the surface again.

"Whoa!" Carl gasped.

"Double whoa!" Jeremy chimed in.

"My God, Becky!" Eric said, with his jaw about to hit the ground. "If I hadn't seen it for myself I wouldn't have believed it!"

"Well, I've seen it a few times and I still don't believe it," she said, shaking her head. "Did you guys understand what the storm said?" she asked, looking at Carl, Jeremy and Eric.

"Yeah, it came through loud and clear in perfectly spoken English," Eric told her, as Carl and Jeremy nodded an affirmative.

For the next hour they all sat on the beach watching the three storms brewing out in the middle of the sea, while trying to figure out what the storm was planning to do to stop a nuclear bomb. Everyone had their own theories, but none of them were believable.

"It's going to take a miracle to stop Madsen," Becky finally surmised out loud to all of them. "It's going to take one heck of a miracle."

"Well, folks, I suggest we all try to get some sleep," Mickey told them. "Tomorrow morning all hell is going to break loose and I don't want to miss one second of it."

"Are there any hotels nearby?" Carl asked, which prompted the rest of them to glare at him.

"You can't be serious," Mickey said. "You can bet your ass there isn't anything open around here for miles."

"Yes, that's right," Doc said. "I was listening to the radio earlier this afternoon and our buddy, Madsen, has everyone so freaked out that they've evacuated northeast as far as they can go away from this area," Doc said. "Besides that, our stormy friend ordered us all to stay put."

"Idiots," Becky said. "Madsen and all of his men are just a bunch of mindless, blind idiots, along with the rest of the people in this country."

CHAPTER 39

Whispers
Softly whispered secrets
Binding your heart to mine
Powerful only
If they are left untold
A secret shared between just two
Is the only true secret
©dp

"What time is it?" Mickey asked Becky through a mouthy yawn.

The two of them were curled up together in the back of the SUV with their feet dangling out the open door. Doc was sleeping soundly in the front seat, although, every once in a while he'd let out a grunt, as he changed positions, trying to get more comfortable.

"I don't know," Becky said. "I can't see my watch in the dark."

"I don't know about you, but I can't sleep," he said. "I think I'm going to take a walk down the beach. Would you like to join me?"

"I'd love to," she said, as she stretched her legs out. "This is the most uncomfortable car I've ever slept in."

"How many cars have you slept in?" he asked her, trying not to laugh too loud.

"Just one," she said. "This one," she added with a chuckle.

Once they got out of the car and closer to the beach, Becky was able to see the tiny hands on her watch, since there was a full moon out illuminating the sky.

"Before you ask me again, it's four o'clock," she said.

"Hmmm...that gives us about one more hour before

Showtime," he said.

"Yep, about one more hour," she mimicked him.

"Come on," he said. "I have an idea."

With that, he grabbed her hand and he led her about a quarter of a mile south along the gently lapping surf. When he rounded a bend toward the left, he stopped in his tracks and he swept her up in his arms with one hand covering her mouth so she wouldn't scream.

For a split second she was scared out of her wits, wondering what the heck he was going to do, but then she looked into his eyes and she knew he meant no harm. On the contrary, when he pulled his hand away from her face, his mouth dove in like a torpedo, as his tongue spread her lips apart.

The kiss lasted for two long, glorious minutes, while they both groped each others' bodies. As soon as he set her back down on the ground, he lifted her shirt up over her head and then he unbuttoned her jeans, sliding them down below her hips. As she wiggled out of them, he was tearing off his own clothes, until soon they were both standing in front of each other in just their underwear.

"Ohh, Becky," he softly said, as he looked deep into her eyes. "I know this is going to sound crazy, but I have fallen in love with you. I don't know what's going to play out here in the next hour. We could be dead, for all I know, but I didn't want to leave this planet without telling you how much I adore you."

Becky was speechless. She didn't know what to say.

"Does he really think we're going to die?" she wondered. "Do I tell him I love him, too? Yes," she thought. "Yes, Becky, tell him. Tell him, you dope."

Mickey didn't wait for a reply, though. He simply lowered her to the ground with his lips on hers and he proceeded to devour her with deep, passionate kisses. As his mouth explored her body from head to toe, she thought she had truly died already and gone to heaven.

As he was yanking on her panties, trying to get them down below her hips, a loud horn started blasting. The way it kept on and on in an obnoxious ear-splitting rhythm, it was clear to both of them that it was an anti-theft device on someone's car.

"Oh, good grief," she mumbled, which made Mickey start laughing, as he rolled off of her.

"Yeah, somebody please turn that thing off!" he yelled, as he tried to catch his breath.

"Hey, Mickey! Where are you?" Doc shouted from the beach about thirty yards away from them. "I can't get that damned car alarm to shut off!"

"Oh, for godsakes," he said, looking into Becky's eyes and shaking his head. "Can you believe this?"

"Yeah, I can believe it. I guess we weren't meant to have this moment together," she said.

"Well, don't worry, we'll have our time one of these days," he told her with a huge smile plastered across his face. "Now, hurry up and get your clothes on before Doc has another heart attack."

"Maybe this is Doc's fantasy coming true," she said, laughing.

"Huh?" he asked, looking dumbfounded, as he slipped back into his jeans.

"Yeah, you remember what he said earlier today about enjoying the pleasures of a woman. Maybe we're living in his fantasy world right now...not ours," she said, giggling as she hurried to get her clothes back on.

"Not in this lifetime," he said, laughing along with her.

BACK AT THE BOMB SHELTER in Miami, Madsen and his men were in full battle gear, watching all the radar and satellite images of the three storms out in the Gulf.

It was T-minus-fifteen minutes before the jet bomber would drop its deadly cargo. Madsen was shaking in his boots, hoping that there wouldn't be another dimwitted pilot in the cockpit. The last thing he needed right now was for his nuclear bomb to be diverted to a different location.

All but a few diehard non-believers had evacuated the coastal cities around the entire Gulf basin. Oddly or not,

the majority of the people in the Keys decided to stay put.
They were and had always been a hardy bunch of folks.
After so many near misses from hurricanes and always
coming out smelling like a rose with only minor damage
and flooding, they had fallen into a pattern of simply
hunkering down to ride out whatever may come their
way. It seemed a triple hurricane threat that was
predicted to aim northward was no more an issue than a
small tropical storm to many of them.

Farther north, however, from Miami to Tallahassee
and all around the Gulf basin, nearly all the residents had
evacuated. Of course, the highways were still congested
with traffic and one accident after the next, but as far as
Madsen was concerned, he didn't care how many people
were in harm's way. If they were stupid enough to be
within range of the bomb, then so be it. Nobody was
going to get in the way of his plans. He had a mission and
a deadline that he was going to keep, no matter what.

He was still giving everybody within earshot a piece
of his mind for not being able to locate Carl and Jeremy,
although, with them out of his hair to question his
judgment, he should have been ecstatic. When he
received a phone call from the local police captain that
there was an all points bulletin out for Wakulla, though,
he went ballistic.

"That sonofabitch better not interfere with my plans!"
he shouted, and then he slammed the phone down. "Has
anyone heard from those other two lame brain idiots?" he
asked, referring to Becky and Mickey.

"No, sir, they haven't been back to their hotel since
they left the hurricane center yesterday," Sergeant
Emerson said.

"What about the professor? Has anyone checked on
him?"

"I spoke to his housekeeper a couple of hours ago and
she said she hasn't seen him in days," Emerson
continued.

"Well, good," Madsen said, switching back into his
almighty gloating mode again. "I hope they're all out

there on the beach when this bomb drops. It will serve them right."

CHAPTER 40

New Journeys
old roads lead to new journeys
far from home then back again
the wandering between
beginning and end
is oft the treasured
©dp

As Mickey and Becky were heading back toward where the rest of the group was now gathered along the beach, Doc was walking alongside them with a big ol' stogie in his mouth and splashing his bare feet in the surf, just like a precocious kid. Thankfully, either Carl or Jeremy had figured out how to turn off the car alarm, so it was peaceful and quiet again.

"Now, just what in the hell were you two up to back there?" Doc finally asked them, but neither Becky nor Mickey said a word. "Ah, never mind, don't tell me. I can see it in your faces," he said, and he started laughing.

"That's good, Doc, because we weren't going to tell you, anyway," Mickey said, grinning over at him. "By the way, I didn't know you smoked those things," he added, wrinkling his nose at the unsightly cigar dangling from his lips.

"I don't," Doc told him. "I gave them up years ago, but my friend Jeremy over there thought I should have one now. He said it would calm my nerves. Ain't that right, Jeremy?" he asked him, as they approached within earshot.

"It always works for me," Jeremy said, and then he popped a grapefruit slice into his mouth.

Carl, who looked like he was still half asleep, along

with Jeremy, who looked as if he'd gotten no sleep at all, were sitting in the sand peeling the rinds off the last two grapefruits. They were both sucking down the fruit as if it was their last meal on earth. Just then, Mickey looked over at Becky.

"I know, I know. You want to know what time it is," she said, and she glanced at her watch. "It's five minutes before five."

Suddenly, everyone froze. Jeremy stopped chewing, Doc stopped puffing, Carl stopped yawning, and Becky and Mickey stood like tin soldiers, staring into each others' eyes.

In the distance, the sound of jet engines high above the sky reverberated in the silent darkness. Then, the sea began bubbling, bringing a thick white foam to the surface as far out as they could see.

"I guess this is it, Becky," Mickey said, as he held her close.

"Yes, this is it," she said, and she let out a long, drawn out sigh.

"Has anyone seen Wakulla?" Doc asked.

"The last time I saw him, he was asleep in my bass boat over there," Mickey said, pointing off to the right.

"I am here," they all heard behind them. "I am here," he repeated, and then he took his place on his knees at the edge of the surf, soon chanting his prayers over and over again.

The jet engines were louder now and through the moonlit haze they all saw the airplane approaching the center of the bay. As everyone stood watching, Mickey had turned aside and he was fumbling with his keychain.

"Becky, I'd like you to have this," he said, and he showed her the sacred Indian tribal ring that he'd been carrying around with him since he was thirteen years old.

"What? Oh, Mickey, I couldn't," she said, but she took it from his hand anyway to look at it.

"Please," he said. "I want you to have it."

The more she looked at the ring, the more stunned she was acting, until Mickey finally asked her what was wrong.

"This is just too amazing," she said. "It's too coincidental."

When she grabbed hold of her necklace and showed it to him, he, too, was taken aback. The stones in the necklace were identical to the stones in the ring.

"Turn it over," she told him and he did.

"Oh, my God," he said. "It's got my initials on it."

When he explained the meaning of the inscription on the underside of the ring, their eyes met in total disbelief. A second later, he slid the ring onto her finger and then he reached down and placed his hands on her face, drawing her in for one last kiss.

Becky then unhooked the necklace and she placed it around his neck.

"I believe this is yours," she said, smiling at him once she got the clasp shut.

"Bombs away!" Doc suddenly shouted, interrupting their special moment.

Becky glanced at her watch again and she shuddered when she saw the minute hand strike twelve. Then, all of them watched in horror as the huge cylinder dropped from the underside of the airplane.

Everyone was holding their breath, as they waited for the moment of impact. When the bomb hit the sea, however, something strange happened. It didn't seem to have any effect on the water. There was no big splash, there was no gigantic mushroom cloud shooting toward the sky. In fact, it seemed to just disappear below the surface.

"I wonder if it was a dud," Jeremy said, looking nervous as a goat, as he waited for something to happen.

"The only dud is that idiot Madsen," Doc said, as they all continued to watch.

About thirty seconds later, the sky lit up in magnificent shades of purple's and gold's. Then, all three of the hurricanes slowly converged into one massive ball, swirling around at a dizzying pace and looking exactly like a huge spinning top.

The air filled with the aroma of freshly squeezed oranges, mixed with the fragrance of a million magnolia blooms. Soft, velvety dust began falling from the sky, as if a trillion balls of glitter had just been released from the heavens.

"I've never seen anything so beautiful before," Becky said, with her mouth agape.

"That doesn't look like any nuclear bomb I've ever seen," Jeremy said in awe.

"Me, neither," Doc said, with his eyeballs about to pop out of his skull.

"It is not," Wakulla said, again in perfect English, and then he turned around to face them. "It is the center of the Universe dispersing its heavenly dust down upon the people. It is giving mankind one last chance to make amends. Our mission has only just begun."

Within minutes, the sea transformed into the most beautiful body of water any of them had ever seen, clear and blue and slick as glass. The three storms had completely dissipated. Moments later, the sky lit up in amazing shades of red and gold, as the morning sun began its ascent toward the heavens.

A few minutes later, Carl jumped to his feet and he rushed back to Doc's car. After he turned the key in the ignition, he switched on the radio. When he found a news station, he turned up the volume so everyone could hear.

For the next two hours, they listened to the news reports, one after the next. The authorities kept stressing to the public that the only people who were allowed into the Gulf coastline area were the military, until the all-clear was sounded that the storm was over. What the majority of the public didn't know, however, was that all those military personnel were wearing full survival gear, as they tested the atmosphere for the presence of nuclear gases and radiation levels.

One reporter from down in Key West, who had opted to ride out this episode with the rest of the Concher's, said that he hadn't noticed any ill effects from the storm.

He went on to say that the party had been going strong all along Duval Street since last night.

A few eyewitnesses stated that they saw an explosion right before the storms suddenly vanished. One person went so far as to say it was like watching a Michael Jackson stage show with a majestic fireworks finale.

Similar reports were coming in from all around the Gulf coast from folks who had opted not to evacuate. Everyone heard the explosion and everyone watched the storms mysteriously disappear. Not one area along the coastline showed any evidence of damage. It was like the hurricane that never was.

"Well, I guess we can all go back to business as usual," Carl said.

Becky just glared at him, and she wondered what had ever possessed her to be so infatuated with him. He seemed to be totally clueless about what just happened, and right now she didn't have the energy to try setting him straight.

"Yeah, Carl, why don't you and Jeremy head back to Miami," Mickey said, picking up on Becky's anger toward him. "Go back and congratulate Madsen for a job well done."

"Yep," Doc said. "That's exactly what's going to happen. Our boy Madsen is going to be hailed as a national hero in the eyes of the ignorant public."

"Well, you have to admit it," Jeremy said. "Madsen lucked out big time with his daring action. A lot of people could have been killed, including us. And you are absolutely correct, Professor Wiggins. Madsen's face will be plastered all over the newspapers and television screens as the man who saved the world."

Twenty minutes later, Carl and Jeremy were in their car heading out of the park, while Becky, Mickey and Doc stood there shaking their heads in disbelief.

"Hey, where did Wakulla go?" Becky asked.

"I'm not sure," Mickey said, "But if I was him, I'd be heading back to Haiti before the immigration authorities decide to throw him back in the slammer."

The three of them searched for him for the next hour, but he had vanished without a trace.

"Well, kids, I don't know about you, but I think it's time for me to hit the road," Doc said. "I don't think I can spend another night sleeping in this car."

"Yeah, good idea," Mickey said. "You go on. We'll be there in a second."

Mickey grabbed Becky's hand and he led her over toward the breaking surf. When they reached the water's edge, he stopped and turned her around to face him.

"I have the most awesome idea," he started, and then he took a deep breath. "What do you think about taking a little trip up the river?"

"What? Are you nuts?" she shrieked.

"Maybe, but I think it would be a lot of fun, and let's face it, after what we've been through the past few days, we deserve a little bit of fun, don't you think?"

"But...I...Mickey, that's crazy," she said. "Do you mean to tell me you want us to get into that bass boat and motor up the river? To where?" she asked.

"To my place," he said. "We'll have to head a ways south first, down to Cedar Key, though, before we can start heading north."

"Hmmm...I still think you're nuts," she said.

"You're probably right, but I'd really like to travel the route that the storm took to get out here in the Gulf. I'm anxious to see if there have been any drastic changes along the river. I also think it's time you met my father. Besides, the world needs some time to digest what just happened, and when they figure it out, you and I are going to be inundated by reporters."

"But what about my rental car? And our things back at the hotel? And..."

"Hey, will you be quiet for just a minute? You worry too much," he told her. "I'll have Doc return the rental and I'll also have him ship our things to us. Carl already gave you back your laptop, which was the most important thing. Trust me, Doc will be more than happy to oblige."

"There you go with that trust me business again," she

said, grinning.

"Yeah, well, maybe one of these days you'll learn to do so."

Becky started pacing back and forth, thinking so hard that her head felt as if it might burst.

"Well? Are you up for it?" he asked again.

"What about supplies? We need food. We need water. We need..."

"Yes, we need lots of stuff and we'll get it. Just tell me you'll do this, okay?" he begged her.

"Well," she said, and then, after another few seconds passed, she shouted, "Okay! Let's do it!"

"Whoo-whee!" he yelled, and then he scooped her up in his arms and he kissed her as he twirled her around.

"Whoo-whee!" she shouted, too.

CHAPTER 41

Scent of Passion
feeling our love grow
blossoming as soft as a rose
scented with passion
©dp

"You know, I still think you're crazy for wanting to do this," Becky said to Mickey, as they motored south in the bass boat toward Cedar Key.

"Yeah, maybe so, but I have a feeling you're going to change your mind soon," he said, smiling at her.

Just as Mickey had told her earlier, Doc was more than happy to take care of business for them back in Miami, as far as returning her rental car, handling their hotel check-out, and shipping their luggage to their respective homes. He also promised to ship the painting Becky had bought to her house. It was a bittersweet farewell, as they watched him leave the park.

Once they made it to Cedar Key about three-and-a-half hours later, they pulled up beside a mom-and-pop bait and tackle shop. After they both took a bathroom break, Mickey went shopping. He bought an extra large Igloo cooler, filled it with two cases of beer, a jug of water, a gross of bologna and cheese sandwiches, and then he filled it with ice. Now, it was time to begin their journey up the river.

"I see we're going to be eating high on the hog," Becky said, laughing at his choice of food items.

"The way I figure it, after we drink all this beer, we won't rightly care what we eat," he said. "Are you ready for a cold one?"

"I've been ready for days," she said. "By the way, did

you see how that guy at the checkout counter was looking at us?"

"Yep, I sure did. Did you see the newspaper racks?"

"No, why?"

"Your picture was plastered on the front page of every one of them."

"Really? Oh, no," she said. "Do you think that guy recognized me?"

"If he did, he wasn't saying anything."

"Well, let's hope he doesn't. I'd hate to have to outrun a herd of reporters in this little boat."

"Hey, don't knock the boat. I've had her for years and she's never let me down yet. Besides, all the focus is on Madsen at the moment. His ugly mug was on the front page, too, evidently being hailed as a hero...just as we all suspected he'd be."

"Idiots," she mumbled, shaking her head.

"Girl, are you sure you're ready for this adventure? It's going to take us a few days to get home," he said.

"Well, it's too late now to change my mind," she said. "Besides, I've done my share of outdoor living, so I think I can handle this."

"Really?" he asked.

"Yeah, back home I did a lot of hiking in the mountains and camping out in the woods. It was fun."

"Ahh, that's nice to know," he said. "Ever since I can remember, me, my brothers and my dad spent just about every weekend on the river. This will be my first time with a girl, though," he added, and then he reached over to kiss her.

"I'll try to do you proud," she said, and she kissed him back.

It did indeed take them several days to get to Mickey's house. Along the way, Mickey played tour guide, pointing out the various tree and plant species, as well as all the critters and birds who made their home along the river.

Each night they camped out in a small pup tent that Mickey had stashed in the boat. It was well-used and torn in a few spots, but it served the purpose. They bathed in the springs each morning and at night they slept beneath the stars wrapped in each others' arms.

Mickey had somehow learned to keep his hormones under control, even though it was killing him not to jump her bones and make mad, passionate love to her. He couldn't explain his attitude change, but it seemed Becky was in the same state of mind. There wasn't even any discussion about it. It just seemed to be the right thing to do. Now just wasn't the right time to get bare naked crazy with one another. There were too many things to think about.

On the last day of their journey, Mickey told her that the river looked more pristine than he'd ever seen it before, but he was afraid it wouldn't stay that way for long. Sadly, she had to agree with him.

CHAPTER 42

The Spell of the Sea
Holding hands in the sand
Waves from the ocean
Touching our toes
The sun and the sea
Smiling down on us
Surreal are the moments
©dp

By two o'clock on the day the bomb was dropped, the all-clear had been given by Madsen to the local authorities that it was safe for all coastal residents to return to their homes. The media wasted no time going berserk with stories about miracles and divine intervention that had stopped the three most deadly hurricanes in history from obliterating the nation. It was front-page news in every newspaper across the country and all the networks were airing the story for days afterward.

Madsen, even though he had admitted to his staff and all his higher-ups that he had no idea how his nuclear bomb took out the storm, to the general public he was taking full advantage of the situation. On orders from his superiors at Air Force headquarters in Washington, however, he was to state that it was a newly developed weather bomb that had dispersed of the three storms. There was to be absolutely no mention of a nuclear bomb.

What Madsen and all the top government officials didn't know at the time, however, was that Carl and Jeremy were telling their side of the story to an underground news reporter. They kept repeating that they had witnessed the miracle of the storm firsthand and that everything Becky Rogers had told the world was absolutely true. Jeremy then let loose with the shocker, telling a newscaster on live TV that Madsen had ordered a nuclear bomb to be dropped into the Gulf of Mexico and that he also had his words on audiotape. He went on to say that he had seen a nuclear bomb explosion before and that this incident in the Gulf bore no resemblance to it whatsoever, which inadvertently got Madsen off the hook, even though that wasn't his intention.

Soon, reports started coming in from the general public that they had seen hundreds of men in full disaster gear swarming the beaches with Geiger counters from the Florida Keys to Mexico not long after the supposed weather bomb went off.

Eventually, a media war erupted and both Carl and Jeremy were placed into protective custody by NASA officials, who had been at odds with the Air Force for the last ten years regarding all their secret missions to interfere with normal weather patterns.

Madsen, of course, was immediately ordered by the President to make a public statement, which he did hours later.

"It is preposterous to think that the United States military would drop a nuclear bomb within its own waters," he said on national television. "What everyone witnessed was a newly-developed weather bomb and that is what took out the storm," he declared.

It was a short five-minute interview with members of the media and he dodged one question after the next about the weather bomb, saying that it was top-secret information.

As to be expected, once his segment aired, there were two equally opposing sides on the top news stations debating Madsen's integrity, the military's actions, and the government's backing of the bomb, as well as whether or not it was a nuclear bomb that was dropped into the Gulf. There was so much conflicting evidence from both sides that the public didn't know who to believe.

Jeremy and Carl had literally disappeared, evidently

burrowing deep into the witness protection program, compliments of NASA officials.

As Madsen's story began to shred in the media, and when he suddenly retired a few days after the bomb incident, never to be heard from again, all the environmental activist groups immediately got back on their bandwagons. Within hours of hearing about Madsen's supposed retirement, every environmental group in the world rallied together. It was the largest conference call in history one afternoon where it was decided to hold a vigil along the beaches of the Gulf coast basin.

Wakulla State Park would be the staging area for the media to cover the event. All week long, Becky's interview that day at the park when she listed the storm's demands, kept replaying over and over on TV. After a while, most everyone across the nation felt that there was too much evidence backing up all that she had said for it not to be true.

When news leaked out that every one of the children from the bus mishap had been magically healed and were now cancer-free, it added even more fuel to their arguments that the storm and the heavenly dust it brought was the reason behind their cure. Each child, along with their doctors, had told their stories on national television, so there was no denying the truth.

Back in Washington, the President had just signed three new laws into the Constitution that miraculously made it through the House and the Senate in record time.

Meanwhile, both Becky's mother and Mickey's father were being inundated with phone calls, letters and visits from members of the media and different environmental groups. Everybody wanted to know where these two incredible people had disappeared to. Even the professor was being asked if he knew where they were, but he kept his promise not to breathe a word to anyone of their whereabouts.

CHAPTER 43

Truth
Lead with words of truth
and her heart will follow you
to the ends of the earth.
©dp

"Well, are you ready to meet the crazy old man?" Mickey asked Becky, after he moored the boat to the makeshift dock behind his house on the river.

"It's now or never," she said.

"Well, would you lookie there!" Brent shouted from the back porch when he saw them approaching. "Where in tarnation have you two been? You've got the whole damned world looking for you!" he added, as he rushed over to greet his son.

Mickey gave him a big bear hug and then he introduced him to Becky.

"Well, Ms. Rogers, it is my pleasure to make your acquaintance," Brent said, putting on a show for her, as he kissed her hand like an English gentleman.

"Please...call me Becky," she said. "It's a pleasure to meet you, too. I've heard a lot about you, Mr. DeRosa."

"Yeah, I'll bet you have," he said, as he glanced over at Mickey. "Don't you believe a word of it, sweetheart. And since we're on a first name basis, I'll let you call me Brent," he added with a smile.

"Okay," she said, smiling back at him.

"Well, don't just stand there, son. Bring the young lady inside for a cold beer," Brent told him.

For the next hour, they sat around the kitchen table talking about everything that had happened, bringing Brent up to date on all of Madsen's atrocities, as well as explaining the miracles of the storm. Afterward, Mickey gave her the grand tour of the house, which she immediately fell in love with.

"I didn't know you were such a "green" advocate. How come you never said anything?" she asked him.

"I'm not sure," he said. "Maybe I wanted to surprise you."

"Well, you did. This is awesome."

"Yeah, I kind of think so, too," he said. 'I've been working on it for years."

Mickey went on to explain that all the furniture fabric was organic and that all the furniture was handmade by him and his father. All three levels of the home were designed with an open floor plan, and each room had skylights for natural light and heat. There were solar windows throughout and ceiling fans in every room. The bathrooms all had tankless water heaters and all the kitchen appliances were high-efficiency Energy Star rated.

When he took her out into the yard, she was even more impressed.

"Is that a windmill?" she asked.

"Yep, it supplies the majority of the house with electricity," he said.

"Oh, I love all these solar landscape lights," she said, when he took her down closer toward the river.

"What do you think of these rain barrels?" he asked her, pointing to the side of the barn.

"Let me guess," she said. "You use the rainwater to do your laundry."

"Yep, sure do," he said. "I also use that clothesline over there, unless we have days and days of torrential downpours. Then I'll use the dryer, but it doesn't happen that often, so I save a lot on the electric bill."

"Wow, this is just so darned cool, Mickey. You have really impressed me with your ingenuity."

"If you really want to be bowled over, follow me," he said, smiling, as he led her over to the side yard.

"Oh, my goodness," she gasped. "You have your very

own vegetable garden!"

"The fruit trees are over there," he said, pointing down a grassy path to the south.

"Why, you little stinker," she said. "And all this time I thought you were just a meat and potatoes man."

"Hey, don't get me wrong," he said. "I still like a good T-bone every now and then."

"Yeah, me, too," she said, giggling. "Every once in a while."

"The cattle are over there," he said, pointing off to the far left. "We've probably got about fifty or sixty in the herd."

"Wow, no wonder you like steaks so much," she said.

"Let's go back inside. I saved the best for last," he said, and he held her hand as they walked back toward the house.

When he took her upstairs to the huge master bedroom she nearly fainted. The view out the gigantic pane glass window above the bed's headboard made her feel as if she was in a fairy tale setting. The romantic Suwannee River was clearly visible through the trees, as it gently flowed downstream.

"Mickey, this is breathtaking," she said in awe.

"It is, isn't it? It's even more beautiful with you standing here next to me."

"Aww, you are such a sweet, wonderful man," she said, as she pulled him close to her.

"Oh, by the way, I promised you something the other day and I never fall back on a promise," he said.

"Oh?" she asked, and then she watched him walk over toward a bookshelf on the other side of the expansive room.

"Here you go," he said, and he handed her a copy of the book he had written years ago. "It's already autographed."

"Oh, my goodness," she said. "You don't have to do this, but thank you."

"You're quite welcome," he said, smiling at her. "Hey, you know what? Maybe you and I could write a book together some day. What do you think?"

"Hmmm...maybe," she said. "But I'll only do it if it's a trashy romance novel. All this history crap gets quite boring after a while," she added with a chuckle.

"Yeah, right," he said, knowing full well she was pulling his leg. "Well, let's get back downstairs. I think Dad could use some help in the kitchen. You do know how to cook, don't you?"

"What do *you* think?" she asked him with a crooked grin. "I'll bet you're not so bad yourself."

"I get by," he said.

That evening the three of them feasted on T-bone steaks, mashed potatoes and gravy, fresh vegetables from Mickey's garden and a bottle of champagne.

During dinner, Brent told them it was good that they came in the back way via the river, because there had been a rash of reporters staked out by the road for days.

"See, Becky? I told you to trust me, didn't I?" Mickey asked her.

"That you did," she said. "I wonder if my mother is going through the same mess with the reporters."

"I'd say to call her, but I have a feeling if you do, it might be our demise if word gets out where we are."

"I agree," she said, after thinking about it.

"By the way," Brent said, interrupting them. "Since when do you wear a straw hat, son?"

Mickey started laughing and then he explained about all the jokes and references to his bald head over the past few days. Then, Becky stood up and she pulled the hat from his head.

"You know what, Mickey? Even though your hair is growing back in, I see a definite large bald spot back here," she said, as she rubbed the crown of his head. "It looks to be spreading quite a bit, too, all the way over to your ears."

"What? Are you serious?" he shrieked, and then he rushed into the bathroom to see for himself.

A few minutes later he came back, all red-faced and with the hat back on his head.

"I think you should keep shaving it," she said, straight-faced.

"Me, too," he said, and then all of them broke out into laughter.

"Okay," Brent said to Becky. "If you'll wash the dishes, I'd be more than happy to dry 'em."

"You've got yourself a deal," she said.

"Ahh, that's perfect," Mickey said. "While y'all are doing that, I'll go secure the boat, so it doesn't float away again."

"Yeah, you do that, son," Brent said, laughing, as Mickey shot out the back door.

When he came back inside fifteen minutes later, Becky and his father were still in the kitchen, so he snuck upstairs to grab a much needed shower, knowing that if Becky got in there first, she'd take forever.

After grabbing a pair of clean underwear from his drawer, he went into the bathroom and started stripping off his clothes, while waiting for the water to heat up. Just as he was about to step into the shower, there was a knock at the bedroom door.

"Aww, geez," he muttered. "I hope that's not Becky wanting the shower."

There was a stack of clean white towels piled on the bathroom vanity, so he grabbed one of them and wrapped it around his waist before heading out to see who was banging on the door.

"Geez," Becky said, as she bounded through the doorway. "You could have waited for me," she added, as she tugged on his towel.

"But..." he started to say, and then Becky grabbed his hand and pulled him into the bathroom.

"God, I can't wait to wash this smell out of my hair! Magnolias and orange blossoms, my ass!" she said, trying to keep a straight face, as she stripped in front of the gorgeous man standing next to her. "How about dog poo, cat urine and fish guts? Blechh!" she said, referring to all their baths in the springs over the past few days.

All it took her was five seconds to remove her shoes

and clothes, and then she pulled the shower curtain aside and she stepped in.

"Ohh, this is heaven!" she said with a loud sigh, as the hot water beat down on her body. "Ohh, Mickey, this is wonderful!"

"It sounds like it," he said, still standing in the same spot and obviously unsure what he should do.

"Hey!" she said, and then she poked her head out from behind the curtain. "Are you getting in here or not?"

"I'm in! I'm in!" he said, and that was all the encouragement he needed.

It took him all of two seconds to rip off his towel and jump into the shower. For a moment or two, though, he just stood there staring at her, as she scrubbed herself down with soap. He couldn't seem to take his eyes off her beautifully shaped naked body, as she poised herself underneath the cascading stream of water. As many times as he had seen her naked over the past few days, suddenly, he was seeing her in an entirely different light.

Becky could feel him gawking at her, but she didn't mind in the least. She knew her body was nearly flawless with not one ounce of fat on her bones, except for a tiny pooch just below her navel that all the sit-ups in the world couldn't seem to make go away.

Aside from that, her pheromone levels had skyrocketed just thinking about being naked in the shower with the laughing author, whom she had fallen in love with. Here she was in an immaculately clean, oversized shower stall, looking at the moon and the stars through an eight-foot square skylight above her, knowing there was an extremely sexual being standing less than a foot away from her. It was just so romantic and titillating she could barely stand it.

All those times they slept together in the woods were wonderful, even though they never engaged in sex. All they did was kiss and hold each other, and it was oddly all she needed and wanted at the time. She suddenly wondered how Mickey managed to control his urges all those nights.

"Would you hand me the shampoo?" she finally asked him, with her eyes clamped shut, as the water beat down upon her head.

"I'll do you one even better," he said. "Turn around."

"Okay," she said, and she opened her eyes to look up at him.

As she attempted to turn around in the shower stall, her breasts brushed up against his chest and it made her nipples tingle. Then, she felt a shot of adrenaline sweep through her body, followed by more tingly jolts of electricity between her thighs. When she lowered her eyes and saw what was protruding below his groin her face broke out into a smile a mile wide.

"You know," she said. "You're really not too shabby down there."

"Thanks," he said, with a grin plastered on his face. "You don't look so bad yourself, Miss Perky Tits. Come on...turn around."

"Yes, dear," she said, and she planted a quick kiss on his lips before doing as he asked.

"Good God Almighty," he said, when he got a fresh glimpse of the heart-shaped behind that he first fell in love with back at the hotel. "You've got one fine ass there, Ms. Becky Rogers."

"Sheesh," she said. "You can take the man out of Fishbend..."

"Yeah, yeah, I know," he said, laughing.

Then, as if he was a seasoned hairdresser, he poured a generous amount of Pantene shampoo into his palm and rubbed his hands together. As soon as he started massaging it into her scalp, she began serenading him with a series of ooh's and aah's, until he suddenly quit moving his hands.

"Ohhh, don't stop, Mickey. That felt so good," she said.

"I was just making sure you were enjoying this," he joked with her.

Soon, she felt his fingers gathering up the rest of her

long brown hair, as he continued lathering the shampoo into a silky smooth pile atop her head. The next thing she knew, his wandering, slippery hands were gliding down her neck, past her shoulders and then around to her breasts, cupping them in his palms and then caressing them as if they were mounds of yummy chocolate. It had been too many years since a man had touched her this way and she was extremely aroused. The laughing author had touched her on more levels than anyone ever had, and in such a short time.

"Oh, goodness, somebody is excited," she said when she felt a definite poking into the small of her back.

"Ummm, yes, there is some definite excitement going on back here," he said, while his hands drifted farther south.

As the water from the showerhead bathed them in a soothing, pulsating stream, Becky was relishing in the feel of his body rubbing against hers. There was no mistaking his level of arousal and she knew he was enjoying the moment as much as she was. She had never had sex in the shower before and she wondered if she'd be lubricated enough to allow him to enter her.

Her fears were laid to rest when he turned her around to face him. It was all so easy to let him slide inside of her, as she held onto his buttocks. As his mouth searched for hers amid the broiling passion between them, all she could think was that she didn't want this moment to end. His soft tongue delved deep inside her mouth, while his body was thrusting in and out of her, gaining momentum, until she felt him reach a feverish pitch. The primal screams that came out of his mouth next were the sounds of a man who had been denied the joys of a woman for much too long.

As they held each other close, she could feel his body go weak in the knees. Then, the steady stream of water bearing down on them slowly washed all traces of soapy suds, shampoo and juices of passion down the drain, swirling around their feet in a pool of white.

"Ohh, Becky, I love you," he said, once his breathing

returned to normal. "Thank you so much for being you and for allowing me to ravage your body. You have no idea how long it's been."

"I think I can render a guess," she said, and she kissed him on the lips with her arms still wrapped around his waist. "I don't think I've ever heard sounds like what came out of your mouth when you climaxed, except maybe when that storm was yelling Dumala," she added, breaking into a giggle.

Mickey started laughing, too, but she figured he was only doing so because he was embarrassed that a woman had seen his dark, passionate side. She didn't mind the laughter, though, because it seemed to be the solid glue that bonded them together as soul-mates. They could laugh at anything, as long as they were together.

Then, all of a sudden, reality crept back in and all she could think about were Dumala's, Wakulla's, presidents, nuclear bombs and the evil Colonel Madsen.

Once Mickey could stand up straight again, she moved out of the way so that he could enjoy the full effects of the hot steamy water, as she soaped him up from head to toe. When she saw him getting aroused again, she figured it was time for both of them to rinse off, get out and dry off, or else they'd never get out of the shower.

While they were getting dressed, all Mickey could talk about was how hungry he was again.

"We just had dinner, silly," she told him.

"Sorry," he said. "Sex does that to me."

"I can see that," she said, laughing at him. "Would you like some dessert?"

"Only if you're the main ingredient," he said, and he kissed her.

After she threw on his oversized robe, she went downstairs. Ten minutes later she came back up to the bedroom with two bowls of vanilla ice cream, topped with fudge, nuts and strawberries. When she offered his to him on her belly, he devoured it like a gentle, yet ravaging wolf.

Late that night, after another round of lovemaking and another quick shower, they lay atop the crisp cotton sheets watching the stars through the skylight above the bed. Soon, and to Becky's utter surprise, something magical happened.

"Ms. Becky Rogers," Mickey started, and then he raised himself up on one elbow, gazing at her with a definite twinkle in his eyes. "Would you marry me if I asked you?"

"What do *you* think?" she asked him with a giggle.

"I think you would," he said, and then he kissed her on the cheek before laying his head back down on the pillow beside her.

"By the way, Mickey, I love you, too," she said, and she smiled, as she reached for his hand.

CHAPTER 44
Dreams
Mysterious visions
Curiosity manifesting awareness
The unknown still unknown
Illusions
©dp

Early the next morning a phone call came in to the DeRosa residence that gave Mickey and Becky renewed hope that all their efforts had not been in vain.

It was the professor calling to tell them about the planned vigil at Wakulla State Park, which was set for the coming weekend. He also told them that Madsen was being brought up on charges of conspiracy and that he'd most likely be spending the rest of his life in prison, albeit a low-security one with outrageous amenities that he didn't deserve.

The three of them were still wondering if the President had supported Madsen's nuclear bomb plan. It was, and would probably stay a mystery forever. In any case, whether he knew about it or not, he had no choice but to vehemently deny it, in order to save face among the American people and also not ruin his chances for re-election.

After a long discussion that morning, Becky and Mickey agreed that they should definitely go to the vigil, in order to support the cause. Even though neither one of them had an overwhelming desire to go back to Wakulla State Park, it was something they both knew they needed to do.

The next several days were quite hectic. First, Mickey went to his friend's jewelry store in town and he picked out a two-carat, pear-shaped diamond engagement ring. The tribal ring he gave Becky was just a promise ring in his mind, and besides, he wanted his wife to have the finest diamond ring that money could buy in the town of Fishbend Creek.

That evening he took Becky down to the river and he proposed to her properly on bended knee, not knowing that his father was secretly watching them from the back porch.

"Whoo-whee!" Brent shouted when he heard Becky say yes. "Finally! Finally, I'm going to have some grandkids of my very own that I can spoil rotten!"

"Grandkids? Come on, Dad!" Mickey shouted to him. "Give us a little time, would you?"

"Yeah," Becky piped up. "Give us some time."

Outwardly, she was smiling, but inside she was cringing, wondering how she was going to tell both of them that she would never be able to bear a child.

The next day, Mickey and Becky drove up to North Carolina, so that Mickey could meet her mother and the two of them could break their exciting news to her together. They only stayed one night and then they drove back to Mickey's house. During that time, Becky was in a panic worrying about the baby issue. If she told Mickey she couldn't have children, it might end their relationship.

"I have to tell him," she thought to herself. "I have to tell him, but not right now. I can't do it now. Everything is too perfect between us."

The following day, Mickey, Becky and Brent piled into Mickey's pickup and they headed toward Tallahassee. It was a short two-hour drive and when they arrived at the park Saturday afternoon, they were shocked to see millions of supporters lined up along the beach. They soon found out that there was one long line of people along the Gulf Coast basin from Key West to Mexico, from every race and nationality. They would all be holding hands together to form a near complete circle.

When the clock struck seven o'clock that evening,

there was an hour-long session of silent prayer for the Universe. Everyone who had gathered for the vigil, as well as those who were watching from home on their televisions made a solemn proclamation that night. They, as a united global people, promised to work as one for the benefit of planet Earth and mankind.

As the sun set in the western sky, it was one of the most beautiful things the world had ever seen. Millions of people were hand in hand with their toes in the sand. Sounds of laughter and tears of pure joy could be heard for miles when a tremendous rainbow filled the eastern sky, as a light tropical breeze softly whispered in the wind.

As dusk turned to night, a spectacular meteor shower graced the heavens above the Yucatan and the entire Gulf of Mexico, as if God was giving his children His Almighty version of a fireworks display. The heavenly scene was breathtaking and mesmerizing. The fireworks show which lasted well over an hour finally reached a climactic conclusion when the great northern lights suddenly lit up the sky as far as one could see.

Everyone who was watching it knew that it was an impossible and inconceivable act of nature. They also knew there was no earthly explanation, other than the hand of God proving his existence. Off in the distance, a blue whale could be heard calling for its mate. Then, dolphins were heard playing and splashing in the water. They were chattering with each other in gleeful squeals, as if they were enjoying the show even more than the humans.

The message was loud and clear to all mankind. If they didn't begin now to make changes to sustain the Earth, then the Earth could not, and would not sustain man.

Mickey and Becky were tightly holding hands throughout the entire spectacle, and they, too, vowed to protect the planet that they had grown to love so dearly. They were now true soul-mates of the greatest kind and it was evident to both of them.

Soon, an overwhelming sense of peace and tranquility seemed to settle over the entire Gulf basin. It was as if the Earth could feel the love radiating from all the humans gathered for this monumental vigil. The Universe, it seemed, was ecstatic. Its work was done...for now.

It was a humbling experience for everyone who was a part of this amazing spectacle. Soon, people around the world would begin to realize that the Universe held a special power to heal and to communicate, but that it also possessed the power to destroy. The humans witnessed its power first-hand when the cancer patients were healed right before their eyes. They watched it again when it destroyed the prison, and again when it annihilated the nuclear bomb. The majority of mankind now viewed all of these extraordinary phenomena's more as a wake-up call than a terrorizing act of nature.

Throughout the coming days, as the world listened to Becky's pleadings, along with Mickey's Aboriginal interpretations of the events that had happened, professors and scientists around the globe began to realize that the storm was trying to communicate a formula for sustained life on the planet.

Becky knew it wouldn't take long before they figured out how landfills could be utilized for clean-burning fuel, how wastewater could be recycled into usable industrial products, how solar power could be utilized by every nation, and how vehicle emissions could be drastically reduced by adding a simple "green" chemical. Interest, she knew, would be sparked around the world as mankind delved deeper into finding new, alternative power sources.

In the mean time, she had been on national television for days afterward, continuously sending out a message to the people. She wanted everyone to know that the hurricanes were really ticked off and they were ready, willing and very capable of destroying civilization if man did not immediately start heeding its warnings.

The Earth, she assured everyone, knew that man

would have shortcomings, but it also knew that mankind was now on a better path.

Wakulla was found in the Everglades days later by a couple of hunters, who blabbed to the cops. He was still living in the same place with his family, and once the media got involved, he, too, was hailed as a hero on international television. He was eventually given a brand new "green" house on Miami Beach and a huge lump sum payment from the government of the United States, which would take care of his entire family for life.

Becky and Mickey, of course, didn't get a dime from the government, but they did garner a lot of notoriety. For the moment, their job was done. They finally got the human race to wise up, which was more priceless than any amount of money in the world.

As for the environmentalists of the world, they continued their efforts to educate mankind on how to make the planet a better place to live. Just getting a few more people interested in their programs and raising awareness of important issues was a small victory for them. They were also praying that when December 21st came around, perhaps, the Universe would rebel again if the human race was still balking at making positive changes for the betterment of the planet. It was their only hope.

For the next two months, Becky and Mickey took turns traveling back and forth from Fishbend Creek to Jubilee Falls in order to spend time with each other. One day, though, Mickey had about enough. All he was doing was driving himself crazy with worry every time she got on the road.

"Becky, let's get married right away," he said to her one evening, as they sat on his back porch. "I can't stand it when you're not here."

"Really? But we've only been engaged for..." she started, but he stopped her.

"I know it, baby, but I worry about you. It's such a long drive from here to your house. The last thing I want is for you to get into an accident. I'd never forgive myself."

"Ummm...well, okay," she said. "I miss you, too, when we're not together, but..."

"I know what you're going to say. Where are we going to live? Here in Fishbend or at your place in Jubilee Falls. Believe me," he said. "I've been wondering the same thing myself. Neither one of us wants to leave our one remaining parent alone, but we'll figure something out. Trust me."

"There you go again with that 'trust me' thing," she said, and she laughed.

"I'll tell you what. Why don't we bring my dad along on a little trip up to your place, so he can at least meet your mother," he suggested. "I think it's about time, don't you? After all, they're going to be in-laws soon. What do you say? We'll leave tomorrow, okay?"

"Okay, I suppose that's a start. Oh, and I can introduce you and your father to Pastor Gutierrez. You're going to love him and I'm sure he would be happy to officiate our wedding."

"Ah, so you want a church wedding, huh?"

"Well, yeah," she said. "Don't you?"

"Yeah, sure," he said with a cocky grin. "I just hope the walls don't cave in when I step inside the church. I haven't been in so, so long."

"Don't worry, honey. God doesn't do those kinds of things to his children. You'll be fine."

Surprisingly, when Mickey asked his father to accompany them on a road trip up to North Carolina, he was all for it. Even more astonishing was the animal attraction that happened between Ida and Brent when they first laid eyes on each other. It was like watching a remake of *On Golden Pond*. All of a sudden, Becky and Mickey's problems didn't seem quite so daunting.

The next day they met with Pastor Gutierrez and a wedding date was set for Saturday, September 22nd, the first day of fall. By mutual agreement between Mickey and Becky, it would be a small gathering of just family and close friends. Becky asked Brent if he would walk her down the aisle and he said he'd be proud to do the honors.

As a budding romance was developing between Brent and Ida, wedding preparations were well under way for the two lovebirds. Brent was a changed man and he was so smitten with Becky's mother it was surreal. He even went so far as to stay in North Carolina for the next few weeks to help Ida with the food preparation for the reception. Mickey, for one, was truly astonished. Again, it was making the residence issue less of a problem than either he or Becky could have hoped for.

The wedding went off without a hitch and it was the most beautiful event of the century, especially when the media got wind of it. Reporters from all over the country and from every major news station pounced on Jubilee Falls to get pictures of the nuptials.

Mickey took his new bride to Costa Rica for a romantic honeymoon in one of the swankiest hotels in the country. For two glorious weeks, the two of them made mad, passionate, glorious, steamy, earthshaking love to one another.

One evening, about five weeks after their wedding ceremony, Becky and Mickey were out on his bass boat for an after dinner moonlight ride down the Suwannee River. They left Brent and Ida sitting on the back porch, having a glass of wine and making goo-goo eyes at each other. All of a sudden, Becky felt extremely nauseous.

"Oh, my God," she said to Mickey, as her face turned green. "I think I'm going to lose my dinner."

A second later, she was puking her guts out over the bow of the boat. When she finished, Mickey started hootin' and hollerin' like a crazy person.

"What the heck is wrong with you?" she asked him, still looking green around the edges.

"You're pregnant! Becky, you're pregnant!" he shouted.

"Are you nuts? I can't be pregnant!" she screamed. "Can I?"

"I think you can and you are," he said. "I can see it in your face. I hope it's twins," he added with a smirk. "That way we can get both of our kids into this world in one fell swoop."

"How do you know it wasn't something I ate that made me sick? How do you know it's not the flu or something?"

"Because I'm a man," he proudly said. "I can spot a pregnant woman from a mile away and you, my dear, are definitely with child."

"I hope you're right," she said. "Otherwise, you can bet your ass you'll be throwing up next."

"I'm not the least bit worried, honey. Not the least," he said, and he leaned over to kiss her just to prove it. "I love you, Becky DeRosa. I love you so much."

"I love you, too, honey. I love you, too," she said, even though her mind was wracked with fear of the unknown future...

Also by Joyce Marie Taylor

Life in San Argle
(Co-written with Kathleen E. Kelly)

Nina's Corner
(Co-written with Kathleen E. Kelly)

joyce's shorts

Kiss Me Darlin'

Forbidden Rendezvous

Sailing On Love

Ruby

Aniratak

Life, Some Rhyme, No Reason

Boys Are Smelly

Rocky Road Love (Coming Soon!)

For more information, log on to
www.joycemarietaylor.com

To learn more about Mike Mullis and his band
WhooWhee, log on to www.dothegatorchomp.com

Made in the USA
Charleston, SC
15 May 2010